"I intend to do exactly what Miss Harding asked me not to."

Chadwick sighed. "I will introduce her to every suitable gentleman I know."

Edgecombe snapped his fingers. "Why don't you introduce her to Lord Crambie?"

"Crambie! The man is a boozer," Chadwick said, shocked.

"All right, what about Lord Taylor?"

"Too boring," Chadwick replied.

"Lord Brookeston?"

"Too fat."

"Well, then, there's only one other person I can think of who might meet all your exacting requirements," Edgecombe said brightly. "Me. I'm the right age and I have no particularly loathsome vices nor am I bad-looking. Further, Miss Harding would become a countess. Shall I commence my courtship at once?"

Regency England: 1811-1820

"It was the best of times, it was the worst of times...."
As George III languished in madness, the pampered and profligate Prince of Wales led the land in revelry and the elegant Beau Brummel set the style. Across the Channel, Napoleon continued to plot against the English until his final exile to St. Helena. Across the Atlantic, America renewed hostilities with an old adversary, declaring war on Britain in 1812. At home, Society glittered, love matches abounded and poets such as Lord Byron flourished. It was a time of heroes and villains, a time of unrelenting charm and gaiety, when entire fortunes were won or lost on a turn of the dice and reputation was all. A dazzling period that left its mark on two continents and whose very name became a byword for elegance and romance.

Books by Gail Whitiker

HARLEQUIN REGENCY ROMANCE
78—BITTERSWEET REVENGE

Don't miss any of our special offers. Write to us at the following address for information on our newest releases.

Harlequin Reader Service
P.O. Box 1397, Buffalo, NY 14240
Canadian address: P.O. Box 603,
Fort Erie, Ont. L2A 5X3

THE BLADE AND
THE BATH MISS

GAIL
WHITIKER

Harlequin Books

TORONTO • NEW YORK • LONDON
AMSTERDAM • PARIS • SYDNEY • HAMBURG
STOCKHOLM • ATHENS • TOKYO • MILAN
MADRID • WARSAW • BUDAPEST • AUCKLAND

If you purchased this book without a cover you should be aware that this book is stolen property. It was reported as "unsold and destroyed" to the publisher, and neither the author nor the publisher has received any payment for this "stripped book."

To Louie, for believing

Published February 1993

ISBN 0-373-31192-3

THE BLADE AND THE BATH MISS

Copyright © 1993 by Gail Whitiker. All rights reserved. Except for use in any review, the reproduction or utilization of this work in whole or in part in any form by any electronic, mechanical or other means, now known or hereafter invented, including xerography, photocopying and recording, or in any information storage or retrieval system, is forbidden without the permission of the publisher, Harlequin Enterprises Limited, 225 Duncan Mill Road, Don Mills, Ontario, Canada M3B 3K9.

All the characters in this book have no existence outside the imagination of the author and have no relation whatsoever to anyone bearing the same name or names. They are not even distantly inspired by any individual known or unknown to the author, and all the incidents are pure invention.

The Harlequin trademarks, consisting of the words HARLEQUIN REGENCY ROMANCE and the portrayal of a Harlequin, are trademarks of Harlequin Enterprises Limited; the portrayal of a Harlequin is registered in the United States Patent and Trademark Office and in the Canada Trade Marks Office.

Printed in U.S.A.

CHAPTER ONE

"MY DARLING GIRL, I love you with all my heart, but I fear you must have bats in the attic if you think your cousin will be happy about coming all the way up here for the wedding! You know how he feels about London. *And* how he feels about me. He made that perfectly clear on the occasion of our betrothal dinner. In fact," the young, good-looking man continued in some agitation, "I wonder at your wisdom in even asking Chadwick to give you away. Would your uncle Alexander not have been a more logical choice?"

The sentiments being expressed to Lady Margaret Glendenning by her fiancé, the Honourable Bertrand Rowsbottom, regarding Lady Margaret's cousin, the Marquis of Chadwick, were hardly unexpected. Nor were they entirely unjustified, given Tristan's unusual behaviour of late, not even to the decidedly biased ears of Lady Margaret.

Tristan seemed to have developed a definite antipathy for Town, shunning the extensive selection of entertainments to be had during the Season and stubbornly burying himself away in the country. And while he dutifully maintained the elegant Town house in Eaton Square as part of the general overseeing of the Glendenning estates, a responsibility which, along with the guardianship of his two young cousins, had passed to him upon the death of the earl and his wife some years earlier, he visited it only when called upon by necessity to do so. Such necessity, it seemed, included the engagement and forthcoming marriage of the eldest of the two girls, Margaret.

All the same, Lady Margaret staunchly refused to entertain any criticism of her beloved cousin and turned to regard her fiancé with a decidedly troubled expression.

"I am sorry to hear you say so, Bertie. I always thought you liked Tristan."

"My dear girl, I hold Chadwick in the very highest regard," Bertie replied, anxious not to trouble the waters of marital bliss before even setting out upon them. "How could I not? The man is a veritable pink of the ton. It is simply that I do not think he and I . . . well, hit it off as well as we might. You must admit, dearest, that your cousin is not the easiest of men with whom to get along."

"Really? I have never found that to be so," Lady Margaret replied sweetly. "Still, I suppose being related does tend to prejudice one's opinion somewhat. But I assure you, Tristan exhibited no signs of reluctance whatsoever when I asked him to give me away. On the contrary, I do believe he was rather pleased," Lady Margaret said, awarding her fiancé one of her most radiant smiles.

When her ploy failed to elicit the required response, Lady Margaret sighed, and pouted prettily at her betrothed. "Oh, Bertie, do say you are not out of curl with me. I understand that you are concerned, and I allow that Tristan has been acting a little . . . curious of late," she conceded, "but that is not because he does not care for you. Tristan is merely . . . different, that's all. He doesn't fall into a definable mould. He never has. Why do you think he has never married?"

"I assume for the same reason the rest of us haven't," Bertie remarked lightly. "Because he hasn't found the right lady."

"Precisely!" Lady Margaret replied, as if the explanation were quite clear. When she saw no answering comprehension in her fiancé's eyes, she shook her head and tried again. "Well, do you not see, Bertie? Tristan could have married a dozen times over if he had wanted to. He's had more than enough opportunity."

"I'm not saying he hasn't," Bertie acknowledged, well aware of the frequent wagers placed down at White's whenever the marquis was seen to be escorting a new lady about Town. "But I fail to see what that has to do with his being different."

"The point is," Lady Margaret explained patiently, "that if Tristan were only concerned with what Society thought, he would have married some suitable young girl years ago and set about raising a family. The fact that he has steadfastly remained a bachelor to such an advanced age clearly reveals that he follows his own feelings, and I, for one, admire him for it."

"Yes, I know," Bertie grumbled enviously. "You, and a good many others."

"Bertie!" Lady Margaret gasped, her eyes widening. "Never say you are jealous of Tristan!"

"Jealous? Of course not." Her betrothed was quick to rally. "It's just that, well, Chadwick is such an admirable fellow that one cannot help but feel somewhat lacking in comparison. Ever since we announced our betrothal, I've heard nothing but what a nonpareil Chadwick is, what a splendid Corinthian, and how his cattle are the best to be had, and his clothes of better fit and quality than anyone else's. It's rather discouraging, to say the least."

Lady Margaret listened to his impassioned speech, touched by the note of uncertainty in it, and smiled, her eyes softening as she laid a gentle hand on her fiancé's arm. "Dearest Bertie, you have no need to take on so. I love you, silly goose. There has never been anyone else for me. In my eyes you are every bit the nonpareil Tristan is. You know that, don't you?"

Bertie blushed uncomfortably. "Well, yes, I suppose . . ."

"Good. Then if you know it, why are you so out of curl over this? Yes, I love and respect Tristan, but that is because he is my cousin, and you of all people should know how close we are. Tristan is the brother I never had. For that reason alone I should hate to see him absent himself from our wedding. Why, I shouldn't be surprised to learn that under that gruff exterior, my dear cousin is actually looking forward to the occasion."

The Honourable Bertrand Rowsbottom, well acquainted with the rumours, if not the fact, of Chadwick's less than complacent views regarding the marriage of his eldest cousin, wisely bit back the retort that sprang to his lips, and muttered instead, "Well, if he is, he is certainly taking pains to conceal it. He struck me as being dashed chilly when we conversed over dinner last month."

"Oh, that." Lady Margaret laughed, her blue eyes sparkling merrily. "I wish you would forget about that silly quarrel. I'm sure Tristan did the moment he left the house. Besides, you should know better than to discuss matters political with Tristan. He has very strong views, and it is bound to cause a stir when your own are so radically opposed."

"I wouldn't say they were *radically* opposed," Bertie objected. "I think we were just observing the same situation from slightly different perspectives, that's all."

"Yes, I am sure that is all it was," Lady Margaret said, her eyes twinkling.

"Still," Bertie continued, his face assuming an expression of wounded dignity, "Chadwick needn't have laughed outright at my sentiments. I was only expressing the popular opinion, after all."

"Yes, I know you were, dearest," Lady Margaret said in a placatory tone as she glanced over the lists strewn about the top of the elegant Hepplewhite writing table. "Unfortunately, that was your second mistake."

"My second?" Bertie quizzed.

"Mmm. Your first was in assuming that Tristan would be in accord with the popular opinion," Lady Margaret pointed out. "My cousin has never been one to fall in with the majority. It simply isn't his way."

"Wonderful," Bertie mumbled under his breath.

"What was that, dearest?" his intended asked, pausing in her hunt for whatever it was she was searching for.

"Nothing, my love, nothing," Bertie hastened to assure her, his face resuming its normal, easygoing expression.

Bertrand watched as Margaret smiled prettily, and then returned her attention to the papers on the desk. He knew better than to continue in his present vein. There would be little agreement from his betrothed regarding the unconventional behaviour of her beloved cousin. Even if Chadwick were to be convicted of some heinous crime, with witnesses ready to condemn him and all manner of indisputable evidence pointing unerringly towards him, Bertie knew that Margaret would still endeavour to defend him. Theirs was simply that sort of relationship, and nothing Bertie could do or say would ever change that—not even marrying her.

Hence, resolutely accepting the inevitable, Bertie shrugged and moved on to another less volatile topic. "Have you heard from Miss Harding yet?"

At the mention of her dearest friend, Lady Margaret's face brightened considerably. "Oh, yes! A letter came just this morning, in fact." She glanced at the daunting clutter of papers in front of her. "Now, I know it's here somewhere. Ah, yes, here it is," she said, triumphantly extricating a single sheet of fine parchment and holding it up. "Emma says that she is eagerly looking forward to coming to London for the wedding, and that she will be arriving Tuesday week on the two o'clock stage. She also asks if someone might be able to meet her at the station." Lady

Margaret put down the letter and smiled at her young man. "You will be a dear and go, won't you Bertie?"

"Yes, of course I will," Bertie replied, his brow furrowing. "But surely Miss Harding is not taking the stage?"

"I'm afraid she is," Lady Margaret replied, perusing the letter again. "And that is why I want you to be there to greet her, Bertie. Emma is going to be unsettled enough by the time she arrives. The least we can do is take good care of her from the moment she steps off the stage. Don't you agree?"

Fortunately, on this matter, Bertie had no qualms about agreeing. Next to his own darling Margaret, he considered Emma Harding to be one of the most genuinely delightful young ladies he had ever encountered, notwithstanding the fact that their acquaintance had been brief and that the occasion of their first meeting had been overshadowed by the gravity of the circumstances.

They had met, or rather, Margaret had introduced them, at the funeral of Emma's father just over a year ago. Emma had been eighteen when her father had passed away, yet she had conducted herself with a dignity and composure well beyond her tender years. Her features, which had been just barely visible through the heavy black net covering her face, were strikingly lovely, and she had stood quietly at her aunt's side, listening to the monotonous voice of the old village curate as he extolled the virtues of a man Bertie did not know, with her head held high, and her eyes dry.

Later, when they returned to the house for refreshments, Bertie had watched Emma move about the room, admiring the grace with which she carried herself. He recalled noting with some surprise that, social position notwithstanding, Miss Harding was treated with respect by many of the older tabbies present. In fact, more than one Society matron was heard to remark that Emma Harding had more sense about her than the entire crop of high-born, giggling debutantes at Court that Season.

Yes, Mr. Rowsbottom acknowledged silently, meeting Miss Emma Harding at the station would be a deuced more pleasant occupation than pondering how best to deal with Margaret's older and decidedly forbidding cousin!

"I suppose I'd best take the landau," Bertie observed. "No doubt Miss Harding and her maid will come laden with the usual assortment of bandboxes, portmanteaus and trunks."

"Actually, no," Lady Margaret informed him slowly. "Emma will not be bringing a maid, Bertie. It seems that my dear friend is coming up to Town on her own."

"On her own!" Bertie expostulated. "Good Lord! Whatever can her aunt be thinking of to let a young lady like Miss Harding travel unchaperoned. It just ain't done!"

Lady Margaret nodded, well aware of the breach of etiquette. "I know, dearest, I know, but it seems that Emma's aunt cannot spare any of the servants to accompany her. By the sound of things, they are terribly busy and trying to manage without adequate staff. Though why Emma hasn't a maid of her own, I cannot imagine," Lady Margaret added, clearly puzzled.

"Humph," Bertie snorted disparagingly. "I doubt Miss Harding has had the wherewithal to do very much at all since her father died in that unfortunate way."

Lady Margaret raised startled blue eyes to her fiancé's face. "What way, Bertie?"

"The way most gamblers do, my dear. In dun territory!"

Lady Margaret gasped, shocked by the unexpected disclosure. "But are you sure, Bertie? I cannot recall Emma's ever having made mention of such a thing."

"I'm sure she did not," Bertie agreed readily. "Miss Harding is too much a lady to let on how things really are."

"And how are things...really?" Lady Margaret enquired hesitantly.

Bertie shrugged, and pulled an ornate snuffbox from his breast pocket. Flipping open the lid, he helped himself to a pinch. "From what little I've heard, not very good. While it may be nothing more than idle gossip put about by servants, it's rumoured that Reginald Harding ran up such a staggering gambling debt before he died that his daughter had no choice but to sell everything in the hope of paying it off. That's why Emma went to live with her aunt in the first place," Bertie explained, returning the box to his pocket. "The bank foreclosed on the house in London."

"Foreclosed! Oh, my poor Emma," Lady Margaret said, her pretty face crumpling. "She never mentioned any of that in her letters. She told me she had gone to live with her aunt because the woman was sick and in need of Emma's care."

Bertie nodded sympathetically. "Yes, Miss Harding probably would say something of the sort. I don't suppose she wanted you to know how bad things really were."

"But why not?" Lady Margaret demanded almost angrily. "Emma is my dearest friend. Surely she knows I would have helped her in any way I could. Why, she could have come to live with us. Aunt Rachel and Elizabeth have always liked Emma, and I would have enjoyed her company immensely."

"And I'm sure she would have enjoyed that too, for a while," Bertie agreed readily enough. "But I fear Miss Harding is not the type to accept charity, my dear, and that is how she would have viewed your offer. To live with a relation when one's circumstances change is one thing, but to impose upon the generosity of a friend—"

"But she would not have been imposing!" Lady Margaret spoke up heatedly. "How can staying with a friend be deemed an imposition?"

"It might not be to you, Margaret, but I assure you it would have been to her," Bertie said gently. "And from what little I know of Emma Harding, it simply would not have been the thing.''

Lady Margaret looked at the letter in her hand, and sighed, her normally untroubled countenance clouding. ''Then I shall do my best to convince Emma that now it *is* the thing, Bertie,'' she announced decisively. ''I want Emma to come here and live with me until she finds a husband. There is absolutely no reason why she should have to bury herself away on that . . . farm, or whatever it is, simply because of a set of unfortunate circumstances beyond her control,'' Lady Margaret muttered.

''Now don't go flying up into the boughs, my dear. You don't know that Miss Harding is all that unhappy,'' Bertie pointed out reasonably. ''I imagine she has her horses and her hobbies to keep her busy.''

''Horses and hobbies? Fiddlesticks to horses and hobbies!'' Lady Margaret snapped with unusual fervour. ''Emma is nineteen years old. She needs more than horses and hobbies to fill her days, Bertie. She needs to go to parties and meet dashing young men. She needs to have them whisper sweet things in her ear and tell her how beautiful she is—to dance attendance upon her every whim. That's what Emma needs. *Not* horses and hobbies! She may have those when she is old and grey.''

Bertie chuckled indulgently. ''So she may, my dear.''

''And now that she is out of mourning, I intend to reply to Emma's letter this very instant and invite her to stay with me here.''

''But she is staying here,'' Bertie said.

''No, no, I mean *after* the wedding, silly goose,'' Lady Margaret chastised him fondly. ''I am going to tell Emma that she may stay in this house for as long as she pleases. And this time, I will not take no for an answer!''

EMMA HARDING sat quietly in one corner of the coach, trying to enjoy the sight of gently rolling hills and verdant pastures visible through the window. The stage was uncomfortably full this morning, and Emma was weary of being confined with her three fellow passengers: the bespectacled, spinsterish woman beside her who carried a well-worn travelling bag and spent the entire trip dutifully reading her Bible as if to ward off the imminent arrival of the devil himself; the florid-faced gentleman who sat directly across from her, wheezing and gasping so frightfully that Emma felt sure he would not survive to the end of the journey; and the amiable young man beside him who had introduced himself as Mr. Joseph Braithwaite shortly after they set out for London.

London. At the thought of the bustling, beautiful city where she had been born and spent most of her life, Emma's mouth curved in a smile of fond remembrance. She had so many happy recollections of living in Town, glorious times when she and her mother and father had been happy.

But, unlike so many other people's, Emma's happy times had not been destined to last. Three years ago, her mother had died after a brief, debilitating illness, and her father, in his grief, had been inconsolable. He had wandered about the house like a lost soul, gradually fading in spirit until he scarcely resembled the charming, gregarious man he had always been. Eventually, he had turned to the bottle for comfort, spending his days in a drink-induced stupor where he had felt nothing and known nothing. But when he had started gambling, Emma had known it was the beginning of the end.

Not surprisingly, by the time Reginald Harding died, his gambling losses were so high that Emma had been forced to dismiss the servants and sell everything they owned in an effort to clear the debts. Everything had gone: the horses, the lovely London house and every stick of furniture within. And Emma, alone for the first time in her life, had found herself relegated to the ignominious position of "poor relation," forced to accept the charity of her mother's elder sister, Georgina; a little-known aunt who lived on a small farm in the south of England, and who, since the death of her husband, had managed to eke out a comfortable living by supplying the local market with eggs, milk and butter.

Emma jumped as the coachman's deep, resonant voice boomed out, startling her from her reverie. They were pulling into the yard of a bustling posting inn to change horses. And where, too, judging by the cluster of people gathered about, all anxiously clutching travelling bags in their hands, they would be taking on extra passengers.

Emma relaxed and leaned back against the well-worn cushions. Thank goodness Aunt Georgina had been good enough to secure her passage to London on an inside seat. Emma well knew that comfort and safety were not always the order of the day on the carriages which travelled back and forth between Brighton and London. Oft-times, upwards of ten people were crowded together on the roof of the carriage, left to endure the rigours of the six-hour trip as best they could. Emma shuddered to think what the state of her appearance would have been had she been required to pass even a small part of the trip in one of those precarious seats. Even now her lovely new gown was crumpled beyond repair.

When the coach finally came to a stop and the steps were let down, Emma impulsively gathered up her skirts and stepped outside for a breath of fresh air. She was eager to escape, if only for a moment, the claustrophobic atmosphere of the crowded vehicle. How she longed for the comfort of a private carriage, well aware, however, that she was not likely to enjoy such luxuries again.

Emma smoothed out the skirt of her stylish new travelling gown of sky blue twilled muslin, and allowed herself a small sigh of pleasure. The gown had been a present from her aunt, the first new dress she had owned since donning her blacks just over a year ago. And although Emma had dutifully reprimanded her aunt for such unwarranted extravagance, she had secretly rejoiced in the gift. She was tired of wearing sombre colours, having, over the course of the past three years, found herself twice in mourning.

Emma had briefly tasted the life of a light-hearted girl when, after the first period of mourning, she had made her belated come-out and taken her place in Society, enjoying what London during the Season had to offer. She had revelled in the musicales and the assemblies, and had danced with many a charming young gentleman.

But, all that had abruptly come to an end when, little more than six months later, her father had died; a father whose grief and drink-induced gambling had resulted in her present financial straits, and Emma had found herself once more in black gloves.

Still, it could have been much worse, Emma reflected with a surge of youthful optimism. Aunt Georgina, the unknown relative who had offered Emma a home, had proved to be a kind, decent woman who had appreciated Emma as much for her companionship as for the help she was able to provide. Emma was not weighed down with menial duties, nor was she ever asked to do anything her aunt would not have done herself. Consequently, the two of them lived in amiable accord, enjoying sparse but comfortable surroundings and accepting their reduced circumstances with as good a grace as possible.

"Miss Harding, perhaps I could escort you inside for some refreshments," Mr. Braithwaite said, suddenly appearing at Emma's side. "The day is warm, and you must be feeling a bit parched after all that travelling, especially given the close confines of the carriage."

Emma turned to regard the gentleman who, like herself, had stepped out to take some air, and smiled uncertainly. He had seemed a personable enough young man when he had introduced himself just after they had set off from Brighton, and out of politeness, Emma had smiled and responded in kind. But once the introductions had been made, she had quickly resumed her study of the passing scenery. Emma was well aware that travelling alone and unchaperoned could encourage unwanted familiarity, and it was for that reason that she now felt a trifle dismayed by his offer.

Still, Emma thought reasonably, what harm could come of it? They were at a busy posting inn where an endless stream of people were bustling to and fro. And she was uncommonly thirsty. Perhaps it would be permissible to go inside just for a drop of refreshment and then come right back out.

"Yes, all right. Thank you, Mr. Braithwaite," Emma responded quietly. "It is very kind of you to offer. I do admit to being rather thirsty. I daresay a glass of lemon water would be most refreshing."

Mr. Braithwaite smiled encouragingly. "I thought that might be the case. Shall we go?"

In response to his engaging smile, Emma bowed her head and turned to precede him into the inn. Had she but seen the speculative gleam which suddenly appeared in the young man's eyes, Emma would have turned and made her way back to the carriage as swiftly as possible. But, as Fate would have it, she did not, and she walked innocently into the inn with Mr. Braithwaite following closely behind.

The noise of laughter and revelry hit them as soon as they opened the door, along with a pungent mixture of odours Emma was unable to identify. Instinctively, she took a step backwards, her eyes widening in alarm. Perhaps it was not

such a good idea that she had come in, Emma thought belatedly, nor that they linger here any longer than was absolutely necessary. The occupants of the bar looked a seedy
lot, some of them appearing downright villainous. Even
now they were eyeing Emma's person with a boldness she
found distinctly intimidating.

"Mr. Braithwaite, I think that perhaps we should—"
Emma began, then stopped as she realized that Mr. Braithwaite had already made his way to the bar and was conversing with the landlord.

The innkeeper, a large, greasy-looking man who glanced
first at the lovely young lady who was regarding her surroundings with growing doubt, and then at the toff who had
come in with her, said something Emma was unable to hear
and then appeared to wait. Looks were exchanged, along
with some coin, and the innkeeper nodded. His slow, leering smile exposed a set of broken, rotting teeth.

"But of course, good sir. You're quite right. This rowdy
bunch is 'ardly suitable company for such a refined young
lady," he said with a grin. "I'll 'ave Mabel seat you somewhere more...quiet, shall I? Mabel!" he shouted, glancing quickly round the crowded pub. "Mabel, where the 'ell
are you, woman!"

The man bellowed in the general direction of a blowzy,
buxom girl who was standing with her back to them, intent
on displaying her ample charms to the occupant of a table
in the corner. She was obviously loath to break off her flirtation for such a mundane thing as work, and for a moment, Emma was not convinced that she would.

But clearly, something in the tone of the innkeeper's last
shout brought her to her duty, and Mabel reluctantly
straightened and made her way back to the bar, her hips
swinging.

"Ah, that's a good girl." The innkeeper grinned as she
approached. "Now, why don't you show this good gentle-

man and 'is lady into the parlour, Mabel? And then take them in some refreshments.''

With an audible sniff at the innkeeper, and a clearly envious glance at Emma's smart new travelling gown, Mabel tossed back her flaming red hair and turned to lead the way to an adjacent room.

'''Ere we are, ducks,'' she announced, grandly throwing open the door to what was clearly a private dining parlour. ''The best as we've got. Make yourselves at 'ome and I'll be back wiv some grub.''

''Food? Oh, no, that won't be necessary!'' Emma proclaimed quickly, growing more agitated by the minute. She had not thought to be left alone with Mr. Braithwaite, and turned to glance at him in dismay. ''I think that perhaps we should go back, Mr. Braithwaite. We really do not have time to eat.''

''Eh?'' Mabel said. ''Then wot you doing . . . ?''

About to ask why she had even bothered wasting her time bringing them to the parlour, Mabel suddenly caught sight of Mr. Braithwaite's face. She saw him shake his head and glance pointedly at Emma, whose attention was still focused upon the barmaid anxiously.

Slowly, a grin not unlike the one which had appeared on the innkeeper's face broke over her own, and her voice became suddenly coy. ''Oh yes, of course, I understands perfectly, miss.'' She winked at Emma boldly. ''Why waste time eating when there's other more important fings to get on wiv, ain't that right?''

Emma stared at the woman in confusion, wondering what she was talking about. Did she not understand that they only wanted something to drink?

''I don't think you quite understand—'' Emma essayed quietly.

''Oh no, love, I understands perfectly,'' Mabel declared, glancing enviously at Mr. Braithwaite. ''Arfer all, we're both women at 'eart, ain't we? And we all need the same fings when it comes right down to it, don't we?''

"Thank you, Mabel!" Braithwaite said, abruptly taking the barmaid by the arm and ushering her somewhat roughly towards the door. "That will be all," he said pointedly.

"Well, I never!" Mabel huffed. "You're as bad as 'er. Why don't you just book a bleeding room for the night? Then you'll 'ave plenty o' time," she called out for Emma's benefit before the door closed swiftly in her face.

"Interfering busybody," Mr. Braithwaite muttered, straightening his cravat. "Now, Miss Harding, why don't we—"

Mr. Braithwaite broke off in midsentence, having turned and caught sight of the face of his companion. "Why, Miss Harding, you've gone quite pale. Won't you allow me to—"

"I shall allow you nothing, sir," Emma said quietly, her deep violet-blue eyes flashing. "And I shall thank you to escort me from this room at once!"

"But my dear Miss Harding, we have not yet partaken of—"

"I am *not* your 'dear Miss Harding'," Emma informed him coldly. "Nor do I intend to partake of anything while in your company, which I do not intend to share any longer. To that end, I repeat that I wish you to escort me back to the carriage immediately!"

Emma's voice was remarkably calm, given the gravity of her situation. She faced him with a composure totally at odds with the fear which trembled in the pit of her stomach. Typically, Emma blamed herself for the awkward situation in which she now found herself. Her aunt had warned her unscrupulous men were always about waiting to take advantage of a female careless enough to put herself at their mercy. And Emma had been just so foolish. She had allowed herself to be taken in by Mr. Braithwaite's practised charm, and now found herself in a decidedly precarious position. She could scream, of course. That would certainly attract attention. But would any of the occupants of the tavern respond? She had only glimpsed their faces in passing, but Emma could not recall having seen anyone there who looked the type to come to the rescue of a lady in distress. And judging by the lecherous look in Joseph Braithwaite's eye, that was exactly what she was about to become.

"I shall scream if you so much as come near me," Emma warned him, slowly backing away. The easygoing expression on Braithwaite's face suddenly assumed a malevolence that frightened her.

"Go ahead. Scream. It won't do you any good," he replied silkily. "Can *you* hear any sounds coming from the bar?"

Emma listened, and suddenly grew frightened. She could hear nothing—not a peep. And the room had been raucously noisy, almost oppressively so. Yet here in this room with the door closed, no sound penetrated. They might have been the only ones in the entire inn!

Emma quickly took stock of her situation. Braithwaite was firmly stationed between herself and the door, effectively blocking her escape from that avenue. She glanced briefly at the window, and then just as quickly dimissed it. The handle was latched, and she knew the man would be on top of her before she managed to get it undone and propel herself through. Where did that leave her? Emma wondered silently. She had to get back outside. She wasn't sure how long they had been in the inn, but she felt sure the coach would be leaving shortly.

The coach! Of course, Emma thought, almost crying aloud with relief. Joseph Braithwaite needed to get back on that coach as much as she did.

"Mr. Braithwaite, I suggest we leave here immediately," Emma said, bravely lifting her chin. "No doubt the carriage will be leaving shortly and we both need to get to London."

"Yes, that's true," Braithwaite acknowledged, taking another step towards her. "But whether I get there today, tomorrow or a week from tomorrow really makes no difference to me. And at the moment, Miss Harding, I'm in no particular hurry to go anywhere."

Emma swallowed, his words banishing the last vestiges of her courage. She was trapped! The coach had been her last resort. If he came at her now, she would have no recourse but to fight him as best she could until eventually his superior strength wore her down.

"So, my dear Miss Harding," he repeated, his voice making her cringe. "Will you make this pleasant for both of us, or am I going to have to...convince you?"

Without warning, Braithwaite lunged forward and grabbed Emma's arm, his fingers bruising the soft white skin above her wrist. Startled, Emma screamed, totally unprepared for the quickness of his attack. "Mr. Braithwaite, let me go!" she cried as he yanked her towards him.

"Not on your life, my little lovely." He laughed harshly. "You're far too tempting a morsel to get away."

Pinning her against the wall with his body, Braithwaite lowered his mouth, trying to bestow a kiss on those inviting lips. Truly frightened now, Emma began to struggle in earnest. "Mr. Braithwaite! Let...me...go!"

She heard him laugh, and opened her mouth to scream, when suddenly, and without warning, the door to the parlour flew open and banged back against the wall. Startled, Braithwaite broke off his assault. He barely had time to look round before a strong hand reached out and seized him by the scruff of the neck. Emma's eyes widened in amazement as she saw a tall, well-dressed man spin Mr. Braithwaite round and hit him squarely on the nose with a punch that would have done justice to John Jackson himself, followed quickly by a second blow to the stomach, doubling him over. One more well-placed punch and her assailant lay on the ground, knocked quite senseless. He hadn't even had a chance to return a strike!

Emma, her breath coming now in shaky gulps, stared up at the man who had rescued her, tears clouding her eyes as she realized just how close she had come to ruination. Her legs felt suddenly weak, and as the room began to spin, Emma slumped forward. The last thing she remembered as blackness descended was a muffled oath, and two strong arms reaching out to catch her before she struck the floor.

CHAPTER TWO

EMMA'S EYELIDS fluttered open, her gaze focussing blankly on a smoke-blackened ceiling criss-crossed with dark wooden beams. She felt weak and disoriented, and for a moment did not move, trying to remember what had happened. She was lying on a settee in a rudely furnished parlour which smelt unpleasantly of stale beer and even staler food. An old, threadbare rug covered the dusty floor, and a wooden dining table and chairs, which had clearly seen better days, occupied the centre of the room.

Emma closed her eyes again, hoping that the fuzziness would clear. Where was she, and what was she doing here? She was supposed to be on her way to London...to Lady Margaret's wedding. She had been on the coach, and then...

"Oh, no!" Emma groaned, lifting a hand to her temple as memory abruptly returned. How could she have forgotten? She had foolishly allowed herself to accompany Mr. Braithwaite into the inn, and there he had attempted to ravish her. And he would have, had a stranger not barged unannounced into the room and thrown her attacker bodily to the floor. But where was the stranger now? she mused fuzzily. And where was Mr. Braithwaite?

Emma sat up and then groaned as a wave of dizziness overwhelmed her, abruptly sending her back to her supine position.

"Steady on, child, don't move so quickly. You've had a nasty fright," a voice said gently from the direction of the window behind her.

Emma gasped, startled as much by the sound of the voice as by its proximity. Resting her hand on the back of the settee for support, she tentatively raised herself into a sitting position and turned round. She shut her eyes for a moment, and drew a deep breath. When she opened them again, she found herself gazing up into the face of a stranger, a face that momentarily took her breath away.

It was a noble face, with its firm, square jaw, high forehead and steely grey eyes under thick, well-shaped brows. Dark hair lightly flecked with grey was swept back and waved in careless disarray to just above the collar of his jacket. The mouth was strong, the lips disturbingly sensual. The man had been gazing absently out of the window, but upon hearing the sound of her moan, had returned to stand by the settee. He now stood gazing down at her, his eyes frankly curious.

"You're quite safe now," he informed her directly. "Your... fellow traveller has taken himself off."

The words were spoken in a refined voice, and while the message itself was comforting, the stranger's deep, mellifluous tones exerted an even stronger calming effect upon Emma's nerves. She continued to gaze up at him, a mixture of confusion and gratitude visible in her violet eyes.

Yes, she remembered him now. Though she had only caught a quick glimpse of him when he had burst into the room, Emma knew he was the man who had rescued her from Mr. Braithwaite's unwelcome advances, the man whose face she had seen just before she had lost consciousness. But how had he come to be there, Emma wondered fleetingly. How had he known that she needed assistance, if the sounds of her struggles were muffled by the thick, soundproof walls?

Abruptly aware that she had been staring at him far longer than was polite, Emma hastily lowered her eyes and felt the colour creep up into her cheeks. She was fully cognizant of the fact that they were alone and that, as a properly reared young lady, she should leave the room at once. But somehow, the thought of doing so without learning more about her mysterious rescuer seemed both ungrateful and vaguely ill-mannered. Consequently, her gaze returned to the man who stood watching her. She noted that while he was casually attired, there could be no doubt as to the quality of his garb. The buckskin breeches which fit smoothly into polished black top-boots looked to have been cut by the finest tailor, and his rust-coloured jacket, open to reveal a snowy-white shirt and skilfully arranged neckcloth only slightly disarrayed, fit his lithe, muscular body to perfection. His attire had more than a touch of Town polish, yet there was nothing even remotely dandified or effeminate about this country gentleman!

Emma, aware that she had been staring again, hastily averted her gaze, chiding herself for her own silliness. She was acting like some starry-eyed schoolgirl rather than the mature young lady she was.

"I owe you everything, sir," she said quietly and with as much dignity as she could muster under the circumstances. "But for your timely intervention, I daresay I should have been ruined. Even now, I fear my reputation is damaged quite beyond repair."

Recognizing that the girl was sufficiently recovered to converse, the man pulled up a chair and sat down. He watched her for a moment, an unfathomable expression in his clear, grey eyes. "What is your name, child?"

Emma bit her lip. At nineteen, she was hardly a child, and the fact that this handsome stranger persisted in addressing her as one disturbed her. "Emma...sir. Emma Harding. And you are...?"

"Tristan Landover," the man informed her after a brief hesitation. "And what, Miss Harding," he probed, "were you doing alone in here with a man?"

His voice was surprisingly gentle, yet Emma detected the note of censure in his tone. "I...that is, he...offered to get me some...refreshment."

"'He,' being?" Tristan enquired.

"Mr. Braithwaite. A passenger on the coach."

"I see. And were you travelling with this Braithwaite?"

"No, indeed I was not!" Emma replied quickly, her cheeks blushing crimson at the very idea. "Until this morning, Mr. Braithwaite was a complete stranger to me. He introduced himself to me shortly after we set off from Brighton."

"I see. Then why did you come in here with him?"

Emma flushed under the intensity of his gaze. "He...offered to procure a glass of lemon water for me. I was so very thirsty, and we still had such a long way to go that I agreed to let him...escort me inside."

"Yes, I saw you come in." Tristan nodded briefly.

Emma's eyes opened wide. "You did?"

"Mmm. Initially I assumed you to be a married couple, given the fact that you were travelling without benefit of a maid, and that you did not object when the serving wench brought you back here."

Tristan saw the magnificent eyes cloud over. "Mr. Braithwaite asked the innkeeper for a...more select area in which to partake of some refreshments," Emma explained, feeling more foolish by the moment. "He seemed so very considerate. I really did not expect him to behave in such a reprehensible manner."

"Pity you did not," the man said narrowly. He glanced at the girl, noticing that her smooth white hands were trembling again.

"Please understand, Mr. Landover," Emma began, desperately wanting him to understand. "I do not normally speak to strangers, especially gentlemen. My aunt has warned me time beyond measure that it can lead to...misunderstandings."

Tristan quickly turned away to hide his smile, all the while wondering what manner of relation would allow such a beautiful young girl to travel unescorted in a public coach. It was little wonder that she had been molested. It would have surprised him more had she not been.

There was no doubt that she was a diamond of the first water, with that perfect face and those amazing eyes. And she obviously came from a good family. The sky blue travelling gown, though not styled in the crack of fashion, was nevertheless cut of good material and bespoke quality. As did her manner of speaking and her general air of refinement. And while he would not have guessed the girl to be any more than seventeen, the curves outlined by her becoming carriage dress were already alluring in the extreme. So much so that Tristan had a sudden, inexplicable desire to see her dressed in fine silks and satins, certain that she would set the ton on its ear.

"So, Miss Emma Harding," Tristan continued brusquely, resolutely putting such frivolous thoughts aside, "now that we have established that you were not travelling with Mr. Braithwaite, perhaps you would be good enough to tell me where you *were* going. And why," he added, his voice purposely stern, "you were travelling there unchaperoned."

Emma felt the warmth creep into her cheeks again and quickly shook her head. "I am—that is, I was on my way to stay with friends in London. And the reason that I am alone is by way of necessity rather than by choice. I do not make a habit of travelling alone, Mr. Landover. Indeed, beyond an occasional shopping trip to Brighton, I travel very little indeed. But this was...is a special case," Emma explained, her eyes pleading. "My very dear friend is getting married in a few weeks, and invited me to come to stay with her. Naturally, I wanted to go, and advised her that I would if I could secure my aunt's permission."

"Which you obviously did," Tristan ventured.

Emma nodded. "Yes. Aunt Georgina felt it would be a bit of a holiday."

"I see," Tristan said, his disapproval evident. "And her idea of a holiday was to send you off to London by public coach without so much as a maid for company?"

Emma quickly shook her head, her smile fading ever so slightly. "You must not judge my aunt so harshly, Mr. Landover. Our circumstances are not all that we might wish them to be. Our own carriage is hardly suitable for travelling outside our village, and even if it were, we do not have the luxury of a spare set of hands," Emma explained, her voice dropping away.

"But surely there was someone from a neighbouring house who could have driven you?" Tristan persisted more gently. "Or the daughter of a friend who might have accompanied you—"

"I saw no need to impose on the generosity of others, sir," Emma interrupted him, her eyes flashing proudly. "I am nineteen years of age and quite capable of travelling on my own. Nor would I consider taking someone away from work which must be done merely to afford me the pleasure of a stay in London! I would rather remain at home!"

Despite her assurances to the contrary, Emma knew how feeble the excuse sounded, even to her own ears. No matter what she said, Emma knew that no lady of Quality would travel without an abigail. It just wasn't done. Witness her present state: she hadn't even been able to get halfway to London without encountering trouble. No wonder her aunt had been so upset by her stubborn insistence that she go to London alone. Now she understood why.

Emma sighed, and the sound of it did the strangest things to Tristan's resolve. He had been fully prepared, in light of her flimsy explanation, to give her a proper set-down for her actions, pointing out that she had been both irresponsible and foolish in choosing to travel to London on her own. But now, as he surveyed the downcast face which followed her brief, momentary flash of spirit, Tristan hesitated.

Nineteen, he reflected silently. *A mere girl*—a regular Bath miss. Yet, it was as much as he could do not to reach out and pull that warm, slender body into his arms and hold her close to his chest, murmuring assurances that everything would be all right.

If the truth were known, Tristan was astonished by the intensity of his attraction towards Emma. He found his sudden, unexpected desire to protect her a new and unsettling experience. Previously, he had viewed females with the practised eye of a man well used to taking his pleasures where he wished. He was known to be a skilled lover, and being both exceedingly attractive and financially well placed, never lacked for willing partners. He was said to be very selective of the ladies he chose to place under his protection, and was sought after by single and married women alike, and though he preferred not to involve himself with married ladies, on the one occasion he had been persuaded to do so, it was with the knowledge that his partner could be relied upon to be the very soul of discretion. It was for this reason that Tristan had been able to enjoy an exclusive and mutually satisfying relationship with Lady Archer for a number of months now, his activities having gone almost unnoticed by the sharp, ever-watchful eyes of the ton.

It was this very complacency, however, which now gave the marquis such cause for concern as he contemplated his inexplicable feelings towards the young and charming Miss Emma Harding.

When Lord Chadwick, seated unobtrusively at a table in the corner of the crowded posting inn, had initially seen the young man and woman come in, he had quite naturally assumed them to be husband and wife. It was incomprehensible to him that a lady possessed of that degree of beauty would be travelling alone with a man who was not her husband or, at very least, her betrothed. In so thinking, Chadwick had paid them no further mind when they were shown into what was clearly a private parlour.

But when the amply bosomed barmaid had returned to the pub, winking lewdly at the innkeeper and voicing remarks that, even to Chadwick's experienced ears, were hardly in keeping with the honourable estate of marriage, he had begun to suspect that all was not well. His fears had been confirmed when he overheard some of their whispered conversation, and realized that the young couple were not married at all.

When Mabel had returned to his table to resume her flirtation, Chadwick had taken advantage of her eagerness and cajoled her into telling him what was going on in the back room. Mabel had been only too happy to impart the details of what was no doubt taking place even as they spoke.

With his darkest suspicions confirmed, Chadwick had wasted little time in reacting. Bursting into the room, he had not been surprised by the scene which had met his eyes, nor had he mistaken the genuine fear he had glimpsed on the young girl's face. Whatever her reasons for accompanying the gentleman into the parlour in the first place, Chadwick knew that she was regretting them now.

The man, having been caught off guard by Chadwick, and not being equal to a man who had spent a good deal of time at Gentleman Jackson's rooms in Bond Street, had been quick to fall. And Chadwick, turning to view the young lady before she toppled forward in a swoon, had been startled to discover that she was little more than a child. A beautiful, winsome child who had touched his heart in a way no London beauty had ever been able to.

When Braithwaite had regained his senses, he had all but run from the room, anxious to escape before more damage could befall him. Ignoring him, Chadwick had picked Emma up and laid her gently on the settee, quickly ascertaining that she was unharmed. She was so beautiful, he thought, with her fair complexion against the burnished gold of her hair. Her mouth reminded him of a soft pink rosebud, enticing in its perfection, while her long golden lashes lay closed against her skin, masking those incredible violet-blue eyes which had looked at him with such despair before she had fainted.

Momentarily, a flash of dark, unreasoning rage suffused Chadwick's face at the thought of this delicate flower being molested. The man should be shot, the marquis growled inwardly, and he was suddenly glad he had thrashed him. Maybe that would make him think twice before bothering a young lady again.

When the girl had finally regained consciousness, Chadwick had been prepared for hysteria and weeping—the sort of behaviour he would have expected in a female of Emma's age. But again she had surprised him. She had acted with a quiet dignity totally at odds with her youthful appearance. And Tristan Edward Landover, Marquis of Chadwick, reputed rake and confirmed bachelor, had fallen hopelessly and quite irrevocably in love, then and there.

Blissfully unaware of any of this, Emma sighed, and slowly stood up, taking care that her legs were strong enough to support her. When she smiled, she was dismayed to feel her lips tremble ever so slightly. "I don't know that I shall ever have the words to thank you, Mr. Landover, but please believe me when I say that I am forever in your debt."

"Your thanks are not necessary, Miss Harding. I only hope," Chadwick replied, "that it has taught you a lesson."

Emma managed a shaky laugh. "Do not fear, good sir, I have learned it well and truly. Although it does not alter my present circumstances," she mused, gazing at him ruefully. "I fear I must continue my journey to Town unescorted, and to that end should return to the coach before it leaves. My friends are expecting me in London this afternoon."

Emma saw him glance towards the window. "I am sorry to disappoint you, Miss Harding, but you will not reach London today by that conveyance," the marquis informed her slowly. "The coach has already departed."

"It's ... gone?" Emma said in a choked voice, her stomach turning over. "But it can't have. I'm supposed to be on it. My aunt paid for passage through to London. Surely it would not have left without me."

"I'm afraid it did exactly that," Chadwick said gently. "About fifteen minutes ago. No doubt the coachman didn't even realize you were not aboard."

As she heard Chadwick's pronouncement, Emma's face fell, and she sank back down onto the settee in a state of abject despair. How was she to get to London now? Granted, there were other coaches making for the city today, but now at the height of the Season, it was doubtful there would be room available for her. She could try getting a message to her aunt, of course, but there was no telling how long that would take. And under no circumstances could she consider staying alone at the inn overnight.

And what about poor Lady Margaret awaiting her in London? Emma thought, well aware of her friend's tendency to worry. How would she react when the coach arrived and Emma was not on it?

"Oh, dear, my valise!" Emma cried, glancing at Tristan in dismay. "All of my belongings were in that bag!"

Chadwick looked thoughtful for a moment. "It is just possible that one of the other passengers may have seen to its removal. I shall make enquiries. But you may have to accept the fact that your valise has carried on to London without you."

Emma stared at him mutely. This, on top of everything else, was just too much, and despite the fact that she was not normally given to such feminine weaknesses as crying, Emma was mortified to feel tears running slowly down her cheeks. She had so desperately wanted to go up to London—to be with her friend and to try to forget all the unhappiness of the past year. Instead, she found herself stranded at a posting inn in the middle of the countryside, with her reputation in tatters and no likely prospect of getting anywhere today. Added to that was the mortification of allowing a complete stranger to see her in this state. It was all just too horrible!

Emma fumbled for her reticule, trying to disguise her tears, when a large white handkerchief suddenly appeared under her nose. Glancing up, she saw Chadwick watching her, his eyes infinitely tender, a fact which only added to her weepiness.

"Th-thank you," Emma whispered, reluctantly accepting the square of fine lawn and dabbing her eyes. "I don't normally cry. It's just that I so wanted to get to London, and now I really don't know how I am to get there. Or how I'm going to get home."

Chadwick watched her, aware once more of an almost overwhelming desire to pull her into his arms and tell her that everything was going to be all right. She was so young, so beautiful. And right now, there was no doubt in his mind that without his help, she was very, very alone.

Abruptly, the marquis rose and made his way slowly back to the window. "Miss Harding, it just so happens that I, too, am bound for London," Chadwick heard himself say.

"One of my horses threw a shoe, and we stopped here to have it attended to. I am merely awaiting the blacksmith's word that it is repaired before we are under way again." He paused briefly. "You are more than welcome to come with me, if you would care to."

Emma's head shot up, her red-rimmed eyes widening in amazement. The gentleman was offering to take her to London? But why? He didn't even know her. And no doubt, he thought her a ninnyhammer for travelling alone and unchaperoned, not to mention dreadfully imprudent for having allowed herself to be found in a room alone with a man, fighting for her virtue.

"It is . . . very good of you, Mr. Landover, but I really cannot accept," Emma demurred, wondering even as she said it what she was going to do if she did not accept his offer.

The marquis, aware that she could not possibly stay here any longer, and being equally aware that he did not want her to, tried again. "Miss Harding, I understand your concern at travelling with a stranger, but consider your alternatives," he pointed out pragmatically. "You cannot stay here another night without some kind of suitable chaperonage. The landlord has already proved himself totally untrustworthy."

Emma nodded, closing her eyes to shut out the memory. "Yes, I know that, but—"

"And you are travelling to London at a very busy time. I don't think I need point out that if you are unable to secure passage on another coach today, you will be obliged to stay here for the night."

"My lord, truly, I . . . I don't know . . . what to say," Emma stammered, clearly at a loss. "I could try to reach my aunt, of course—"

"You could." Chadwick nodded slowly. "And I would be more than happy to help you. But even then, it's not likely that she will be able to send someone to fetch you in time to prevent your having to spend the night here. *If,*" he stressed, "she is able to find anyone at all. After all, you yourself told me how shorthanded she was."

Emma nodded, a fresh wave of despair washing over her. Everything Tristan said made perfect sense. If she didn't leave with him, she was very likely to be stranded here for at least one more day. Yet, even knowing that, dared she go with him? It hardly seemed the thing to do. After all, look where trusting a stranger had landed her in the first place! But on the other hand, what alternative *did* she have?

Lord Chadwick, assuming Emma's hesitation stemmed from her reluctance to travel alone with him, hastened to reassure her. "Miss Harding, if you are anxious about travelling alone with a stranger, set your mind at rest. You have my word as a gentleman that you will be safe. I shall ride up next to my coachman, and you shall have the privacy of the compartment to yourself. Upon our arrival in London, I shall take you directly to the house of your friends. Further, if you wish to partake of refreshments before we leave, I shall secure them for you myself now."

The words were so earnestly spoken that Emma felt some of her reluctance dissolve. For some unknown reason, she trusted this man—completely. She didn't really know why, but she knew for a certainty that he would not harm her.

"Mr. Landover, I do not know how to thank you," Emma whispered softly. "First for what you did . . . before, and now for offering to take me to London. I am truly in your debt."

"You owe me nothing, Miss Harding," Chadwick replied quietly. "In fact, you will be doing me a great favour by agreeing to come with me."

"Oh?" Emma replied, startled. "How so?"

"Because if I were to leave you here now, knowing that you would be forced to fend for yourself, I should rob myself of any kind of peace of mind I might hope to have for years to come," he replied with a teasing smile. "And since I already have sufficient annoyances in my life, I surely do not wish to add to them!"

The explanation was so unexpected, and the look in his eyes so tragic, that Emma reluctantly felt a gurgle of laughter bubble up in her throat. "Then far be it from me to evoke such feelings, sir," she replied in mock solemnity, her bright eyes sparkling. "When you put it like that, I see that I have scarcely any choice but to accompany you to London."

Her words brought an unexpected lightness to the marquis's features, and he quickly turned his head away to hide a smile. She was so young, he thought absently. So young and trusting. Yet there was a dignity about her that was strangely poignant. As though she had been pushed out of childhood before the proper time. "Then, shall we go, Miss Harding?" Tristan said, rising and extending his hand.

Emma glanced at the hand opened to her, and tentatively put her own in it, utterly unprepared for the tremor which coursed through her slender body as their fingers touched. Her eyes lifted innocently to his, wondering if he had felt it.

The marquis, however, seemed not to have noticed anything untoward and bent to retrieve her reticule from where it had fallen onto the floor. He escorted her to the door and then through into the taproom, shielding her with his body when he felt her begin to tremble. He threw some coins on the bar and glared at the innkeeper, aware by the way the man flinched that he knew his chicanery had been discovered. Once outside, Chadwick took his coat and draped it protectively about Emma's shoulders, his manner almost brusque. He could not allow her to see how shaken he was by the simple touch of her hand.

"Wait here," he ordered, pulling the collar up over her shining hair. "And speak to no one. Do you understand?"

Emma nodded, too breathless to speak. She watched him stride away, admiring the long, well-shaped legs in the close-fitting breeches, and the broad shoulders outlined so advantageously in the well-cut jacket. He was tall and proud, this stranger who had suddenly become so important in her life. He commanded respect, and Emma was not surprised to see him return within the space of five minutes, a smile of satisfaction on his handsome features. "The carriage will be brought round directly. The blacksmith was just finishing. And I have good news. It seems someone did remove your valise from the stage before it departed. I have given instructions that it be placed on board my own carriage. Now, before we set off, is there anything you would like?"

Only to be with you, Emma mused, astonished by the temerity of her thoughts. But of this she said nothing. "I should like a glass of lemon water, if it is not too much bother. And then to be away from this place, and on our way to London again."

Tristan seemed pleased by her answer. "Then so we shall, little one."

Within minutes, an impressive Town coach drawn by four perfectly matched greys pulled up in front of them. Emma, observing the coat of arms emblazoned on the doors, glanced up at Tristan in surprise. It seemed there were a great many things she did not know about this stranger who only identified himself as Tristan Landover.

After procuring Emma's glass of lemon water, and then assisting her to board, Chadwick, true to his word, swung up beside his coachman and stayed there for the duration of the journey. The horses, refreshed by their brief stop, set off at a lively pace, and as Emma watched the inn recede into the distance, she sat back against the luxurious velvet seat and breathed a heartfelt sigh of relief.

Thank goodness she was on her way to London again, with her reputation still intact! Emma knew she would have some explaining to do when she reached Town, given the fact that she would be arriving late and in a stranger's coach, but that was nothing compared to what she might have had to explain, Emma reflected ruefully. And if she had to arrive with a stranger, at least it was with a very impressive, and obviously titled, one at that!

THE CARRIAGE made excellent time. It was a pleasure to ride in Tristan's well-sprung, comfortable equipage and, as they drew nearer Town, Emma sat forward, straining to catch a glimpse of the city where she had first drawn breath.

London, she thought fondly, feeling a frisson of excitement run up her spine. It was such a lovely city, with its beautiful architecture and tempting shops. There was always so much to do, especially during the Season! There need never be a moment spent doing anything that was not pleasurable. And now that she was out of mourning, those pleasures were available to her once more. And like any pretty young girl, she was looking forward to them immeasurably!

Briefly, Emma experienced a pang of guilt as her thoughts returned to her aunt. Dear Aunt Georgina. She was so dreadfully short-handed on the farm right now. The growing season was off to a good start, but reliable farm hands and skilled workers were in short supply. Jeb, one of the fine, strapping young sons from the farm next door, had offered to lend a hand when he could, but Emma knew there was far more work than even Jeb could manage. She also knew it was largely because of his attraction to her that he had offered. If only they'd had the money to hire on a few extra workers, Emma thought sadly. There were plenty of good men to be had, but they couldn't be expected to work for nothing. Not this year, when they had their choice of farms.

For all their impecunious circumstances, however, Aunt Georgina had refused to countenance Emma's not going up to London for Lady Margaret's wedding. She had assured her niece that come what may, the farm would be maintained, pointing out that Jeb could easily take over the work of two of her smaller lads, freeing them to perform chores around the house. Under no circumstances was Emma going to miss the excitement of a London Season again!

Even the matter of suitable attire had been taken care of. Lady Margaret had written to say that there was to be a shopping excursion shortly after Emma's arrival to procure a gown for her for the wedding, as well as to outfit her with the other necessary accoutrements for any young lady taking her place in Society.

Emma, of course, had taken silent exception to that, knowing that there was precious little money for such extravagances as silk gowns and fancy slippers. She had enough money set aside for perhaps one or two day dresses which could be used when she returned to the country, but she knew her funds would not run to the purchase of an elaborate ball gown. Besides, she would hardly need such things once she was back on the farm. And if she did, she could no doubt make some slight alterations to the gown she would be wearing in Lady Margaret's wedding. She was not unskilled with a needle, and she knew that by changing a few of the ribbons, and adding some lace, she could alter it sufficiently to make it look like an entirely new gown!

When the carriage suddenly slowed and came to a halt, Emma looked up in alarm, wondering at the reason for the stop. She knew they were still on the outskirts of the city, and could only hope they had not encountered some manner of trouble. She was about to call out when the door opened and Chadwick smiled in at her.

"Is everything all right, Miss Harding?" he asked solicitously. He saw the sparkle in her eyes, and the tremulous smile which formed upon her lips.

"Everything is fine, my lord," Emma said, suddenly fearing that she may have been in error merely calling this man *Mr.* Landover. "But why have we stopped?"

"It occurred to me that I need the address of your friend's home so that we might take the correct route," Chadwick explained. "Since the London stage will already have arrived, I see little point in taking you to the station. No doubt whoever was awaiting your arrival will have left. Therefore, with your permission, I shall take you directly to your final destination."

Grateful for his generous offer, Emma smiled, and felt her heart begin to pound. Perhaps if Tristan knew where she was staying, he would call upon her once she was settled. "But of course," Emma replied. "I shall be staying with a Lady Hatton in Eaton Square."

For a moment, Emma wondered if Tristan had heard her. He stood stock-still, his face unmoving, his eyes glued to her face. Then, ever so slowly, he began to smile. "You wouldn't by any chance be here for the wedding of Lady Margaret Glendenning, would you, Miss Harding?" he ventured.

Astonished that his guess should prove so remarkably accurate, Emma blinked and nodded. "Why, yes. Lady Margaret is a dear friend of mine. It is she who has invited me to be one of her bridesmaids."

"What a remarkable coincidence." Chadwick chuckled. "It seems that we are intent on the same purpose, Miss Harding. I, too, seek the house of Lady Hatton."

Hardly able to believe her good fortune, Emma stifled her gasp of pleasure and strove to maintain a calm appearance. "I can scarce credit such a coincidence, my lord. Do you claim acquaintance with Lady Hatton or Lady Margaret?"

This time, the marquis could not contain his laughter. "I am well acquainted with both estimable ladies, Miss Harding, and as such, I think it is time I made a more complete introduction. I am, as I told you, Tristan Edward Landover. However," he continued, dark eyes flashing, "as the eighth Marquis of Chadwick, I am also Lady Margaret Glendenning's cousin!"

CHAPTER THREE

THE HONOURABLE Bertrand Rowsbottom sat atop his curricle and grumbled all the way back to Eaton Square. Having set off from his club in sufficient time to retrieve Miss Harding, Bertie had been obliged to cut short a very enjoyable dinner he had been having with his old friend, Bunker Didlington. Bunker had been regaling him with tales of the lavish expenditures and outrageous goings-on of the Prince Regent down at Brighton, and Bertie, while not enjoying as close a relationship to the Regent as Lady Margaret's cousin, Lord Chadwick, nevertheless enjoyed being able to say that he and the Prince had exchanged pleasantries the last time Bertie had been down on the coast.

It was also during this agreeable conversation in the comfortably masculine ambience of White's that Bunker let slip the latest on-dit regarding the illustrious Marquis of Chadwick.

"It's rumoured, you know," Bunker said with the air of one about to impart a secret of monumental importance, "that a certain celebrated marquis, who shall go unnamed given the fact that he shall soon be related to one of us, has been seen keeping company with the very charming Lady Archer. And that Lady Archer was observed to be sporting a rather glorious diamond-and-emerald parure at Lady Sefton's assembly, which, by all accounts," he added smugly, "was said to be a gift from a devoted admirer."

Bertrand, who in all fairness was reluctant to entertain gossip regarding his fiancée's cousin, shook his head and

took a sip of the very fine French cognac Bunker had felt
disposed to order. "Bunker, you of all people should know
better than to discuss Chadwick's female companions so
loosely. You've lost more money betting on who the marquis's eventual wife will be than the rest of us put together.
I thought you would have learned your lesson by now."

"Dear boy, did you not hear what I said?" Bunker
drawled. "I said Chadwick was seeing Lady Archer. Not
some ballet dancer from Covent Garden. The eminently respectable and most definitely *married* Lady Archer."

"Yes, I heard you," Bertie retorted, giving his friend the
benefit of a telling look. "But what of it? What woman in
her right mind would not take Chadwick over Archer?
Granted, Archer's rich as a nabob, but as a gentleman, he's
hardly in Chadwick's class. Nor, I hasten to point out, has
he ever been the most faithful of husbands himself. His ex-
ploits with pretty young actresses in particular have been
very well publicized."

"Tut, tut, you're missing the point, old man," Bunker
objected, shaking his head. "Chadwick is associating with
a *married* woman. Married! And we all know how fastidi-
ous Chadwick is. He doesn't normally entangle himself with
married ladies. Goodness knows, he's turned down offers
from enough of them," Bunker added, a trifle enviously.

Bertrand sipped his drink, trying to appear unconcerned
by this latest bit of gossip. In truth, he was surprised to hear
rumours of a liaison between Chadwick and Jane Archer,
who was regarded as both a beautiful and refined woman.
That she would show an interest in Chadwick was hardly
surprising, given the fact that her husband's peccadillos
were so well known. But knowing that Chadwick, who was
reputed to be discreet in his liaisons, was actually dallying
with a married woman did not sit well with Bertrand . . . not
well at all. He could only imagine how shocked Margaret
would be if she were to hear such tittle-tattle. And Bertrand

knew it was very likely that she would. There were more than enough malicious chatterboxes about Town who would delight in imparting such a juicy piece of gossip regarding the Marquis of Chadwick to his adoring cousin, given half the chance.

At this point, Bertie, who had been diligently watching the clock, abruptly ended the discussion by rising. "Sorry, Bunker, must run."

"What? So soon?" Bunker protested. "But I was just getting to the good part."

"I'm afraid you'll have to save it," Bertie advised him good-naturedly. "I have to meet someone at the station."

"Eh? And who might that be?"

"Miss Emma Harding," Bertie informed him, downing the rest of his cognac and shrugging himself into his coat. "She's coming up for the wedding. Old friend of Margaret's."

"Harding. Emma Harding. Oh, yes, I remember her now," Bunker said, his features brightening. "Quite a diamond, as I recall. Staying for the Season, is she?"

"If Margaret has any say in it, yes." Bertrand laughed fondly. "My fiancée is determined that Miss Harding shall not return to the country without a husband in tow."

"Well, I shouldn't think that would prove too difficult an undertaking." Bunker chuckled agreeably. "Tempting little chit, Miss Harding. Had the opportunity of standing up with her once or twice myself. Amazing eyes, as I recall. Haven't seen much of her in the last year, though."

Bertrand shook his head. "She has been in mourning since her father died. Lives with an aunt down in Sussex."

"I see. Well, perhaps I shall take the opportunity of calling once she has had a chance to settle."

Assuring his friend that there would be ample opportunity to do so before the wedding, Bertrand rose and posted off to meet Miss Harding. Fortunately, the traffic was light, and he arrived in plenty of time to meet the appointed stage. Lightly springing down from his seat, Bertrand handed the ribbons to his tiger with instructions to "walk them," and then made his way to the door of the White Horse Inn. When satisfied that Miss Harding had not surprised him by arriving early, Bertrand stationed himself just outside the door, and waited for the next coach to arrive. When it did, filled to overflowing with passengers, he watched in anticipation as each person alighted, expecting at any moment to see the daintily shod foot of Miss Harding set forth from within.

Surprisingly, however, it did not. The last person stepped off the coach with no sign of his charge. Not even a valise! And as the next coach arrived, Bertrand watched again, hoping to spy the young lady he had been sent to collect. But this, too, proved to be in vain.

Strange, Bertrand reflected, trying to come up with a logical explanation as to why Miss Harding was not on any of the coaches. He knew Margaret had not given him the wrong day. He, too, had read Miss Harding's letter, wherein she had specifically said it was today she was coming, and upon which stage she would be arriving.

So what then, he mused. Could she have missed the coach at her end? Conceivable, Bertrand admitted, though to his way of thinking, highly unlikely. He couldn't imagine anyone being careless enough to miss a departure time. Punctual himself, he blessed everyone else with a similar partiality to time.

No, there had to be some other reason, Bertie concluded. The only problem was that for the life of him, he couldn't think of what it might be. And now he had to return to Eaton Square and try to explain to his fiancée, her sister and her aunt, the whereabouts of Miss Emma Harding, who, by all rights, should have been sitting next to him at this moment!

The curricle drew to a halt in front of the Hattons' elegant Eaton Square residence, and it was not without some trepidation that Bertie climbed down. After handing his hat and gloves to Higgins, Bertrand made his way to the drawing-room. There he found Margaret, her younger sister, Elizabeth, and Lady Hatton all anxiously awaiting his arrival.

"Bertie, you're back!"

Lady Margaret had risen at his entrance and rushed forward, her face wreathed in smiles. But when Bertie walked into the room alone and closed the door behind him, all three ladies glanced at him in consternation.

"But where's Emma?" Lady Margaret asked as Bertie sank down into the chair.

"That's a very good question, my dear," Bertrand replied, shaking his head. "And one for which I do not have an answer. Miss Harding was not on the stage."

"Not on the stage! But that's impossible!" Lady Margaret squeaked. "She must have been. Are you sure you met the right one?"

"I met the appointed one and the one after that," Bertie said patiently. "I saw the— Ah, yes, brandy if you don't mind, Higgins," Bertie said in answer to the butler's silent question. "I think I rather need one."

Lady Margaret waited until Higgins had returned with her fiancé's drink and then withdrawn before resuming her interrogation. "You saw the what, Bertie?" she prompted.

"I saw the stage that Miss Harding was supposed to be on arrive, and I watched each and every passenger get off. Miss Harding was not one of them. I then stayed and watched the next stage come in, with the same result."

"But this doesn't make sense, Bertrand," Lady Margaret said, the use of his full name a sure sign that she was agitated. "Emma's letter clearly stated that she was arriving today. I know I didn't make a mistake," she added defensively.

"Calm yourself, child, no one is saying that you did," Lady Hatton said placidly. "Are we, Mr. Rowsbottom?"

"Not in the least," Bertie replied in a conciliatory tone. "I read Miss Harding's letter too, Margaret, and it clearly stated that she would be arriving today and upon which stage she was booked."

"Then what could have happened to her?" Lady Margaret cried, truly beginning to worry about her friend. "I know she would have sent word if there had been a change in plans. Emma is not the sort to leave loose ends."

"Perhaps she suddenly took ill, Meggie," Lady Elizabeth said helpfully. "She does live by the seaside, after all."

"Oh, Lizzie, what a silly notion," Lady Margaret chastised her sister. "What does Emma's living by the coast have to do with making her ill? If anything, the sea air is reputed to be quite restorative. Why do you think the Prince Regent spends so much time down there?"

"I am sure I do not know," Lady Elizabeth replied innocently. "But I have oft heard cousin Amelia say that *she* feels quite indisposed when she goes down to the seaside. And she says she never gets sick in Town."

"The only reason Amelia gets sick when she goes to Brighton is because she eats too much," Lady Hatton pointed out bluntly. "She gets it into her head that she is on holiday, and takes to eating whatever is put in front of her. She just likes to blame it on the sea air, that's all." Lady Hatton's mouth twisted sardonically. "I hardly think Miss Harding would suffer from a similar overindulgence."

The sound of a carriage drawing to a halt outside the front gates momentarily halted the flow of conversation, and hurrying towards the window, Lady Margaret peered out, her nose pressed against the glass. Lady Hatton, observing her niece's characteristic impulsiveness with resigned forbearance, shook her head and tutted audibly. "Margaret, how many times must I remind you that a lady does not show such marked eagerness at the sound of a carriage arriving. You must wait for Higgins to announce—" Lady Hatton recited, only to be interrupted by Lady Margaret's equally unladylike squeal of delight.

"It's Tristan. He's here! Oh, how marvellous—I hadn't expected him for days yet," Lady Margaret cried, clapping her hands. "But how strange," she murmured, her smooth forehead creasing. "I wonder why he's riding up front with his coachman? He doesn't usually—"

Lady Margaret halted abruptly as she watched her cousin hand over the ribbons and then lithely swing down. She watched him open the door and extend his hand to someone within. "Gracious," Lady Margaret gasped, "I do believe Tristan has brought someone with him. And if I am not mistaken, it appears to be a lady!"

"A lady!" Bertie echoed in surprise, wondering for a fleeting moment if it might be Lady Archer. "By Jove!"

"Lizzie, Auntie, do come and look!" Lady Margaret beseeched them. "I am sure it is a female, and I'm in a positive fidge to find out who it is!"

Lady Elizabeth, followed more circumspectly by Lady Hatton, joined Lady Margaret at the window and peered through the glass, all three trying to make out the identity of Tristan's companion. Given the slight stature of the person, it seemed that a lady had indeed stepped out of the coach. But dressed as she was in a rather voluminous cloak with the hood drawn closely about her face, it was impossible to make out her features.

It wasn't until Higgins opened the door and Lady Margaret was able to get a better look at the unexpected visitor that her look of curiosity gave way to one of surprised delight.

"Emma!" she cried. "Oh, Emma, I am so very glad to see you. We've been so dreadfully worried. Where have you been? Why weren't you on the coach? And Tristan, dearest!" Lady Margaret said, turning before Emma had a chance to reply. "We weren't expecting you for another week. What are you doing here so early? And how on earth did the two of you come to arrive together?"

Suitably bowled over by Lady Margaret's enthusiasm, Emma and the marquis stepped in through the front door and exchanged knowing smiles.

"It's a long story, puss," Chadwick answered, grinning affectionately. "And one with which I'm sure Miss Harding will be only too happy to regale you another time. Good evening, Higgins," the marquis said, turning to greet the largely ignored butler. "I hope my somewhat early arrival will not cause you any undue inconvenience."

"Not at all, my lord," that unflappable fellow said, taking the marquis's hat, cloak and gloves with admirable composure. "Mrs. Hart made your room up fresh this morning. I trust you had a good journey, my lord?"

"An interesting one, I'll wager," Bertie observed, stepping forward to shake the marquis's hand. "Chadwick."

For once, Bertrand's presence did not irritate him unduly, and Chadwick was able to smile back with marked civility. "You might say that, Rowsbottom," he replied, glancing at Emma. "You might indeed say that."

Emma, bashfully returning the smile, was suddenly filled with a wondrous sense of joy and relief. The journey was over. She was here at last, safe in the home of her dearest friend. And on top of it, the man who had been responsible for her safe deliverance, in more ways than one, was here with her. She couldn't possibly have been happier.

"But come along, Tristan," she heard Lady Margaret badgering. "Tell all! What are you doing here so early? And how did you come to arrive with Emma? Bertie was quite beside himself when he went down to the station to meet her and she wasn't there! We were all worried sick, weren't we, Bertie?''

"Indeed!" Bertie said, not quite sure which question he was supposed to agree with.

Emma merely smiled, however, and grasped Lady Margaret's hand. "Lord Chadwick is right, Meggie. It is a long story, and one I shall be happy to tell you—some other time." She glanced at Tristan shyly. "Let us just say that Lord Chadwick happened along at a most auspicious moment and kindly offered his assistance."

Lady Margaret glanced from her friend to her cousin, and back again. "Now that is an intriguing statement! I sense a mystery here."

"No mystery about it, puss," Chadwick explained lightly. "And just so you don't pester Miss Harding about it all night, which I can see is very like to happen," he continued with a grin, "let me set your mind at rest by saying that Miss Harding simply missed getting back on her coach when it stopped to pick up passengers. I've seen it happen before. The coachman is anxious to be off and neglects to attend to who gets on and who gets off. And, as I also happened to be at the inn having one of my horses reshod and eventually discovered Miss Harding's plight, it seemed the perfect solution."

By this time, they had reached the drawing-room. Higgins reappeared shortly with some light refreshments, while Emma enjoyed an enthusiastic reunion with Lady Hatton and Elizabeth, commenting on how well they both looked.

Turning in the direction of Lady Margaret, Emma then extended her hand to the gentleman who stood quietly by her side. "I must officially extend my felicitations to you, Mr. Rowsbottom," Emma said with a warm smile. "It has been a while since last we met, and you and Lady Margaret were not officially engaged at the time."

"No, we were not, Miss Harding," Bertie replied earnestly, bowing over her hand. "And indeed, the circumstances of our meeting were not the most pleasant. It is gratifying to see you looking so much happier now, and I welcome the opportunity of our getting to know each other better now that you are here."

Emma laughed, the sound of it light and charming. "I fear I have the advantage in that regard, Mr. Rowsbottom. Lady Margaret has told me so much about you that I feel I already know you quite well."

"Really? Oh dear." Bertie chuckled. "I confess I've oft wondered at the nature of the things which fly back and forth between young ladies."

"Rest assured they were only the most admirable of sentiments, Mr. Rowsbottom," Emma replied, laughing.

Lady Margaret, watching them, pulled a face. "As if I would say anything unkind about you, dearest," she teased her fiancé playfully.

Chadwick, standing by the fireplace, his arm resting on the mantel, slowly raised his glass and took a sip of port, studying Emma over the rim. Until now, he hadn't seen the sparkling side of her nature. The circumstances of their meeting had been far from frivolous, and as he had spent the entire journey on top of the carriage, he had had no chance to converse with her.

But now, as he watched, Chadwick caught a glimpse of the real Emma: seeing evidence of the sparkling, vivacious girl she was. And not for the first time that day, Chadwick experienced an unexpected feeling of regret; regret that he was not a callow, bright-eyed youth eagerly awaiting what life had in store for him; regret that he could not be closer to her in so many ways; regret that he was not younger!

"Well, if the rest of you will excuse me, I shall retire to my room to clean up before dinner," Chadwick said, downing the remainder of his drink in one swallow. "I cannot speak for Miss Harding, but I for one am quite done in."

Lady Margaret abruptly set her glass down and rose guiltily. "But of course, dearest. How inconsiderate of us to keep you here talking." Impulsively, she crossed to her cousin and threw her arms about his neck. "Dear Tris," she whispered, her eyes shining. "It's so good to have you here. Thank you so very much for coming."

Tristan, surprised and not a little touched by Margaret's unexpected show of affection, brusquely returned her embrace and kissed the top of her dark, glowing hair. "You know I wouldn't have missed it, puss," he said softly.

Emma, watching the affectionate encounter between them, was surprised to find her eyes suddenly misty, and hastily glanced away. The trip must have tired her more than she had realized, Emma decided, blinking. Family scenes didn't usually affect her in such a manner.

Before leaving, Chadwick stopped to brush a kiss on his aunt's cheek. "Dinner at eight?" he asked.

"Well, of course," Lady Hatton said, as though surprised he would ask. But the softness in her eyes belied the sternness in her voice. "Though I can alter it if you like."

"What? And throw off years of tradition? I wouldn't hear of it," Chadwick replied, winking at Emma. "Eight o'clock will be fine. That will give me more than enough time to wash away any lingering traces of my journey."

"Speaking of which," Lady Margaret said, glancing now at Emma, "you must be as eager as Tristan to rest after your journey, Em. Come, I shall show you to your room. I have put you in the one next to mine. Oh, we're going to have the most wonderful time!" Lady Margaret beamed. "I can hardly believe you're finally here!"

The girls locked arms and made their way upstairs just ahead of the marquis. At the top of the stairs, Chadwick made them a gracious bow and then turned to the left and started along the corridor to what was obviously his own suite of rooms.

"Aunt Rachel always has Mrs. Hart keep Tristan's rooms ready, just in case he arrives home unexpectedly," Lady Margaret informed Emma, turning to the right. "Aunt Rachel may not show it, but she dotes on Tristan. Almost as much as he does on her. Here we are," she said, throwing open the second door and ushering Emma inside.

Emma glanced around the large, spacious room and smiled in genuine delight. The room was decorated in her favourite shade of pale lavender, the carpet and bedspread being of a slightly deeper hue. The pale-pink-and-lavender carpet picked up the colours of the room and covered nearly the entire expanse of floor. Along with a magnificent four-poster bed, the room contained an exquisite Sheraton writing desk and mirror, a love-seat upholstered in pink-and-white-striped satin, and a large dressing-table with drawers.

"The balcony looks out over the gardens," Lady Margaret informed her, indicating the door partially hidden by the curtains. "You'll see them in the morning. They're simply breathtaking right now. Aunt Rachel had the whole garden rearranged in the spring."

Emma nodded, and glanced at her friend fondly. "Everything is just lovely. Thank you, Meggie. And thank you for inviting me. I am so looking forward to the wedding. It is clear to see that love agrees with you."

Lady Margaret blushed, and giggled irrepressibly. "Oh Em, I am very happy. Even more so, now that you're here. I've missed you so much since you went down to the country," Lady Margaret informed her sincerely. "I missed sharing all the wonderful things that were happening to me."

"But you did share them with me," Emma corrected her, smiling. "Your letters were all so wonderfully descriptive that I almost felt I was right here with you. Especially at Lady Heddleston's party when Lucinda Bedley knocked over the punch-bowl.''

Lady Margaret gave a whoop of delight. "Oh, Emma, I wish you could have seen her face! Poor Lucinda went as red as a poppy. And her mother was having fits! Especially as Lord Markham just happened to be standing right there. And she hoping for a match.''

"I take it the good baron was not impressed," Emma ventured.

"I think you may safely assume so," Lady Margaret responded, laughing. "Oh, but Emma, now that you're here, we're going to have the most marvellous time. There are so many wonderful things to do. And you simply must stay here until Bertie and I return from our wedding trip to Italy. I know Aunt Rachel will be most grateful for your company. Poor dear. I daresay she shall find it dreadfully quiet after we go. And then once we return, I shall require your assistance in so many ways. You always were the organized one. Just imagine how lovely it will be, Emma. You can stay on here and come and visit us whenever you please. Oh, Emma, pray tell me that you do not intend rushing back to the country the moment I am wed.''

For a moment, Emma was silent, lost in her own private wanderings. How different they were now, Emma reflected. Her dearest friend was about to get married and set up her own house, whereas Emma was only just shedding her blacks. Dear Margaret had never had to worry about anything at all, whereas Emma, out of necessity, had been moved to worry about everything.

She knew, of course, that Margaret meant well in asking her to stay, and Emma knew that she would, at least until the wedding was over. But once it was, and Margaret and her new husband left on their wedding trip, Emma knew she would have to leave. After all, Lady Hatton would still have

Lady Elizabeth to bear her company. More important, Aunt Georgina had need of her. Dear Margaret would never be able to understand what an inconvenience it was to be poor. Emma had not realized it herself until she had found herself in just such a position.

Having once been part of a loving family, able to come and go as she pleased, and have whatever she pleased, Emma had felt the sudden lack of both with painful intensity. She had learned very quickly the meaning of frugality, recalling Aunt Georgina's admonition that frugal didn't necessarily mean stingy; it simply meant being mindful of the quality received for the money expended.

Emma liked that. It seemed so much nicer than telling people you were poor, and she had kept it in mind whenever she had been called upon to deal with the many tradespeople who had come to see her after her father had died.

Emma sighed again. Yes, she and Margaret were very different now. And given that Lady Margaret would probably be starting a family soon, their worlds would drift even further apart. What could she possibly have in common with a married woman with a husband, a home and children to care for?

"When are you going to tell me how you encountered my cousin today?" Lady Margaret said, abruptly breaking into Emma's thoughts. "La, I was that put about to see you stepping out of Tristan's carriage. How did you come to get off the stage anyway?"

Emma, preferring to forget all about her unfortunate run-in with Mr. Braithwaite, shook her head, her eyes silently pleading. "Meg, I hope you don't mind, but it has been a long day, and I really would prefer to put my journey behind me. You know I'm not the best of travellers, and now that I am here I just want to enjoy every day I have with you."

If Lady Margaret was surprised by her friend's reticence, she kept it well hidden. Like Emma, she was happy just to have her friend there, and suddenly, how she arrived or what might have happened on the way seemed unimportant.

"You're quite right, dearest," Lady Margaret said, beaming. "And that's exactly what we shall do. We have two weeks before the wedding, and we have so many things to do before then I hardly know where to start. The main thing is that you are here. Oh, and since you weren't able to bring a maid along, I have engaged one for you. Her name is Fiona and she is ever so sweet."

Emma, upon hearing this, gasped in dismay. "Never say you've done such a thing, Margaret!" she cried, horrified to think of the inconvenience it must have put everyone to. "You know that I am quite capable of managing on my own."

"Yes, I know you are," Lady Margaret replied calmly. "But this is not the country, Emma, and you are going to be very busy over the next few weeks. You will need a lady's maid of your own to help you get ready for everything. She will also dress your hair and bring you your tray in the morning. You simply won't have time to attend to such things yourself. Now I'm going to let you rest," Lady Margaret said, rising. "Fiona will be up shortly to unpack for you, and then she can help you dress for dinner. We're informal tonight, since we are just family. Oh, I am so glad you're here Emma," Lady Margaret whispered, hugging her friend again. "It's going to be just like the old days. You'll see!"

WHEN EMMA GLANCED at her reflection in the mirror a little later, she hardly recognized the fashionably turned out young woman staring back at her. With her hair freshly washed and arranged in an elegant cluster of curls on top of her head, a few wispy tendrils escaping to fall softly around her face, she looked quite different from the dusty, travel-worn young girl who had arrived earlier. The dress, one Lady Margaret had brought in, looked lovely on her, the soft pink shade enhancing the creamy smoothness of her complexion.

"I knew it! It's perfect on you," Margaret had pronounced, standing back and viewing Fiona's quick alterations with satisfaction. "Do you like it?"

"Well, yes, of course, it's lovely..." Emma began.

"Good. It's yours."

"Oh, no, Meggie! I couldn't," Emma said, shaking her head. "It looks almost new."

"It is," Lady Margaret replied, her tone evincing a complete lack of concern. "But I never should have bought it. I look terrible in that shade of pink. It's far too soft for me. But with your colouring, it's perfect. Isn't it, Fiona?"

"Aye, my lady, it is," the young Scottish girl agreed. "And I've got a wee smidgen of lace that will just fill in that neckline beautifully. Just to make up for the slight...difference in your sizes," she said tactfully.

Lady Margaret, glancing first at Emma's delicate outline and then down at her own generous bosom, started to giggle. Emma, colouring, joined in, and soon all three of them were laughing. Thus by the time Emma descended the staircase, the lovely pink gown having been skilfully altered to flatter her slender figure, she felt much more returned to her normal good spirits. Margaret was right, Emma thought brightly. It was good to be back. She would enjoy every day to the fullest. She would worry about the future when she had to. And not one moment sooner!

"Well, you certainly look different from the young lady I rescued earlier today." A familiar voice cut into her thoughts. "And I thought you looked fetching as a damsel in distress!"

The teasing voice could only belong to one person, and Emma drew in her breath as she caught sight of the marquis standing at the foot of the stairs. He, too, had changed and bore little resemblance to the carelessly elegant country gentleman she had seen at the inn that afternoon. Tonight, Tristan looked every inch the aristocrat in a perfectly tailored coat of dark blue superfine over cream-coloured pantaloons and soft shoes. A brilliant blue sapphire nestled in the snowy-white folds of his cravat, glowing like a captured piece of the night sky.

Emma felt her cheeks blush pink. She had never been in the presence of a man who could fluster her merely by smiling. Was this how Margaret felt when her Mr. Rowsbottom was about?

"I was surprised by the warmth of the welcome you received earlier, Miss Harding," Chadwick said, his eyes crinkling attractively. "I had no idea you were such a close friend of the family."

"Lady Margaret and I were at school together," Emma replied.

"Ah, that explains it." The marquis chuckled.

"Explains what?"

"Why I never saw you around the house. By the time Margaret was of an age to go to Miss Langford's, I was away in France."

"Yes, I remember Margaret telling me about your leaving," Emma said, drawing level with him. "I remember how frightened she was when the lists used to come back, and how relieved she was when she found your name was not on them."

"And would you have been frightened for me, too, Miss Harding?" Chadwick asked before he could stop himself.

Emma met the questioning look in his eyes and nodded slowly. "Yes, my lord, I think I should have been very concerned, had I known you then," she replied simply.

The marquis, expecting a flirtatious answer, was stayed by the gravity of her response. How easy it would be to drown in those eyes, he suddenly found himself thinking, seeing them clearly for the first time that day. Their deep violet blue reminded him of the pansies which grew wild in his country garden. And how quickly they would attract the young men, the marquis reflected, finding himself annoyed by the thought. They would swarm around her like bees around a newly opened bud, while he stood by and watched her like some crusty old toad.

Chadwick smothered a sudden impulse to laugh at his own analogy and ruefully shook his head. *A crusty old toad indeed,* he thought drily. What on earth had motivated such a ridiculous comparison? He knew he was still viewed as a prize matrimonial catch. Hadn't Jane told him that just the other day? Then why was he standing here thinking himself over the hill, just because he was confronted with a mere slip of a girl?

For once, Chadwick did not have an answer. And as he was moved to think guiltily of his present mistress, his smile faded ever so slightly. Jane's charms had began to pale of late, though in all fairness Chadwick knew it had nothing to do with her. Jane was nothing if not a willing and talented partner in bed. She had never once failed to please him. And yet, after the last few times they had been together, Chadwick had been aware of a definite feeling of ennui, a sense of something missing.

Typically, Chadwick blamed himself for the rapid demise of his latest relationship. He was growing tired of having one beautiful woman after another. He wanted more. And glancing down at the petite young lady in front of him, Chadwick found himself wondering whether he might not have found exactly what he was looking for.

No, it was sheer foolishness, Chadwick admonished himself, angry that he had even allowed himself to contemplate the thought. Emma Harding was but a child. She deserved better than the likes of him. He was too old for her, apart from the fact that he had led the life of a rake and a gambler—a man who had fully earned his well-deserved reputation as a ladies' man. What could he possibly offer a sweet, untainted girl like this? She deserved so much, he thought sadly, glancing down into the face that was raised in such a trusting fashion to his. *If only,* he thought sadly, pushing the thought aside. *If only.*

Dinner was a convivial meal, beautifully prepared and served while conversation flowed as freely as the fine wines which accompanied each course. Chadwick was unusually gregarious, entertaining them all with light-hearted stories about the farms on his estate and the tenants who drew their living from them. By the end of the meal, however, it was all Emma could do to keep her eyes open. It was as though everything which had happened had finally caught up with her. Dutifully, she accompanied Lady Hatton and her nieces to the drawing-room while the gentlemen leisurely partook of their port and cigars. But almost immediately upon their return, Emma rose and asked if she might retire.

"But of course, my dear," Lady Hatton said graciously. "How selfish of us to keep you up so late talking. You must be exhausted after your long, tiring journey. I know I always am. I've often said to Tristan how inconvenient travel is. But then, we must get about, mustn't we?" she said, laughing. "We see little enough once we're dead, as my late husband was wont to say."

Chadwick nodded, and winked mischievously at Margaret, who hastily turned away to hide a smile. Emma, intercepting that look, smiled, too. At times, Tristan seemed so young and boyish, not at all like a man who appeared to be well over the age of thirty. But then, Emma had had so little experience of men, young or old, that she hardly knew what constituted normal behaviour. Perhaps all older men acted that way, she reflected thoughtfully.

Emma bade them good-night and made her way upstairs. She climbed the stairs slowly, so weary that she found her legs almost too weak to carry her. She paused about halfway up and had just reached out to grasp the railing when a sudden noise at the bottom alerted her to the presence of another person. Turning, she was surprised to see Lord Chadwick standing at the bottom of the stairs watching her.

"Do you need some help, Miss Harding?" he enquired softly. "You seem to be having a bit of difficulty climbing those last few stairs."

His tone was light and teasing, and despite her exhaustion, Emma's face dimpled. "Thank you, my lord, but as you have already come to my rescue twice today, I scarcely think I have the right to ask for your assistance a third time. I shall marshal my strength and carry on."

"As you will, Miss Harding," he replied, bowing. "Good night."

"Good night, Lord Chadwick," Emma replied. She turned and continued up the stairs, aware that his eyes were still on her. She could almost feel the intensity of his gaze on her back. And while she didn't look back again, she knew that he watched her until she turned the corner at the top of the stairs and reached her room.

Later, as she lay in bed, Emma thought back over everything that had happened to her that day. What an amazing day it had been, she reflected. First her unfortunate encounter with Mr. Braithwaite, and then her meeting with Lord Chadwick. Or rather, her rescue by Lord Chadwick, Emma amended guiltily. One could hardly call collapsing at a stranger's feet a meeting, she thought ruefully.

Still, it had all worked out in the end. She was here with Margaret and had a wedding to look forward to. And for the first night in a very long time, Emma closed her eyes and drifted off into a deep, peaceful sleep, unaware that her lips curved upwards in a smile of anticipation.

CHAPTER FOUR

FIRST AND FOREMOST on the list of things to do was shopping. Since Emma had bought precious little in the way of fashionable clothing over the past year, her wardrobe was sadly lacking, a fact which Lady Margaret was quick to recognize and comment upon.

"But Meggie," Emma protested when her friend proposed the outing over breakfast a few days later. "You have already given me your pink gown, the pale green muslin with the matching bonnet and that lovely sprigged cotton walking gown. Surely I cannot require any more than that for the brief time I am here."

"Dearest Emma, you simply cannot go abroad in fashionable Society without being dressed in the very height of fashion, whether you are here for a few days or a few months!" Lady Margaret informed her, preparing yet another list. "You know how the ton love to talk. Why should you be the one to suffer their barbs just because you are recently out of mourning, and have not yet had occasion to visit a fashionable modiste?"

Not being able to find a reasonable answer to that, or at least not one that Margaret would consider acceptable, Emma shrugged and silently nibbled a piece of toast. Lady Elizabeth, who had briefly looked up from her book at the onset of the conversation, smiled at Emma sympathetically before returning her attention to the absorbing romantic novel she was reading.

The girls were seated in the cosy breakfast room which gave view onto the rose garden. It was a glorious morning, albeit a trifle warm, and not even the wispiest feather of a cloud drifted by to mar the cerulean blue of the sky. Emma and Margaret were seated at the table opposite the window and sipped their chocolate in companionable silence broken only by the sound of Margaret's pen. Lady Hatton generally took breakfast in her room, and as Chadwick had already left to go riding, the girls were able to enjoy the peace and serenity of the morning all to themselves.

"I think we shall go to Madame Broussard's for the gowns first," Lady Margaret said, jotting down a note on the piece of paper already covered with her fine scrawl. "She is making my wedding dress and the dresses for you and Elizabeth, which as I said in my letter are my gift to both of you. I told her I would be bringing you to be measured for a gown just as soon as you arrived."

"Margaret, it is very generous of you, but there really is no need—" Emma began awkwardly.

"Hush! there is every need," Margaret interrupted her. "Since you are here at my request, and for a very special reason, I would not dream of having you pay for your own gown. What a dreadful idea! I want to hear no more about it. Then we shall go along to Mrs. Woodrow's for gloves and silk stockings. And suitable underpinnings, of course. I think, however, that we shall save Mrs. Wilbury's for another day. Now, as to what else you will need, I should think a new walking gown, a carriage dress and perhaps a morning gown. And I don't think another habit would come amiss, perhaps in a deep blue velvet—"

"Margaret!" Emma gasped, now growing seriously concerned at her friend's impetuosity. "Forgive my saying so, but do you not think all that is just a little excessive? I shall only be in London for a few weeks."

Lady Margaret glanced at her friend in surprise. "Well, yes, I know that, Emma, but as I have already said, it doesn't alter the fact that you must dress the part while you are here. Next," she said, carrying on as though Emma hadn't spoken, "you shall require a gown for Lady Fortescue's ball. From what I hear it's going to be a dreadful crush, so you must look absolutely stunning."

Emma couldn't prevent a chuckle. "I must?" she teased. "Why? If it's like to be that much of a crush, I doubt anyone will see what I'm wearing."

"That's no excuse. You must look wonderful."

"Indeed you must, Emma," Lady Elizabeth piped up helpfully. "Meggie has told any number of people that you were coming up for the wedding."

In the act of lifting the cup to her lips, Emma hesitated. "Oh? What kind of people?"

Margaret sent her sister a quelling glance. "Read your book, Lizzie. Don't worry, Emma," Lady Margaret continued. "They are all people with whom you are acquainted. Or at least, most of them are. I still keep in touch with some of the girls we went to school with. You remember, Lady Vyne's three girls, and the Misses Clyde. And then of course there are my cousins Daphne, Phoebe, Rachel and Mary. And a few...others."

"Others?" Emma probed, eyeing her friend with a hint of suspicion. "What others?"

"Well, I did mention it in passing to a few gentlemen at Lady Stanley's tea last—"

"Margaret, you didn't!" Emma gasped, blushing.

"Well, yes of course I did." Lady Margaret laughed, amused by her friend's reaction. "Why are you so surprised? Surely you didn't think I was going to let you languish away at home while you were here."

"No, of course I didn't, but—" Emma replied, aware that she had been thinking exactly that.

"Good. Oh, now don't look so mopish, Emma. There would have been little point in bringing you up to London well before the wedding and not introducing you around. You need to get out and enjoy yourself! And don't think the gentlemen have forgotten you," Lady Margaret said. "They all remember you very well. Indeed, I don't think you realize how popular you were. Lord Edgecombe was most delighted at the prospect of seeing you again."

"Lord Edgecombe?" Emma's cheeks coloured becomingly. She was flustered that Margaret should mention the name of the gentleman who had been so kind to her after her father's death, and lowered her eyes, missing the sudden rush of colour to Lady Elizabeth's pale cheeks at the mention of the handsome earl. "In truth, I am surprised he even remembers me. We only conversed a few times."

"Well, he remembers you just the same," Lady Margaret continued, clearly satisfied. "And if his recollection of you while you were in mourning is that clear, imagine what an impact you will make now. Oh, I am in an absolute fidge for the ball!"

"Margaret, I do think you're getting a little ahead of yourself again," Emma chided her friend. "You mustn't think that just because you are bethrothed, it is your sworn duty to inflict a similar state on me."

"Tosh! That's not the way of it at all, and you know it," Lady Margaret replied, not in the least chastised. "I simply want you to start going about in Society again, Emma. After all, you have a lot of time to make up for. Who knows? Perhaps you won't be going back to the farm as soon as you think," Lady Margaret said, her eyes sparkling mischievously. "Perhaps you will meet some devastatingly handsome young man who sweeps you off your feet and proposes marriage right out there in the rose garden. In which case this run-up with me will be of endless benefit to you when your own time comes!"

Emma, listening to her friend plan both her engagement and her marriage, turned away to hide a smile. Dear Margaret. She hadn't changed at all over the past two years. She was as hopelessly impulsive and kind-hearted as she was when they had been at school together.

After Elizabeth left to fetch a new book from her room, Margaret beamed at her friend. "Oh, Emma, I'm so glad you're here. It's going to be wonderful having someone to confide in again." Margaret hesitated, and looked at her in sudden earnestness. "And your being here will help all of us. Especially Tristan."

"Lord Chadwick?" Emma quizzed, trying to ignore the sudden, intensified beating of her heart. "How in the world does Lord Chadwick require my help?"

Lady Margaret smiled a touch sadly. "To be honest, he doesn't know that he does, and that's why I wanted to speak to you alone. You see, Emma, Bertie and Tris don't get on very well together. They never have. And it's made things terribly awkward for me at times."

Lady Margaret saw the surprise and doubt in Emma's eyes, and nodded. "I know it seems strange, and you may not have noticed it yet, but you will as time goes on. They are really most uncomfortable in each other's company."

"But why?" Emma said, gazing at her friend in dismay. "Did something happen between them?"

Lady Margaret shook her head. "I don't think so. I have a feeling it is because Tris and I have always been so close. He's always been so protective of me and now I think he's concerned that Bertie isn't good enough for me." Lady Margaret paused, and glanced at her friend awkwardly. "He's even intimated that Bertie only courted me for my money."

"But surely that isn't true," Emma argued, justifiably upset. "From what I saw last evening, it is obvious to me that Mr. Rowsbottom adores you."

"Of course he does," Lady Margaret said, blushing. "Dear Bertie. He's really terribly sweet once you get to know him. And to be honest, I really don't believe Tristan meant the remark."

"Then why would he have said such a thing?" Emma asked, completely mystified. "How could he come to dislike your fiancé so intensely?"

"I don't think it is a case of Tristan's not liking him *per se,* but rather that Tristan has some silly notion that I could have done better for myself. He says I should have married the son of a duke or a marquis at the very least. He's even hinted once or twice that I am too young to wed, but you and I both know how silly that is. After all, I am nineteen years old. If I were not wed by the time I reached twenty, I should think myself quite on the shelf," Lady Margaret pronounced defiantly, momentarily forgetting that Emma was exactly the same age and not even betrothed.

Emma, however, not in the least offended by her friend's oversight, shook her head, trying to rationalize this latest and most unexpected development. She was having trouble believing that Lord Chadwick would object so strenuously to his cousin's marrying someone he did not deem suitable. Mr. Rowsbottom seemed a pleasant enough young man. Not for a moment had he struck Emma as a man desperately seeking a rich wife.

"Personally, I think it's just because Tristan is so much older than the rest of us," Lady Margaret said finally. "He's never truly been in love, or he could sympathize with Bertie."

"How old...is your cousin, Meggie?" Emma asked as nonchalantly as she could.

"Positively old!" Lady Margaret sighed. "Eight-and-thirty last birthday. And still not married. Aunt Rachel positively despairs of him! As do most of the other Society matrons. Especially those with marriageable daughters!"

Eight-and-thirty, Emma thought. *Dear me.* Whatever would Aunt Georgina say? "Well, whatever Lord Chadwick's reasons for not wanting you to marry, Meg, I still don't see how my being here will be of any help," Emma replied in a matter-of-fact manner. "It won't alter the relationship between Mr. Rowsbottom and your cousin."

"No, but I thought your being here might help to keep Tristan occupied."

"Occupied? Whatever are you talking about, Margaret?" Emma asked.

"Well, the two of you are going to be together at the wedding," Lady Margaret said. "And I should think you would be happy to get to know Tris a little better before the actual day. Just so you don't feel uncomfortable with him."

"I don't feel uncomfortable with him now," Emma protested, trying to ignore the way her pulse quickened at the thought. "What would make you think that I was?"

"Oh, I don't know," Lady Margaret replied in an offhand manner. "Mayhap because I saw the way you blushed when he came into the room last night. And then, there is this mysterious meeting you refuse to tell me about."

"I am not refusing to tell you about it, Margaret," Emma interrupted her guiltily. "I simply do not wish to dwell on it, that's all. And please believe me when I say I am *not* uncomfortable in your cousin's presence. Lord Chadwick has done nothing to make me feel even remotely uncomfortable since we met," Emma said, praying her face would not give her away.

"Good. Then that's all the better. By spending time in your company, Tristan will be in less frequent contact with Bertie, thereby avoiding the possibility of any undue...clashes of temperament," Lady Margaret said, trying to phrase it as subtly as she knew how.

"Clashes of temperament?" Emma repeated slowly. "Good heavens, Margaret, you make them sound like mortal enemies. Have your cousin and Mr. Rowsbottom...clashed?''

''Not in the physical sense, no. But Tristan has given the occasional verbal thrust in Bertie's direction. At our betrothal party, for example, they got into a rather heated discussion over that abysmal situation at Walcheren. Tristan maintained that it was a stupid mistake on the part of the government, and that it would end up being nothing but a dreadful fiasco.''

''Which it was,'' Emma felt obliged to point out.

''Yes, I know,'' Lady Margaret agreed, ''but Bertie argued that the government had no choice but to try to beat Bonaparte back wherever possible, and that our men had to be prepared to fight and die for the cause. Well, you can see the potential for sparks.'' Margaret's concern was evident. ''Tristan was noticebly cool for the remainder of the evening, and I don't think Bertie has felt comfortable with him ever since. That's why I thought your being here might be helpful to all of us. After all, if Tristan is with you, he won't be running aground of Bertie, will he?''

The reasoning made sense, Emma admitted, but it seemed to her that Margaret had overlooked one very important point. ''And just how do you intend to make your cousin spend time with me, Margaret?'' she asked quietly, endeavouring to keep her voice steady. ''I can hardly just walk up to Lord Chadwick and say, 'Excuse me, Lord Chadwick, but your cousin desires that I keep you and Mr. Rowsbottom apart, so would you be so good as to take me out somewhere,' now can I? Nor do I think Lord Chadwick would, of his own accord, approach me. At best, our acquaintance is slight, and as you have already informed me, your cousin is very much concerned by differences in age and social position.''

''I know,'' Lady Margaret conceded. ''But we also agreed that the two of you should come to know each other a little

better before the wedding. And I have no qualms about
putting that suggestion to him in just such a way. Besides,
it will give Tristan something to do,'' Lady Margaret added
quite honestly. ''He gets so terribly restless when he's in
Town for more than a few days that I begin to feel positively uncomfortable around him. Taking you out and
showing you the sights will afford him the opportunity of
passing the days until the wedding more pleasantly, for I'm
sure that the moment the day is over he will flee back to the
country as though the devil himself were at his heels. Lord
only knows where he derived this strange antipathy for the
city!''

AT THAT VERY MOMENT, the gentleman in question was enjoying a hearty gallop through the Park, recalling all too
well exactly why he had chosen to leave London in the first
place. It was simply too crowded—too over-populated by
people concerned solely with what they did, when they did
it and how well they looked while doing it. And God help
you if you did something that was not quite acceptable by
ton standards. Even riding in the Park had to be done ac-
cording to fashion, Chadwick lamented. It seemed that early
morning was now the only time he could enjoy a decent
gallop along the inviting, tree-lined alleys. Lord knew, it
would create havoc if he raced his spirited black stallion any
later in the day. Once the Fashionables were out taking the
air, as it was called, the Park became positively tiresome—
nothing more than a place to see and be seen. But then, was
that not the underlying motive for being in London during
the Season in the first place?

Feeling that he had answered his own question, the marquis checked the stallion's powerful stride, and eased him
into a walk, reining in under the shadow of a clump of large,
spreading trees. Kicking free the stirrups, Chadwick dismounted and ambled about for a while, leaving Diamanté,

named for the white blaze of colour on his forehead, to forage contentedly, though always in sight of his beloved master, while Chadwick's own thoughts returned to the events taking place in the house in Eaton Square.

There was no doubt in his mind that Emma Harding was a thoroughly delightful young lady. Even now, he found it hard to believe that she was the same age as Margaret. There seemed to him a world of difference between the two girls. His past experience of young ladies that age had taught him that most of them still belonged in the schoolroom.

But Emma was different somehow. She was quiet, yes, but not awkwardly so. She did not chatter for the sake of making conversation. She spoke only when she had something intelligent to say. That trait alone commended her, Chadwick admitted ruefully, recalling some of the inanities he had heard spewing forth from the mouths of many simpering young females.

"Well, bless my soul, is it really the elusive Lord Chadwick I see day-dreaming before me, or merely a shadow who bears his resemblance?"

So deep was the marquis in thought that the approach of the smiling gentleman on horseback had gone unnoticed. Now, however, as the jocular voice cut through his reveries, the marquis grinned, and shook his head.

"'Tis no shadow, Jeremy, though I can well understand your thinking it might be," he said, extending his hand to the man who had dismounted and crossed the grass to greet him. "Damn, if you're not a sight for sore eyes. How long has it been?"

"Dashed longer than I care to remember," Lord Edgecombe said, affectionately grasping the extended hand and shaking it. "When did you arrive in Town?"

"Just a few days ago," the marquis informed him. "I was planning to call round but I had a few things to attend to first."

"No matter," the young earl replied easily. "The important thing is that you're here."

The marquis nodded, and the two men fell into step. Lord Edgecombe was one of the few men the marquis truly considered a friend, and though they had spent relatively little time together over the past few years, their friendship was deeply enough ingrained to outlast their prolonged separations.

Several years younger than Chadwick, Edgecombe was a handsome man with a trim, athletic figure and a face that caused many female hearts, both young and old, to beat a little faster at his approach. He was witty, clever, warmhearted and, as the marquis well knew, generous to a fault. It was probably that openness of nature which had first impressed Chadwick, being of similar disposition, and the friendship between the two men, the one as blond as the other was dark, had been firmly cemented years ago. While both men had enjoyed considerable success with the ladies, never once had one trod on the toes of the other, each being careful not to trifle with a lady already engaged.

"I assume you're here for the wedding," Edgecombe ventured as they settled themselves on a bench. "Less than a fortnight now, isn't it?"

The marquis nodded, his mouth lifting ruefully. "Ten days, as Margaret keeps informing me. Wretched girl," he mumbled affectionately. "Would that she were marrying someone like you rather than that unlicked cub Rowsbottom."

"Come now, Tris," Lord Edgecombe said affably. "From what I hear, Bertrand's not a bad fellow. A little immature, perhaps, but then, weren't we all at his age?"

"Pray tell me we were not," Chadwick disclaimed drily. "I don't recall you ever being that callow."

"I'm sure I had my moments." Lord Edgecombe laughed. "But enough of Mr. Rowsbottom, how are the rest of the family? I saw Lady Hatton passing by Hatchard's the other morning, but I wasn't close enough to speak with her.'' His eyes twinkled in merriment. ''She looks well. Still as cantankerous as ever?''

''Worse,'' Chadwick responded, the rumble of laughter deep in his throat. ''I swear she thrives on plaguing me. Starts in the moment I arrive.''

''Mmm. No doubt you're up to it,'' Jeremy said knowingly. ''And what about Lady Elizabeth? Still addicted to her books?''

''Ever so, though I can hardly believe how she's changed.''

''Oh?'' Jeremy enquired. ''In what way?''

The marquis chuckled appreciatively. ''Obviously you've not seen my younger cousin recently. Like the ugly duckling, she has turned into a veritable swan. A beauty with a halo of golden hair and the most bewitching green eyes I've seen in a goodly while. I think it's just as well I came to London when I did.'' The marquis sighed.

He paused, and turned to glance at his friend candidly. ''To be honest, Jeremy, I sometimes despair of the pair of them. You're quite right, of course, Rowsbottom's not a bad sort. It's just that I wanted more for Margaret. I would have liked to have seen her with someone more worthy of her.'' He glanced back at his friend. ''Someone like you.''

''Never had eyes for me, old fellow,'' Edgecombe replied with a trace of laughter in his voice. ''Which is hardly surprising, given the way we grew up. Looking back on it now, I venture to say Lady Margaret probably thought of me as a brother more than anything else. Lord knows, we were never much apart.''

''Yes, isn't that the truth.'' The marquis chuckled fondly. ''Remember the time Margaret's bonnet blew into the lake and you tied a rope around her waist so she could lean in and get it?''

"Don't I just!" Edgecombe laughed, his brown eyes crinkling. "Unfortunately I also remember being the one who let go the rope, sending her face first into the water. She never forgave me for that."

The marquis's answering laugh was delightfully warm and natural. "It wasn't your fault a bee stung you on the arm just as Margaret was about to grasp the bonnet."

"Maybe not, but that wasn't the way Lady Margaret looked at it. As I recall she was wearing a brand-new gown of which she was uncommon proud. It was her birthday, wasn't it?"

The marquis nodded. "It was, now I come to think of it. Damn, I'll never forget the sight of her walking back up to the house, dripping wet, and with that silly bonnet perched all askew."

Jeremy smiled, his eyes softening. "No, nor shall I. Looking every inch the lady—and spitting like a kitten. No, I doubt she will ever forgive me for that."

They stopped talking for a moment and nodded to a fellow rider who seemed to be enjoying the silence of the Park as much as they.

"Speaking of lovely young ladies," Jeremy said, turning to regard his friend again, "I understand Emma Harding is staying with you for a while."

"Yes, she's to be one of Margaret's bridesmaids," Chadwick replied, purposely keeping his voice level. "But I'm surprised you already know about it."

"Lady Margaret informed me of Miss Harding's impending arrival a few days ago. Now there's a beautiful and charming young woman," Jeremy added gallantly.

"Yes," the marquis replied, wondering why he should feel so put out that his best friend would speak highly of Emma. "I wasn't aware you knew her so well, Jeremy."

"I don't. I danced with her a few times when she made her come-out, of course, but I really didn't become well acquainted with her. It was not until I visited her in the country that I came to know her better. I happened to be in the area when her father died and occasionally visited her. You know, trying to cheer her up a bit. And what I saw of Miss Harding then, I liked very much. She was very comfortable company, notwithstanding the fact that she was in mourning. And there was something so very honest about her. She always struck me as being older somehow,'' Jeremy commented idly, unaware that he echoed the marquis's own thoughts. ''Charming girl. I'm looking forward to seeing her again.''

Chadwick purposely said nothing, afraid that if he did the tone of his voice might sound more curt than was warranted. He had no right to feel even the least bit annoyed by what Edgecombe was saying. No doubt other gentlemen of the ton would soon be echoing those very sentiments, and then he would be forced to listen to them. For now, however, Chadwick was aware of a growing desire to keep Emma's presence in his house a little-known fact. Let him enjoy her company while he could. Soon enough, he knew, there would be a steady stream of visitors to the house.

After chatting a little while longer, the two men parted, agreeing to meet for dinner at their club the next evening. Riding back in the direction of Eaton Square, the marquis ruminated on his unexpected encounter with Edgecombe. While he was happy at having met his good friend, he was nevertheless a trifle uneasy about Jeremy's eagerness to see Emma again. It was clear that Emma had made a notable impression on him. But had Jeremy made a similar impression on Emma? the marquis found himself wondering. Would she, like him, be anticipating their next meeting with barely concealed impatience?

It was a disturbing thought. Edgecombe was an extremely eligible fellow, and like Chadwick, considered a prime catch. But Edgecombe still had youth on his side, being that much younger than his friend. And, surely, being closer in age to Emma would give him more in common with her, thereby making him the more likely candidate of the two.

Grudgingly, the marquis admitted that it did, and the knowledge that it bothered him immensely was nothing more than a further source of aggravation!

CHAPTER FIVE

THE PLANNED shopping expedition took place two days later. Emma, with Lady Margaret seated beside her and Lady Hatton and Lady Elizabeth opposite, set off for Bond Street, all in high anticipation of the day. Lady Margaret was armed with her ever-present list, and as they went from shop to shop, dutifully marked off what had been achieved and what had yet to be accomplished.

During their first stop at Madame Broussard's, they were entertained with tea and iced cakes while Madame's assistants bustled in and out with a dizzying array of fabrics and fashion plates for their perusal. Madame herself was a quiet, diminutive Frenchwoman whose keen eyes assessed a client's strengths at a glance and then enhanced them with a suitably styled and coloured gown.

Thus, while Lady Margaret was having her wedding gown fitted, Emma, who found herself leaning towards a bolt of newly arrived silk from Paris in a pretty shade of pale mauve, was quickly diverted by Madame Broussard herself.

"*Non, mademoiselle,* zat is not for you," the modiste said, shaking her head. "You need something to flatter your colouring. Perhaps ze apricot, or *la soie huître,*" she said, holding both swatches against Emma's fair complexion. "See how zey bring out ze bloom in your cheeks."

"Madame Broussard is quite right, Emma," Lady Elizabeth agreed. "The mauve sarcenet does nothing for you."

Emma, who did see the difference, nevertheless turned away from the mauve fabric somewhat reluctantly to study the two other lengths of material being held out for her inspection. "Oh, dear, I really don't know which one I ought to choose," she said, glancing from one to the other. "They are both so lovely."

"In that case, take both of them," Lady Margaret piped up, solving the problem for her. "The apricot will make up into a lovely dinner dress, and the nakara silk will be perfect for Lady Fortescue's ball. Do you not think so, Aunt Rachel?" she said, addressing the older woman who sat in a comfortable armchair watching the proceedings.

"I think both would look quite fetching on Miss Harding, Margaret," Lady Hatton agreed placidly, and glanced at Emma. "Do you like them, Emma?"

Emma, both surprised and touched that Lady Hatton should ask, reluctantly nodded her agreement. "Well, yes, of course, Lady Hatton. There is really no question that they are both quite beautiful, but I really do not think..."

"Good, then we shall take the nakara silk and the apricot as well, Madame," Lady Hatton announced, brushing aside Emma's protestations. "And the blue, made up in the style we discussed for the wedding. Now, as for the riding habits..."

The modiste nodded, and the process continued. More samples were brought forth, this time for riding habits for both Emma and Lady Elizabeth, Lady Margaret's having already been ordered. The fabrics were chosen, and then extensive measurements taken and marked down in a little book. By the time they quit the tiny salon, Emma's head was spinning. Never had she imagined that shopping could be such a tiring undertaking!

"Oh, Aunt Rachel," Lady Elizabeth said as they made to get back into the carriage. "Do you think we might stop for

THE BLADE AND THE BATH MISS   81

a moment at the library? I should so like to pick up a volume of Lord Byron's new poems.''

"You would do better to spend more time on your dancing lessons than on reading silly romantic poetry, Lizzie,'' Lady Margaret observed tartly. "What will you do if a dashing young gentleman asks you to dance a quadrille at the ball? Quote verse to him?''

"I shall explain to the dashing young gentleman that my feet are quite worn out from participating in the dances I do know how to do, and ask him to sit and talk with me,'' Lady Elizabeth replied, not in the least flustered by her sister's bullying. "And no doubt, I shall have a much better time of it for doing so.''

"Lizzie, you are impossible!'' Lady Margaret sighed. "How do you ever expect to attract a husband if you are not suitably educated?''

"Perhaps in the same way you did, Meggie,'' Lady Elizabeth replied, looking now at Emma. "By tripping over my skirt and falling right into his arms!''

"Elizabeth!'' Lady Margaret exclaimed, her eyes wide. "You promised!''

"Girls, girls, enough!'' Lady Hatton said abruptly. "I shall thank you both to remember yourselves.'' She glared from one to the other. "Elizabeth, you may collect your volume of poems from the library. Margaret, you and I are expected at Wedgwood and Byerley to go over dinnerware. Emma,'' she said, turning to regard the other girl, "perhaps you would be so good as to accompany Elizabeth into Hookham's. After that, we shall meet you back here and return home for a light nuncheon before going on to Mrs. Watling's this afternoon.''

The arrangements being suitable to all concerned, the party separated. Emma did not miss the pointed look Lady Margaret sent in her sister's direction before they parted, but waited until they were alone before quizzing her about it.

"You mean Margaret never told you how she met Mr. Rowsbottom?" Lady Elizabeth replied, an eyebrow arching expressively. "I am surprised. I know how close the two of you are."

"It may have just slipped her mind," Emma offered. "Judging from her letters, Margaret was maintaining a rather hectic schedule at the time."

"Yes, she was." Lady Elizabeth dimpled prettily. "Still, I think it was all terribly amusing. It was at Lady Tinsley's musicale that they met," Lady Elizabeth began, locking her arm with Emma's as they started towards the library. "A shockingly crowded affair, as most of them are, with everyone who was anyone in attendance. We, unfortunately, arrived a little late, and Mr. Rowsbottom was already there. To be fair, I have to say that I do not know precisely how it happened," Lady Elizabeth conceded. "My sister is not usually so clumsy and I think it may have had something to do with the floor at Tinsley Hall."

"The floor?" Emma repeated blankly.

Lady Elizabeth nodded. "Yes. Being uneven. You see, Lady Tinsley had recently had men in to repair some water damage, and I think they must have missed something because as Margaret was making her way between the rows of chairs towards a group of friends, she suddenly stepped on the hem of her gown and pitched forward."

"Oh, dear, I hope she didn't hurt herself?" Emma asked, immediately concerned.

"Not a bit," Lady Elizabeth said with a laugh. "Because she never did actually fall. Mr. Rowsbottom caught her as she very nearly tumbled headlong into his lap!"

"His lap?" Emma replied, clearly amused. "Oh, my goodness! Had they been introduced?"

"No," Lady Elizabeth said, her silvery laughter again rippling forth. "And that's what I found the funniest. Just after we arrived, Margaret noticed Mr. Rowsbottom chatting with a friend and asked me if I knew who he was. When I said I did not, she told me that she thought him quite the most handsome young gentleman in the room."

"So it was love at first sight." Emma smiled.

Lady Elizabeth nodded. "It certainly was for Meg."

"But not for Mr. Rowsbottom?"

Lady Elizabeth shrugged eloquently. "To be honest, I cannot say. He certainly looked a bit dazed when she finally straightened up, though whether that had to do with the manner of their meeting or with Margaret herself, I'm not sure. Having a young lady suddenly fall into your arms would tend to...startle one, don't you think? Mind, she was very graceful about it," Lady Elizabeth acknowledged. "Margaret never did anything that wasn't graceful. But I remember how terribly embarrassed she was when she righted herself. La, her cheeks were as red as Lady Tinsley's curtains. Still, it obviously didn't bother Mr. Rowsbottom overmuch. He called round the very next day, and almost every day after that." Lady Elizabeth sighed, not a little enviously. "I suppose it was, as you say, love at first sight."

Emma nodded, finding the story highly amusing. No wonder Margaret had been reluctant to disclose the details of her first meeting with Mr. Rowsbottom. Given its rather comical nature, it was hardly surprising that she had preferred to gloss over it. And no doubt she would be mortified now if she knew that Lady Elizabeth had taken it upon herself to impart the information. But ever mindful of others' sensibilities, Emma decided not to tell Margaret that she knew. Margaret had been kindness itself, and Emma had no intention of repaying her with laughter. Besides, in the end everything had worked out perfectly. The unfortunate incident had initiated a set of circumstances which had ultimately resulted in a proposal of marriage. What could be better than that?

Secure in the knowledge that her awareness of the situation would not harm her friendship with Lady Margaret, Emma accompanied Lady Elizabeth into Hookham's. Once inside, the girls parted company, Emma to browse amongst the beautifully illustrated art and nature books, while Lady Elizabeth quickly made her way to the section where Lord Byron's work was to be found.

Emma soon discovered that it was here, ambling amongst the book-lined shelves of the great circulating library, that Lady Elizabeth was at her happiest. While never consciously intending to become a bluestocking, Elizabeth had discovered reading to be such a delightful and enlightening pastime that over the past year she had found herself indulging in it almost to the exclusion of all else.

Elizabeth knew very well that her sister despaired of her, and tried to make up for it by attending any manner of social function Margaret asked her to, but even then, she felt rather like a fish out of water. Unlike Margaret, Elizabeth possessed no sense of rhythm, and consequently, her movements on the dance floor appeared, at best, stiff and uncoordinated. Her dancing teachers had valiantly tried to instill some measure of grace into her steps, but all to no avail. They had given up, informing Lady Hatton that in their opinion, Lady Elizabeth would do better to sit out the dances and try to make pleasant conversation, as she would never move around the floor with the grace and aplomb of her sister.

Fortunately, at the time, the tutors' comments had given Lady Elizabeth and Lady Hatton no real cause for concern. Being painfully thin, and with a mop of blond hair that steadfastly refused to do anything but curl after its own infuriating fashion, Lady Elizabeth had been the recipient of very few gentlemen callers. Shortly after that, a miraculous transformation had taken place. Over the course of six months, Lady Elizabeth had blossomed into a beautiful young woman, her wayward hair relaxing into gentle waves which worked to perfection under the skilled hands of her maid. Her figure, which had previously been dubbed long-legged and gangly, was unexpectedly transformed into one that was slender and lissome and Elizabeth suddenly found herself in demand at every ball and assembly she attended. The same girl who had never stood up for more than two dances on the best of nights now had more partners than could be accommodated on one dance card.

Unfortunately, where Lady Elizabeth's outward appearance had improved immeasurably, her dancing skills had not kept pace, and it was the brave gentleman indeed who asked her for a second dance. Being aware of this, Elizabeth did her best to spare both herself and her partners the painful ignominy of appearing with her on the floor. Other than the few country dances she had managed to learn, she consented to dance very few others, preferring to sit out and converse. Thankfully, the decision was a happy one; the gentlemen were only too happy to spend a few precious moments alone with the beautiful Lady Elizabeth, enjoying her undivided attention, while she was spared the painful embarrassment of having to apologize every time she trod on her partner's foot.

Lady Elizabeth walked along the row now, her eyes scanning the titles. She knew that Byron's books were usually kept on one of the uppermost shelves, and had to strain her neck to see them. So it was that she failed to notice the small piece of wood sticking out of the floor, nor see it catch in her hem. It wasn't until she finally espied the coveted volume of poems on the top rack and went to reach up for it, that she felt her skirt tug ominously, and felt herself pitch forward. Emma, coming around the corner of the aisle at that very moment, saw Lady Elizabeth begin to lose her balance, and quickly moved forward, knowing even as she did that she was too far away to be of any help.

"Elizabeth!" Emma cried, watching horrified as Lady Elizabeth fell forward, calling her name as she saw her heading towards the polished wooden railing.

What happened next was little more than a blur in Emma's memory. Everything happened so fast. She remembered running forward, trying to reach Lady Elizabeth before she fell, when someone suddenly stepped directly in front of her, completely obliterating her view of Lady Elizabeth, and stopping her dead in her tracks. Emma felt as though she had run into a brick wall, and knew that had it not been for the two arms which quickly reached out to steady her, she would have fallen, knocked backwards by the sheer force of the impact.

"Good Lord, what the—Miss Harding! Are you all right?"

The voice was familiar, and slowly opening her eyes, Emma recognized the face of Lord Chadwick staring down at her. Her head was spinning, and she could feel the warm colour stealing up into her cheeks. "Oh, my...lord, forgive...me," she said, trying to catch her breath. "I...did not see...I was running..."

It was nearly impossible for Emma to continue. Her breath was coming in short gasps, and she was conscious of a dreadful buzzing in her ears. Her collision with Lord Chadwick had all but knocked the wind from her, and she found it a most unpleasant experience indeed to have to draw in shallow gasps of air merely to remain standing. "Lady Elizabeth...did she..."

"Don't talk now," the marquis ordered abruptly. "You've had the wind knocked out of you. My fault, I'm afraid," he said ruefully. "I didn't see you coming. I heard

Elizabeth's cry and was on my way to see her. Fortunately, Edgecombe got there first.''

The marquis continued to regard the pale face in front of him and then carefully guided her to a nearby chair. ''Here, I think you had best sit down,'' Chadwick advised, pressing her firmly but gently into it. He had seen the tell-tale perspiration break out on Emma's forehead and knew that if she didn't calm her breathing in the next few seconds she would faint. ''Now breathe with me, Miss Harding,'' he instructed. ''In...out. In...out. No, slowly, don't rush it. In...out. Don't hold it, Emma. That's better. In...out.''

Emma nodded, trying to regulate her breathing as he directed, all the while aware of how foolish she must look, sitting here gasping for breath. How could she have done something so unladylike, running towards Elizabeth. Anyone could have stepped out and collided with her. But then, as Lord Chadwick had just said, it wasn't totally her fault. Chadwick had heard Elizabeth's cry and had reacted instinctively, just as she had. He simply hadn't seen her. If anything, it was amazing that she hadn't been knocked flat on her back!

''Lady Elizabeth...she was...falling,'' Emma wheezed. ''I—''

''Elizabeth is quite well,'' the marquis informed her quietly. ''Lord Edgecombe saw her falling and managed to catch her before she struck the railing. She's fine.''

Relieved that her friend had come to no harm, Emma nodded and closed her eyes, trying to still the frantic pounding of her heart, which had nothing to do with her own clumsiness. Lord Chadwick had come to her rescue yet again, she realized dimly. And he had called her Emma.

''I am...sorry, Lord...Chadwick...'' Emma said, the words coming out more coherently, though still with some degree of difficulty. ''It was most unladylike of me to go...running through the library. I should have been...looking where I was going."

Aware that the marquis's hands still rested lightly upon her arms, Emma sat up a little straighter and smiled in confusion. "Th-thank you, my lord, I think I can...stand now."

"Are you sure?" the marquis remarked, his eyes teasing. "I seem to have a distinct knack for catching you when you're off balance."

"Yes, and I seem to have been off balance a good deal lately," Emma murmured drily. "I am not normally so...accident-prone."

His hands fell away and Emma couldn't help but notice the sudden cold where the warmth of his touch had been. To cover her embarrassment, she stood up and turned in the direction of Lady Elizabeth. To her amusement, Lady Elizabeth seemed to be suffering a similar predicament. She was supported by Lord Edgecombe's arms, her pale, anxious face evidence that she was thoroughly shaken.

"Are you all right, Lizzie?" Chadwick asked, moving towards her now. As they approached, Lord Edgecombe slowly removed his arms, but not before receiving Lady Elizabeth's tremulous assurances that she was capable of standing alone. In answer to Chadwick's question, however, Lady Elizabeth merely nodded, her crimson cheeks indicative of her acute embarrassment.

Tristan glanced round the library. "Are Margaret and my aunt here, too?" he said, addressing Emma.

Emma shook her head. "No. They took the carriage over to Wedgwood and Byerley."

Tristan nodded, his mouth twitching. "Well, I suppose I had better keep the two of you company until they return. I daresay you've both had enough excitement for one morning."

With Lord Edgecombe following close behind, Chadwick escorted the ladies outside to wait. By the time Lady Margaret and Lady Hatton returned a short while later, the girls were more than ready to depart.

"Well, this is a most unexpected development," Lady Hatton commented, eyeing the assembled crowd in astonishment. "I had not expected to see Elizabeth out of the library for a good while yet and here you are, obviously ready to depart. And Tristan," she said, further surprised to find her nephew and Lord Edgecombe present. "This is a pleasant surprise. I would not have thought to find either of you here at this time of day," she added with a gracious nod towards the other gentleman. "Is something amiss?"

Emma and Lady Elizabeth exchanged anxious glances, and when no one spoke, Lady Hatton's eyes narrowed suspiciously. "Do my senses lie, or has something happened. Tristan?"

"Your senses are as sharp as ever, Aunt," Tristan murmured. "We had a slight…incident in the library, and both of the young ladies were somewhat shaken. I was merely keeping them company until you returned."

"Incident! What incident?" Lady Margaret cried before Lady Hatton had opportunity. "Elizabeth, what have you been up to this time?"

"It's really nothing to be alarmed about . . ." Lady Elizabeth began uncomfortably, finally finding her voice. "I merely . . . tripped."

"Tripped?" The dismay in Lady Hatton's voice was patent. "Dear me, and I thought we had cured you of that unfortunate tendency."

"Aunt Rachel, I really didn't mean—"

"Elizabeth, you are a beautiful girl," Lady Hatton interrupted with a long-suffering sigh, "but what gentleman is going to look seriously upon you if you cannot even carry yourself erect in a dignified manner."

"Please, Lady Hatton, it wasn't Lady Elizabeth's fault," Emma spoke up quickly. "There was a piece of wood—"

"There is always something, Emma." Lady Hatton sighed again. "A loose hem, an uneven stretch of floor, a piece of wood." The older woman glanced at both Margaret and Elizabeth reprovingly. "The pair of you seem to suffer the same debility, and I fear I shall have to spend from now until the wedding attending to it. Lord knows, I cannot have one or the other of you tripping on your way down the aisle and making a proper spectacle of yourselves. What would people say!"

Aware that both Margaret and Elizabeth were now blushing hotly, Tristan smoothly broke in. "Rest assured, Aunt, the only spectacle people are going to be discussing on Meggie's wedding day is how beautiful the bride was, and how graceful and charming were her attendants. And now, I think perhaps you should be starting back to Eaton Square."

As always, Tristan's words had a remarkably calming effect on Lady Hatton, and she said nothing more as he handed the girls up into the carriage. Lady Margaret, having remained silent during her aunt's tirade, suddenly turned a brilliant smile on her cousin and Lord Edgecombe. "I do not think, Tristan," she said pleasantly, "that Lord Edgecombe has received a very good impression of us, standing out here in the middle of the street. Perhaps you would care to bring him to tea later so that we may make amends."

"On the contrary, Lady Margaret," Edgecombe said with a smile. "My impressions are that of a very close and affectionate family. And while I may have had a less than proper re-introduction to Lady Elizabeth, I assure you it shall remain all the more memorable for its uniqueness."

"A less than proper re-introduction?" Lady Hatton queried. "Tristan, do you mean to tell me that you did not make suitable introductions?"

"Actually, Aunt," Chadwick hedged, having trouble keeping a straight face. "Circumstances being what they were, there really wasn't much time. By the time I turned around from greeting Miss Harding, I found Lord Edgecombe... already conversing with Elizabeth."

"Already conv—! Dear me," Lady Hatton moaned, closing her eyes and shaking her head. "Hoydens! I have raised hoydens! Whatever am I to do with the two of you?" She stared at the girls a moment longer before directing a pained look towards Lord Edgecombe, who, like Chadwick, was having trouble keeping his laughter at bay. "Lord Edgecombe, what can I say? I fear I must apologize for such shocking behaviour on the part of my entire family. Perhaps you would consider joining us for dinner tomorrow evening, that we might endeavour to make up for this rather... unfortunate oversight."

This time it was Tristan's turn to grin, while Lord Edgecombe bowed gallantly. "I should be delighted to take dinner with you, Lady Hatton, though please do not feel it is in any way necessary."

"It is, and I do," Lady Hatton replied brusquely. "I am anxious to put to right whatever lingering doubts you have regarding the propriety with which we conduct ourselves. Shall we say half-past seven?"

There seemed little Lord Edgecombe could say to dissuade Lady Hatton, and aware that he did not really wish to, the earl smiled gratefully. "Half-past seven it is. Until tomorrow, then. Your servant, Lady Hatton, ladies," he said, smiling up at Lady Elizabeth, Emma and Lady Margaret. "Chadwick," he added, winking devilishly at Tristan before turning back towards the library.

When Lord Edgecombe was out of sight, Lady Hatton breathed an audible sigh of relief. "Well, thank goodness that little fiasco is over. I only hope Lord Edgecombe is gentleman enough not to put it about that Lady Hatton's nieces are ramshackle girls who cannot see to put one foot in front of the other without falling forward on their noses," Lady Hatton observed tartly. "And I'll thank you not to laugh, Tristan," she added in answer to her nephew's outright guffaw. "I see nothing remotely funny about this."

"Forgive me, Aunt, but I'm afraid I do," Chadwick said unabashedly. "However, if it will set your mind to rest, I can assure you that Edgecombe is a man of honour and would not consider sullying our good name by putting forth such gossip. Especially in light of your most generous invitation to dine."

Lady Hatton sniffed, but appeared somewhat mollified. "I shall endeavour to mend Lord Edgecombe's opinion of us, and I hope I may count on both of you to be on your best behaviour tomorrow evening," she said, eyeing Elizabeth and Margaret.

Noting that both girls wore suitably chastised expressions, Lady Hatton sat back in relative complacency. "Are you returning with us, Tristan?" she enquired, settling the rug over her legs.

"Not immediately, Aunt," Chadwick said, nodding to the driver. "I've a few more things to take care of. I shall see you at home later."

Emma, surreptitiously watching the marquis from beneath her lashes, was aware of a curious feeling of disappointment that he was not returning with them but studiously schooled her features not to show it. She had felt Margaret's eyes on her more than once during the recent conversation, and while she wasn't sure if it was her reaction to Lord Edgecombe or to her cousin that Margaret was seeking to divine, Emma knew it would not do to let her see she was particularly interested in either gentleman. If she did, her assurances that she was only here for the wedding would mean nothing.

As they made their way home, Emma continued to ponder her growing awareness of Tristan Landover as a man. He was so very fine, she thought wistfully, much more so than any of the younger gentlemen of her acquaintance. Unfortunately, she was also well aware that Lord Chadwick thought of her as little more than a child, and the knowledge that he did not view her as an alluring woman caused her more grief than she cared to admit.

But how could she change that? Emma wondered, a frown marring the smoothness of her brow. How was she to make a sophisticated gentleman like Lord Chadwick look seriously upon a green girl like herself, when all she seemed capable of doing was involving herself in situations from which he was constantly having to rescue her?

Unfortunately, the more she thought about it, the more Emma was inclined to admit that there was very little likelihood that she could.

CHAPTER SIX

IT DID NOT TAKE LONG for Lady Margaret to discover that whatever had happened at the library was clearly a source of great embarrassment for both girls. Every time she mentioned it, Elizabeth suddenly became very involved in a book, and Emma, dear Emma, who had never kept anything from her before, blushed like a schoolgirl and adroitly changed the subject. Both of which combined to make Lady Margaret all the more curious about what had actually transpired.

Still, Lady Margaret was far from stupid, and knew better than to belabour the point while it was still fresh. She would merely let it appear to be forgotten until a time when she could bring it up more propitiously. Thus, by the following morning, she seemed once again intent on her wedding plans. Over coffee she informed Emma that Bertie had also been invited to join them for dinner that evening and that it would no doubt prove to be a diverting meal.

"But you will remember your promise, won't you, Emma?" Lady Margaret asked, peeking at her friend hopefully.

"My promise?" Emma repeated, her own expression blank.

"Yes, silly. Your promise to help keep Tristan occupied."

Emma's eyes widened in alarm. "Margaret! I did not promise such a thing. As I recall our discussion concluded with my asking how you expected me to engage Lord Chadwick's interest for more than a few minutes."

"Yes," Lady Margaret replied amiably. "And I recall telling you, that Tristan was already interested in you and that holding his attention should not prove difficult in the least."

Emma coloured hotly. "I cannot imagine what would persuade you to say such a thing, Margaret. I agree that Lord Chadwick has been politeness itself, but I think you are making a mistake in trying to read anything more than simple courtesy into his actions."

Lady Margaret, appearing to consider this, paused in the act of spreading Cook's superb raspberry jam on one of her equally superb tea biscuits. "Dearest, Emma, forgive my pushing you. Come to think of it, things might go passably well tonight. Lord Edgecombe will be here and he always seems to keep Tristan in good spirits." She paused and glanced at Emma thoughtfully. "By the by, what did you think of Lord Edgecombe? I noticed him smiling at you."

Emma, who had been expecting the question ever since they had parted company the previous day, now affected a look of casual disinterest. "He is as pleasant as ever."

"And very handsome, don't you think?" Lady Margaret added, watching her friend closely.

Emma nodded, but said nothing, studiously pouring cream into her coffee.

"Hmm. Well, did you feel...anything when he looked at you?" Lady Margaret pressed, gazing at Emma expectantly.

"Feel anything? No, I don't recall having done so," Emma replied thoughtfully. She lifted her cup to hide her smile. "Should I have done?"

Lady Margaret was clearly disappointed. "No, I suppose not." She sighed. "I was only curious, that's all."

Aware that it would not do to raise Emma's suspicions, Lady Margaret decided to let matters lie, and turned her attention instead to the silver salver Higgins had just brought in, bearing the morning mail.

Emma, meanwhile, relieved that her friend had apparently lost interest in the subject, relaxed her guard and reached for a scone. It was quite obvious to her that Margaret was intent on matchmaking, and while Emma had originally believed Lord Chadwick to be the intended quarry, she now began to wonder whether it wasn't Lord Edgecombe that Margaret had in mind for her. She also began to consider whether Margaret's matchmaking intentions extended to Elizabeth, and was determined to find out at the earliest opportunity.

The opportunity presented itself that very afternoon. Lady Margaret had gone out to the Park with her fiancé and Lady Hatton was having a nap, leaving Emma and Lady Elizabeth alone in the drawing-room. They had both been sitting quietly with their needlework when Emma noticed Elizabeth's hands slowly drop into her lap. Glancing up, she observed a secretive, almost wistful smile curving the girl's lips.

"Elizabeth, you look miles away," Emma observed with a smile. "What are you thinking about?"

Startled, Lady Elizabeth picked up her tambour, and endeavoured to work a length of deep rose silk. "Nothing," she replied quickly. "I was just wool-gathering." But after she pricked her finger twice with the needle, she sighed and slowly let it drop again.

"Elizabeth, you're blushing like a schoolgirl," Emma commented. "Whatever is going on in that dear little head of yours?"

"Emma, do you think I was clumsy in the library yesterday?" Lady Elizabeth blurted out.

Emma stared back at her in surprise. "Clumsy? No, dearest, I don't think that at all. Your gown became fast on a piece of wood sticking up out of the floor. We all saw it, don't you remember?"

"Then you do not think it was just me tripping over my own feet?" Lady Elizabeth asked earnestly. "Because I am clumsy and uncoordinated?"

"No, of course I don't think that," Emma replied. "Anyone could have tripped over it. Unfortunately, it just so happened that you were the one who did."

"Yes, well, I should like to think that was the case," Lady Elizabeth answered, doubt still clouding her eyes. "But I don't know."

"Elizabeth, what's wrong?" Emma asked softly. "What is really bothering you?"

"Oh, I don't know," the girl moaned. "It's just that, well, I sometimes wonder whether Aunt Rachel isn't right, after all. Perhaps I am just a hopeless clunch. It's true what she says about my not being able to dance. I've had tutor after tutor try to teach me the steps, but I just could not master them. And I know how annoyed Meggie gets when I stumble, but I really cannot help it. I just cannot be as graceful as you or Meg."

"But it has never bothered you before, Elizabeth," Emma said quietly. "You said you prefer to sit out the dances."

"I do," Lady Elizabeth said despondently. "But that is only because I don't know how to do them properly."

"But I thought . . . !" Emma exclaimed.

"Yes, I know." Lady Elizabeth's voice held a note of exasperation. "You thought that I did not like dancing. Well, I do. The only reason I say that I do not is because I cannot. It is easier to say I do not like to dance than have to admit I have two left feet and about as much grace as a goose."

"Fiddlesticks!" Emma remarked firmly. "Anyone can learn to dance if she truly wants to. It is not as though you have no sense of rhythm at all. You know how to do some of the dances."

Lady Elizabeth looked disheartened for a moment. "The simpler dances, yes, but not the quadrille, or the waltz."

"Well that's hardly surprising," Emma was quick to reassure her. "The quadrille is a difficult dance for even the most accomplished young lady to perform. As for the waltz, that is quite a different matter altogether. Given the somewhat . . . close proximity of your partner, it is necessary to know more than just how to execute the steps. A lady has to know how to follow a gentleman's lead at close range rather than how to execute the steps at a distance."

As she was speaking, a tiny suspicion began to form in Emma's mind. "Of course, there are good and bad dancers amongst gentlemen, too," she pointed out casually. "And the skill of your partner can have a direct bearing on how well you acquit yourself of a dance. Not all gentlemen are equally adept at leading a young lady through the intricate steps."

"I suppose not." Elizabeth sounded doubtful. "Though Tristan doesn't seem to have any trouble in that regard. I have seen him dance with Lady Archer any number of times and they look wonderful together."

The casual remark caused Emma an unreasonable stab of jealousy, but she forced herself to ignore it. "Lord Chadwick has been many times at Court and would need to be an accomplished dancer," she said levelly. "Now, take Lord Edgecombe, for example. I am sure he would also be a skilled partner."

"Oh, yes, he is." Lady Elizabeth nodded, blushing. "A very good one indeed."

Her response was so soft that Emma could barely make out the words, but one look at Lady Elizabeth's glowing face was all Emma needed to confirm her suspicions. The girl was harbouring a tendre for Lord Edgecombe, and taking into account the fact that he was one of Tristan's closest friends, probably had been for some time. The question was, of course, was her interest in the gentleman returned?

Suddenly thinking back to the incident at the library, Emma was moved to recall a particular moment which until now had not stood out forcibly in her memory. It was just before Tristan had bade her sit down. She remembered glancing over at Lady Elizabeth and Lord Edgecombe and noticing, even in her dazed state, that Lord Edgecombe was being particularly solicitous of Lady Elizabeth, as though she were a delicate porcelain doll to be handled with the utmost care.

His expression, too, had given Emma a moment's pause. There had been fondness in that look, fondness mingled with respect and admiration, and perhaps even with the beginnings of something more. And now, as Emma glanced at the wistful face of Lady Elizabeth, the meaning of that look became quite clear. "I think, Elizabeth, that if it is of such concern to you," Emma said, setting aside her own needlework, "perhaps what you need is a few more dancing lessons."

Lady Elizabeth glanced up, the look in her eyes suddenly hopeful. Then, just as quickly, the look faded. "I fear it is too late, Emma. Aunt Rachel simply will not engage any more tutors for me. She's had too many tell her that I'm quite hopeless."

"I wasn't referring to a tutor, Elizabeth. I was referring to myself."

"You!" Lady Elizabeth gasped. "Emma, you cannot be serious."

"Of course I'm serious." Emma laughed, warming to her idea. "Why shouldn't I be? I can do all the dances, and I don't see any reason why I can't teach them to you. Most of them are quite simple once you catch on. And besides, if we practise when Lady Margaret and your aunt are out, who's to know?''

For a moment, Lady Elizabeth dared to look hopeful again. ''Do you really think I could learn, Emma?''

''Yes, I do. As I said, anyone can learn if she truly wishes to. And if I'm not being presumptuous,'' Emma said with a gentle smile, ''I think you may have a very good reason for wishing to learn them—now.''

The rosy stain that appeared on the girl's cheeks was answer enough, and Emma nodded in satisfaction. Yes, she would start that very afternoon with Elizabeth's dancing lessons. And this time, Emma had the utmost confidence that not only would Elizabeth learn the intricate steps, but that she would excel at them!

THAT EVENING, Emma stood in front of the cheval glass, anxiously examining her appearance one last time. She knew they were awaiting her downstairs, but was reluctant to leave her room until she had assured herself that everything was as it should be. Tonight was her first formal dinner with the family, and she wanted to look perfect for Lord Chadwick.

Emma was looking forward to him seeing her in her finery. The first of her new outfits had arrived just that afternoon, and there was no denying that the gown of rich, apricot silk over a filmy underskirt of paler peach accentuated the perfect curves of her figure and brought out the dewy radiance of her skin. Fiona had swept Emma's thick, glorious hair up in a style which drew attention to her high cheekbones and slender nose, then fastened a spray of delicate rosebuds amongst the golden curls. Her eyes, rimmed with the lightest touch of burnt cork, seemed larger and more luminous than ever, and the soft sweep of warm colour on her cheeks and lips added a new sophistication to her appearance. Indeed, she bore little resemblance to the distraught young girl the marquis had found so fortuitously that day at the inn.

A knock on the door, accompanied by a quiet "Emma, are you ready?" alerted Emma to the fact that there was no more time to spare. At her nod, Fiona opened the door and Lady Elizabeth entered, looking breathtakingly lovely herself in a gown of pure white sarcenet edged with gold embroidery. Her shimmering gold hair was styled *à la greque,* while a strand of creamy white pearls had been woven in amongst the curls.

Lady Elizabeth's eyes widened in admiration as she watched Emma walk towards her. "Oh, Emma, you look quite beautiful!"

"Then I daresay we shall make quite an entrance." Emma dimpled. "For you, my dear Elizabeth, look radiant. Indeed, I pity poor Lord Edgecombe tonight."

Lady Elizabeth glanced at her in dismay. "Lord Edgecombe? Whatever do you mean?"

"I mean, dearest," Emma replied, gently pressing the girl's arm, "that once Lord Edgecombe sees you, he will be so smitten that he won't care a fig whether you can dance a step or not just so long as he's beside you."

Lady Elizabeth's response was to blush a brilliant red and scold Emma for her presumptuousness. But the sparkle in her eyes robbed the words of any possible sting, and the two girls descended the stairs in the best of spirits.

"Ah, there you are at last, the pair of you," Lady Margaret said as they entered the salon. "I was beginning to think you were lost and was about to send Higgins to find you."

"No need," Emma replied, stepping forward to brush Lady Margaret's cheek with her own. "We are here now, and apologize most sincerely for our tardiness."

"I hardly think apologies are necessary," Lord Chadwick interjected, "given the way both of you look. Clearly the results more than justified the wait."

Emma turned and found herself smiling up into eyes so dark that she felt she was looking into the night sky. Her pulse quickened in response. "My lord is too kind," she murmured.

"Oh, good, and here is Lord Edgecombe," Lady Margaret said, as Higgins announced the earl's arrival. "Now we are all here."

As Lady Margaret moved away to greet Lord Edgecombe, Tristan turned back to Emma. The admiration in his eyes was plain, and his words, when he spoke, were for her alone. "I hope, Miss Harding, that you will permit me to say how very lovely you look this evening. Indeed, I would scarce have recognized you as the same young lady I met at The Horse and Hound only a few days past."

To her dismay, Emma felt her cheeks glow. "I fear you did not see me at my best the first time we met, Lord Chadwick."

The marquis smiled, his eyes twinkling devilishly. "In more ways than one, I venture to say, though thankfully no harm was done."

"Thanks to you," Emma acknowledged softly.

"Here, Tristan! What nonsense are you whispering to that girl?" Lady Hatton barked from her chair by the fireplace. "Don't you know it is *mauvais ton* to monopolize a pretty young lady?"

"Now, Aunt, I think you're just feeling a little jealous that your favourite nephew isn't dancing attendance upon you this evening," Lady Elizabeth said with a laugh. "Truly, Emma, I don't know who spoils whom more."

"Spoil? Fiddlesticks!" Aunt Rachel snorted. "Not my way to spoil family. Softens them," she announced. "Look what it's done to Margaret."

"I rather resent that remark, Aunt Rachel," Lady Margaret said, pretending injury as she walked back arm in arm with Lord Edgecombe. "I am not in the least spoiled, am I, Emma?"

"Of course you aren't, dearest," Emma responded dutifully.

"There, you see," Lady Margaret said triumphantly. "Emma says I'm not spoiled. And Emma would not lie."

"Miss Harding may not lie," the marquis interrupted, handing Edgecombe a glass of wine, "but neither would she willingly offend. A true friend never would."

"I do not think I like what you're insinuating, either, Tristan," Lady Margaret rebuked him. "Bertie, tell them I am not spoiled."

"Of course you are not spoiled, my love," Bertie said, uncomfortably aware of Chadwick's eyes on him. "It is not your fault that you're used to getting everything you want when you want it."

There was a moment's horrified silence, before Tristan suddenly started to chuckle, the sound emanating from deep within his throat. Hearing it, Lady Elizabeth began to titter, and Emma, who was having trouble containing her own laughter, finally gave way as well, until all of them were laughing, Lady Margaret included.

"Thank you, Bertrand, I shall remember that," Lady Margaret said drily when the laughter had died down. "And you, Tristan Landover, it is no wonder you are still single," she said, playfully slapping him on the shoulder. "I pity the poor girl who will have to suffer that wit of yours for the rest of her life."

"I daresay she will need to be pitied, having to be possessed of a similar turn of mind," the marquis retorted, his mouth still twitching. "However, as I doubt many young ladies are cursed with such an affliction, I think I may venture to say that I shall remain a bachelor for a good while yet.''

"Well, I, for one, refuse to believe it," Lord Edgecombe spoke up. "Not with the number of matchmaking mamas after you, old boy. You're still one of the prize catches on the marriage market.''

"Yes, but as a match for the mothers or the daughters?" Lady Hatton piped up. "Lord knows, Tristan, if you wait much longer, you'll be catching some of the mamas on their second time round. There are already a bevy of rich widows from which to make your choice. Speaking of which, I understand from Lady Kettleton that Lady Thorold is back in Society, and that her late husband left her very comfortably fixed, indeed.''

"Ah, yes, Letty," Lord Edgecombe said, finding it hard to refrain from smiling. "Quite a stunner, Tris, even if she is somewhat long in the tooth.''

"Long in the tooth, my eye!" Lady Hatton retorted acerbically. "She is no more than eight-and-twenty. Besides, my nephew is not getting any younger, either. Look at him. He's already going grey.''

"That," Chadwick said, proudly stroking the silvery sprinkling of hairs at his temples, "is what comes of having two younger cousins to launch into Society, with all its accompanying trials and tribulations. Anyone would go grey trying to keep up with these two.''

"Tosh, Tristan, you would think us a terrible handful the way you go on," Lady Margaret chided him fondly. "I'm surprised Lord Edgecombe hasn't run for his very life rather than be caught keeping the company of two such onerous females.''

"On the contrary," Lord Edgecombe said, his glance causing Lady Elizabeth to blush prettily, "fleeing such delightful company would have to be the last thing on my mind.''

"And what about you, Miss Harding?" the marquis enquired of Emma. "Given your tender age, you must find me dreadfully old company to be keeping. No doubt you would prefer to be associating with gentlemen a good deal younger."

Emma met his pentrating gaze with equanimity, despite the fact that her heart was beating like a drum. "Sadly, my lord, as I have had precious little experience of gentlemen of any age, I cannot say that I have a strong preference one way or the other. I think I can say, however, that if one is attracted to a man whose heart and mind are true, the age he bears is hardly a consideration."

"Well spoken, Miss Harding," Lord Edgecombe said. "Very well spoken, indeed. Your sentiments reflect my own."

"That may be so, Lord Edgecombe, and it is all very well to say," Lady Margaret said mischievously, "but if you had the choice, Emma, would you not rather fall in love with a young man than an old one?"

The topic of conversation was becoming decidedly dangerous, and Emma, aware that more than one pair of interested eyes were focussed upon her, was profoundly grateful for Higgins's timely announcement that dinner was served. With a sigh of relief, Emma watched as Tristan offered his arm to Lady Hatton, after flashing her a decidedly wicked grin, while Bertie hastened to escort his fiancée.

"It seems that I am to have the great privilege of escorting two lovely ladies in to dinner this evening," Lord Edgecombe said, gallantly offering an arm to both Lady Elizabeth and Emma. "I think I shall endeavour to dine here more often."

The smile he gave Lady Elizabeth was especially gentle, and Emma saw the transparent joy on the girl's face. Yes, things were certainly progressing in that quarter, Emma mused, deciding that the dancing lessons, which had out of necessity been postponed this afternoon, really had better commence the very next day!

Dinner was a light-hearted, jovial affair which, contrary to Lady Margaret's fears, did not set Tristan and Mr. Rowsbottom at each other's throat. In fact, Tristan was noticeably more agreeable to Bertrand than he had been upon any previous occasion. So much so, that by the time the ladies withdrew to leave the gentlemen to their port, Lady Margaret felt sure that some of the barriers between her cousin and her fiancé had finally fallen.

"After all, it is exactly as I have been saying all along," Lady Margaret commented as she settled her skirts about her on the settee. "Tristan can be a perfect gentleman when he wants to be."

Lady Elizabeth, having seated herself at the pianoforte, ran her fingers lightly over the keyboard and glanced at her sister in surprise. "I cannot think what you mean, Meggie. I have never seen Tristan act in any way other than that befitting a gentleman."

"Tosh, Lizzie, how can you say that after Tris gave Bertie such a setdown at our betrothal dinner? It was quite embarrassing."

"It was nothing of the sort, Margaret," Aunt Rachel corrected her elder niece. "Your Mr. Rowsbottom was merely being argumentative."

"He was not!" Lady Margaret retaliated. "It was Tristan who was being difficult. I think his attack on Bertie was totally unjustified. Besides, he's always being difficult these days. I don't ever recall him being so opinionated when he was younger."

It was probably as close to a criticism of her beloved cousin as Lady Margaret was likely to come, but had Mr. Rowsbottom been privy to it, it would have been enough to make him feel considerably more appeased. As it was, when the gentlemen rejoined the ladies shortly thereafter, it was immediately obvious from Tristan's faintly contemptuous expression and Bertie's injured one that another contretemps had taken place.

"I think, Lady Hatton, that I shall beg your early leave," Bertie said, his voice nearly as stiff as his posture. "Thank you for a lovely evening."

"Bertie!" Lady Margaret implored. But when he looked at her, Lady Margaret flushed and turned accusingly towards Lord Chadwick. "Tristan!"

"Your betrothed need not leave on my account, Margaret," the marquis interrupted mockingly. "I was just leaving myself. I feel the need to associate with a slightly less puerile crowd."

"Tristan!" Lady Hatton reprimanded him sharply.

The marquis paused, and bowed sardonically. "Present company excepted, Aunt Rachel."

Chadwick turned to leave and in doing so came face to face with Emma. Her troubled expression momentarily gave him pause, but in his present frame of mind, it did not serve to alter his course. "Good evening, Miss Harding. I hope *you,* at least, did not find my company too tedious."

The tension was visible in his body and Emma could see the fire burning in his eyes. "I think you know that I did not, my lord," came the quiet reply. "I am only sorry you feel the need to deprive us of your company so soon."

Tristan hesitated. As always when in her company, he felt torn: torn by his desire to be close to her, yet equally torn by the need to put her away from him. He was too old for her. Wasn't that what that obnoxious upstart Rowsbottom had just insinuated?

And yet, as much as Chadwick wanted to turn away from Emma, he knew he could not. She played on his heartstrings the way a harpist plucked her instrument. She moved him in a way no other woman had ever been able to, and he yearned to pull her exquisite body into his arms, to feel the warmth of her skin against his. He longed to spark a fire in those incredible violet eyes. Even more, he yearned for her companionship... for quiet evenings spent by the fireside with her head resting against his shoulder...to see her grace his table, her beautiful face smiling serenely back at him. All this he wanted . . . and knew he could never have.

"Ride with me tomorrow," he ground out, hating himself for the weakness which made him ask it of her.

Emma was startled by the intensity of his request, but there was no hesitation in her reply. "I should be delighted."

Studying her face a moment longer, the marquis abruptly nodded. Then he turned and walked out, the bang of the front door signalling his exit.

An uneasy silence filled the room after Lord Chadwick's departure and effectively put an end to the light-hearted mood of the evening. Mr. Rowsbottom, evidently not pacified by the marquis's departure, left in a huff himself, and Lord Edgecombe took his leave shortly thereafter, though not before extracting a promise from a bemused Lady Elizabeth to drive with him in the Park the following afternoon.

The ladies, thus robbed of their male companionship, made desultory conversation amongst themselves for a while before making their way to bed. Margaret's face wore a decidedly grim expression. She had spoken briefly with her fiancé before his departure, and was clearly upset about it. Lady Elizabeth, on the other hand, climbed the staircase with a rather dreamy expression in her eyes, due no doubt to Lord Edgecombe's unexpected invitation.

Lady Hatton, not bothered by the intricacies of romance, and well used to the vagaries of her favourite nephew, prepared to retire in her normal untroubled frame of mind. She kissed each of the girls good-night, and bade them sleep well, though Emma secretly doubted that any of them would. Consequently, it did not come as any surprise to Emma when, barely ten minutes after closing her door, she heard a knock and turned to see Lady Elizabeth standing in the doorway.

"I can't sleep, Emma," the girl whispered, advancing into the room. "May I talk to you for a few minutes?"

Like Emma, Elizabeth was dressed for bed in a flowing white nightgown that was prettily embroidered around the neck and cuffs. Her long fair hair hung down to the middle of her back and framed a face that seemed almost ethereally lovely in the flickering candlelight. "I hope I'm not disturbing you," she whispered.

Emma shook her head. "I'm not particularly tired, either," she admitted. "Come, sit on the bed and we shall talk."

Lady Elizabeth nodded gratefully and set the candle down on the bedside table. Her lovely features were clearly disturbed. "Did Margaret say anything to you about what happened between Mr. Rowsbottom and Tristan this evening?" Lady Elizabeth asked. "It must have been serious for them both to want to leave so quickly."

The same thought had occurred to Emma, though she was reluctant to say so. "I don't know that she had much opportunity to speak with him to find out. Mr. Rowsbottom left almost immediately after Lord Chadwick." Emma fingered the delicate lace on the edge of the bed sheet, her expression thoughtful. "Elizabeth, why does Lord Chadwick dislike Mr. Rowsbottom so much? He really doesn't seem such a bad fellow, and Margaret clearly loves him."

"I know," Lady Elizabeth agreed with a sigh. "To be honest, I really do not know why there has always been this distance between them."

"It is terribly upsetting for Margaret," Emma said sympathetically. "I know how fond she is of Lord Chadwick."

"She adores him," Lady Elizabeth admitted. "When we were growing up, she would not leave him alone. Especially after Mama and Papa died. Poor Tris, I'm sure it must have been rather trying for him at times, knowing that from the moment he came here Margaret would hound his every step. And yet, do you know, Emma, he never once said a word about it. Never complained. And that went on for years."

Emma said nothing, trying to imagine a younger Tristan Landover going about Town with a bright-eyed Lady Margaret in tow.

"Still," Lady Elizabeth continued, "at least matters will improve once Margaret and Mr. Rowsbottom are married. They will go off and live somewhere else, and no doubt Tristan will return to the country, where he is the happiest."

"Leaving only you and Lady Hatton to entertain poor Lord Edgecombe," Emma teased, tactfully changing the subject.

At the mention of the earl's name, Lady Elizabeth blushed prettily. "He asked me to go driving with him tomorrow, Emma."

"Yes, dear, I know." Emma smiled indulgently.

"Do you think I ought to?"

Emma blinked, surprised by Lady Elizabeth's uncertainty. "Well, of course I think you ought to. Don't you wish to?"

"Yes."

"Then why the hesitation?"

"Well, because—" Elizabeth stopped, and glanced at Emma for approval. "Is it proper?"

"Of course it is proper," Emma replied, an impish twinkle appearing in her eyes. "Lord Edgecombe has invited you to drive in the Park, silly, not run off to Gretna Green with him."

Lady Elizabeth blushed furiously at the very idea, but fixed a smile on her face regardless. "Yes, I suppose you're right. No doubt I'm making too much of it. All right, I shall go. Thank you, Emma," Lady Elizabeth said, impulsively leaning over and giving Emma a quick hug. "It is so nice having someone to talk to again. Since Meggie's engagement, we don't seem to spend much time together anymore."

"I know, Elizabeth, but you have to remember that Margaret will be a married lady soon," Emma reminded her gently. "She has a great deal to be concerned with."

"I know. And I don't begrudge her a moment of happiness. Nevertheless, I am glad *you're* here. And now, I shall bid you good-night and allow you to retire, for your eyes are nearly closing as it is."

Emma was weary, but not for the world would she have admitted it to Lady Elizabeth. She had known instinctively that the girl needed to talk and Emma was well aware that losing a sister to marriage would be a lonely experience for the warm-hearted Elizabeth.

Once Elizabeth left, however, Emma closed the door and padded softly back to bed. Her head was spinning with all that had happened, but she knew there would be plenty of time to think about it in the morning. At present, all she wanted to do was sleep. Settling herself in the big comfortable bed, Emma pulled the coverlet over her and was about to blow out the candle when there came another knock at the door.

"Emma? Emma, are you still awake? Please open the door, I must speak to you!"

This time it was Lady Margaret, and there was no mistaking the urgency in her voice. Her weariness vanishing, Emma threw back the covers and sprang out of bed. She hurried to the door and opened it, then gasped. "Margaret, whatever is the matter?"

Lady Margaret stood on the threshold with tears streaming down her cheeks. "It's over, Emma," she sobbed, stepping forward into the room. "I am going to call it off. I am not going to marry Bertrand Rowsbottom!"

CHAPTER SEVEN

IT TOOK A MOMENT before the words sank in, and when they did, Emma's eyes grew as round as saucers. "Not marry Mr. Rowsbottom!" she repeated incredulously. "Margaret, you're not serious?"

"Oh, Emma, how can I marry him when every time he and Tristan see each other they quarrel!" Lady Margaret wailed. "What kind of life will that be for any of us?"

Lady Margaret held a handkerchief to her eyes as a fresh stream of tears poured forth. Emma, helpless to know what to say, drew her inside and patted her friend's hand, waiting for the sobbing to ease. "There, there, Margaret, I'm sure it's not as bad as all that."

"It is!" Lady Margaret retorted, delicately blowing her nose. "You saw what happened tonight, Emma. They can't even bear to be in the same room."

"I saw that there was a rather stiff parting, yes," Emma admitted, "but you don't know why. You can't say whose fault it was until you know what happened."

Lady Margaret admitted that she could not. "But what does it matter if I know whose fault it was, or what the reason was?" she persisted, turning bleak eyes towards Emma. "It doesn't alter the fact that every time they meet they argue about something. One day it's politics. The next it's fashion. At this rate, they soon won't even be able to discuss the state of the weather with any degree of civility."

Though Emma found that a little hard to credit, she had to acknowledge that Lady Margaret was correct on the other points. It seemed that Tristan and Mr. Rowsbottom were destined to be at loggerheads.

"I can understand your feeling the way you do, Meggie, but I do not see any need to call the wedding off. Once you and Mr. Rowsbottom are married, you will move away and set up your own household. And your cousin will no doubt return to the country. Why, I shouldn't expect that you would see each other more than a few times a year at best."

"I know that, Emma. And I've thought about it, believe me." Lady Margaret drew a deep breath and turned bright blue eyes towards Emma. "Oh, this is all so dreadfully confusing. I love Bertie, Emma. I really do. Oh, I know he is not dashing and gallant like Lord Edgecombe, or able to write romantic poems like Elizabeth's Lord Byron, but he is ever so good to me. He is kind and he is gentle. I never really wanted anything more than that." Lady Margaret glanced at her friend, the despair visible in her eyes. "But I love Tristan, too, and I know he doesn't approve of my marriage, and that hurts me. Terribly. I cannot bear the thought that every time I see him he will be stiff and antagonistic."

"But you don't know that he will be!" Emma said urgently. "You're only assuming that things will always be so. After all, Margaret, he was quite pleasant to Mr. Rowsbottom all during dinner. It wasn't until after we left the gentlemen that things changed. Obviously something occurred which we don't know about. Did you have an opportunity to speak with Mr. Rowsbottom before he left?"

Lady Margaret shook her head, her dark eyes focussing on the ring on her finger. "Not really. I did ask him, but he wouldn't tell me. He said he would rather not go into it at the moment, and then stormed out. Oh, Emma," she said, her bottom lip beginning to quiver again, "what am I going to do?"

Emma drew a deep breath, and looked Lady Margaret straight in the face. "You are not going to do anything, my dear. And you are certainly not going to cancel the wedding! There must be a logical explanation for Lord Chadwick's behaviour. All we have to do is find out what it is and then work at overcoming it."

"That's all very well for you to say, Emma," Lady Margaret replied bleakly. "But I know Tristan. And I know how difficult it is to get him to talk about matters he prefers not to discuss."

"Difficult, but not impossible," Emma replied with a confidence she was far from feeling. "Perhaps Lord Chadwick will find it easier to talk to a stranger, and I shall endeavour to give him the opportunity of doing so in the very near future. But in the meantime, I want you to promise me that there will be no more talk of calling off the wedding."

Lady Margaret sniffed and nodded, albeit reluctantly. "I promise. Perhaps you're right. Maybe the only thing I can do is stay away once we are married," she whispered, her voice little more than a sigh. "I think it will be best for everyone concerned. I fear Tristan has left me no other choice."

As the tears welled up and began to roll down Lady Margaret's cheeks, Emma patted her hand again, trying to think of something comforting to say. In truth, she could think of nothing. How could she say with any degree of certainty that the animosity between Margaret's fiancé and Lord Chadwick would ever resolve itself?

It was a daunting thought and one Emma brooded on long after Lady Margaret had finally dried her tears and returned to her room. How could Lord Chadwick be so kind and solicitous to her, yet be so uncaring and callous towards his own cousin's fiancé? Surely he could see that Margaret was in love with Mr. Rowsbottom, and he with her? Was that not reason enough to try to get along with the man?

Emma sighed as she stared up at the ceiling. If there was a good reason for Lord Chadwick's antipathy, perhaps she could discover what it was and help to resolve it in some way. After all, he had asked her to ride with him tomorrow, so he must not be utterly indifferent to her. Could she not put that inclination to good use for the sake of her friend?

It seemed that she must. She only hoped that Lord Chadwick would see her concern and understand the reason behind it. She had no desire to turn cousin against cousin, any more than she wished to turn Lord Chadwick against herself!

"NOW YOU WON'T have Emma back late, will you, Tristan?" Lady Hatton said as Chadwick waited for Emma to appear for their ride the next afternoon. "We mustn't be late for Lady Fortescue's ball. I've no doubt it shall turn into a dreadful crush early on, and I do want Elizabeth and Emma to be seen before it becomes impossible to see anything!"

Chadwick smiled at his aunt's admonition and drew on his smooth leather riding gloves. As usual, the two had made up their differences the moment Chadwick had returned home.

"The Park will be dark long before it is time for us to leave for Lady Fortescue's, Aunt Rachel, but rest assured, I shall return Miss Harding in plenty of time to attend to the required primping. Need I remind you that I, too, must attend to my appearance before we leave."

"You need remind me of nothing," Lady Hatton said with a chuckle. "It is well known that gentlemen do not take near the time a lady does to complete her toilette."

"For which I can only be thankful," Tristan replied sardonically. "Where ladies acquire the patience to spend that much time in front of the mirror, I'll never know."

"You may not understand it," Lady Hatton said, turning at the sound of Emma's light footstep on the stairs, "but I've no doubt you appreciate the end results. Ah, Emma," she said, pointedly addressing the girl. "How lovely you look, dear."

And indeed Emma did. In a superbly cut velvet riding habit, in a colour almost as deep as her eyes, and with her shimmering, burnished-gold hair swept up and pinned under a rakish hat, Emma looked a picture of elegance. Lightly holding on to the rail with one delicate hand, she gracefully descended the staircase with her crop and a handful of the long, flowing skirt grasped in the other. She felt her breath catch as Tristan turned and gazed up at her, darkly handsome in a deep rust jacket over fawn-coloured pantaloons and highly polished Hessians. In fact, he looked remarkably similar to the way she had first seen him at The Horse and Hound.

"I hope I did not keep you waiting, my lord," Emma said shyly as he extended his hand to her. She saw the gleam of admiration in his eyes, and felt uncommonly flustered as she finished her descent.

"You did not, Miss Harding, and I compliment you on your punctuality." Tristan levelled an amused glance at his aunt. "I was just remarking to my aunt on the inordinate amount of time some members of your sex spend preparing themselves for an outing."

Emma's laugh was light and charming. "Yes, no doubt many of them do, my lord. But given the size of my wardrobe, it does not take me long to dress. I probably should be just as hopeless as any other, given an equally extensive choice."

"Somehow I don't believe you would, Miss Harding," the marquis replied enigmatically. "Shall we go?"

Not being sure how to answer his remark, Emma wisely made no reply. She bade good-day to Lady Hatton and preceded Lord Chadwick outside, where a groom stood holding their respective mounts. Catching sight of the lovely dapple-grey mare Tristan had chosen for her, Emma breathed a sigh of delight, and her eyes glowed up at him with unconcealed warmth. "Oh, she is beautiful, my lord. Thank you!" Emma said.

"I think you will find her satisfactory, Miss Harding," the marquis observed. "Antoinette is in all ways a lady, but there's spirit there, too. And something told me you might prefer a mount not quite so docile as some."

"I'm sure we shall get along famously," Emma declared, admiring the fine line of the mare's head and running a knowledgeable eye down her legs.

The marquis smiled. Emma was so easy to please compared to some of the ladies with whom he had been acquainted. Indeed, he could not imagine Lady Archer looking so delighted had she been presented with a gift far more valuable than the mere loan of a dapple-grey mare.

As he watched, Emma moved forward to the mare's head and gently stroked the velvety nose, whispering words he was not able to hear. He wasn't to know that the mare so resembled Emma's own little Guinevere that for a moment she wondered if they might be one and the same. But then, Guinevere had been sold long ago, Emma remembered, sobering . . . along with the house and all its contents.

"Miss Harding, you look unexpectedly sad," the marquis commented, noticing the sudden wistfulness in the girl's eyes. "Are you not pleased with Antoinette?"

Emma stroked the mare's silvery withers and shook her head. "Forgive me, my lord. My mind was wandering for a moment. She is a delightful little creature. Antoinette, you said?''

Tristan waited until the groom had assisted Emma into the saddle before swinging up into his own. ''Yes, I named her after a very courageous young lady I met while I was in France. A nurse, actually,'' he added. ''She helped save the life of a very good friend of mine.''

Emma smiled, surprised to discover such a sentimental side to the marquis. ''Then I am doubly honoured that you have chosen her for me,'' she told him. *For in meaning something to you, she must equally mean something to me,* Emma added silently.

They set off at a pleasant trot, enjoying the warmth of the early-summer day. As they approached the Park, Chadwick, who had pulled ahead of Emma, waited until she drew level with him again.

''Tell me, Miss Harding,'' Tristan began casually, ''what did you think of Lord Edgecombe last evening?''

His question caught Emma off guard, given the fact that Lord Edgecombe was the furthest thing from her mind at that moment. ''Lord Edgecombe? Why do you ask, my lord?''

The marquis was careful to maintain a detached expression. ''No particular reason. Just curious, I suppose. He's a fine man, you know.''

''Yes, he is,'' Emma replied distantly.

''My closest friend,'' Chadwick continued in that same indifferent tone, ''and an excellent catch. You—that is, any woman—would do well to marry him.''

Emma heard the unintentional slip and felt her breath catch, scarce able to believe what she was hearing. Was Chadwick, like Lady Margaret, trying to effect a match between herself and Lord Edgecombe? It certainly appeared that way, Emma admitted, her heart sinking. Why else would he be extolling the traits of another, obviously more suitable bachelor?

"Yes, I have heard much good spoken of Lord Edge-combe, and have always found him to be a most kind and considerate man," Emma replied, purposely keeping her eyes fixed on the path in front of them. "Indeed, he was most solicitous of me at the time of my father's death. I have no doubt he would make an excellent husband."

The forthright statement brought the marquis's head around abruptly. "Indeed?"

Emma cast a surreptitious glance towards her companion. "You sound surprised, my lord."

Chadwick glanced at her quickly, his face falling. "Do I? I did not mean to. Shall we ride on, Miss Harding?"

Emma pressed her lips together and urged her mare forward, wishing, not for the first time, that she had some knowledge of the workings of Chadwick's mind.

They rode for a while in silence, passing through the gates and into the Park proper. It was a beautiful day, and not surprisingly, a large segment of fashionable Society had already gathered to stroll about the grounds, eager to see and be seen. A number of carriages were clustered near the entrance, and Emma was surprised to find herself hailed by old friends and acquaintances all of whom expressed their genuine delight at seeing her back in London again.

Chadwick, of course, drew his own share of attention, especially from Society matrons with pretty young daughters who glanced at Emma with barely concealed curiosity. When they were informed by Lord Chadwick that Miss Harding was in London for Lady Margaret's wedding, their relief was patent.

"May we expect to see you at Lady Fortescue's ball this evening, then, Lord Chadwick?" Lady Moreby asked hopefully, her smile as wide as those of her two daughters, seated on either side of her. "After all, I should think with all this talk of weddings at Eaton Square, it might put you in mind of entering that noble estate yourself. There are many lovely young ladies at Court this Season.''

By not so much as a flicker did Chadwick's expression change. "There are, indeed, Lady Moreby," he replied in silken tones, "and no doubt I shall see many of them at Lady Fortescue's this evening. However, I do find that one wedding in a household is quite enough for me. And, as I am more than anxious to see *both* Lady Margaret and Lady Elizabeth happily wed, I can assure you that thoughts of my own nuptials are far from my mind. Good day, Lady Moreby. Ladies," he added, bowing slightly from the waist before moving off.

Emma, who had watched the entire episode in silence, now gave vent to the laughter which she had admirably managed to contain during the conversation.

"I fail to see what you find so humorous, Miss Harding," the marquis murmured stiffly.

"Do you, my lord?" she responded, smiling. "Then pray, forgive my outburst. It is just that...well, Lady Moreby was so...so..."

"Determined?" he supplied drily, his own features succumbing to a reluctant smile. "Dashed if it ain't getting more and more difficult to remain a bachelor as time goes on. It seems the older I get, the more desperate they become," he added irritably.

Emma chuckled. "That may well be true, my lord. But a man's eligibility is not diminished by his age, as I think you well know," she remarked.

Tristan gave her an appraising glance. "Granted, my age may not preclude me from marriage as a whole, Miss Harding, but even you must agree that it seriously narrows the field from which I have to choose."

Emma's lips curved in a smile the marquis found distinctly alluring. "I'm afraid I must disagree with you, my lord. To me, the field looks wide open, indeed."

If Chadwick had not been so well acquainted with the character of his companion, her comment might have drawn a quizzical glance. As it was, he shook his head resolutely. "I hope, Miss Harding, that you are not mocking me."

Emma drew her mare to a halt, forcing him to do the same. "Mockery was the furthest thing from my mind, Lord Chadwick," Emma replied quietly. "Though I begin to wonder whether it is not the issue of marriage which you find so distasteful, rather than the question of whom you might marry," she ventured casually. "Is that, perhaps, why you are so reluctant to see Lady Margaret wed?"

It was a daring question, but Emma knew she must risk it. She had to discover why the marquis held marriage to Mr. Rowsbottom in such aversion. Besides, there was nothing she could do now to retract the words. She watched the marquis's face harden momentarily, and when he looked at her again, the dark eyes were steely.

"I have nothing against the institution of marriage, Miss Harding," he replied distantly. "Indeed, I do know one or two people who are actually quite happy in the estate. Sadly, however, they appear to be in the minority. For the most part, I see marriage for a man as a necessity of life, especially for one in a position such as mine. I must marry to ensure continuation of the line."

"But surely there are other reasons for marrying—" Emma began.

Chadwick continued, as if he hadn't heard. "Margaret, on the other hand, may suit herself. Her future is secured and she will never want for anything. Having said that, I must say that I cannot understand why she has chosen to leg-shackle herself to a younger son who has little hope of acceding to the title, and with little more than a stipend as a yearly income. Where, I ask you, is the sense in that?''

In the unexpected flurry of words, Emma realized that Chadwick had told her a great deal, probably a great deal more than he realized. "I understand your reasoning, my lord," Emma remarked calmly. "But does love have no place in your definition of marriage? Granted, many marriages in the past have been arranged, and many yet are. But oft-times, two people meet and fall in love and choose to marry for that reason alone. And love, when it is strong and true, stands the test of time and hardship. Would you not see Lady Margaret happily share her life with someone of her own choosing, albeit not, perhaps, in the grandest of styles, rather than be condemned to a loveless but socially acceptable alliance?''

Chadwick sniffed disparagingly. "You, like so many others of your sex, make marriage out to be a romantical dream, Miss Harding. What can you know of happiness in marriage? Why do all young women view marriage as a fairy tale—as some wonderful new way of life which requires nothing more taxing than planning dinner parties and paying calls? It doesn't always turn out that way.''

"I am quite well aware of that, my lord," Emma replied quietly, "just as I am aware that not every marriage is idyllic. But neither do I believe that a few bad examples give you the right to condemn the institution as a whole. I, too, know couples who are very happily married, and they feel quite free to say so. When a lady marries, she gains the love and respect of one man, and the chance to become a mother to his children. And what woman does not long to cradle her own babe in her arms, my lord? What woman does not long to fulfil the role for which she has been trained, that of being a wife and a mother with the right to maintain her own establishment in the way she sees fit?'' Emma's voice became impassioned. "Is that such a poor reason for wanting to be married, my lord?"

The marquis glanced at her in surprise, his eyes probing hers as if to discover the secrets of her soul. "Is that the reason you would wish to be married, Miss Harding?" he asked so quietly that she almost thought she hadn't heard him properly. "Is that what you would look for in a relationship with a man?"

Emma opened her mouth, dismayed to find that the words would not come. Her heart was racing, every nerve in her body tingling in response to him. "Yes, my lord," she whispered falteringly at last, turning away from those burning eyes. "That is that I would look for. What . . . I hope one day I may find."

The time seemed endless until his reply came. "Then I hope you find it, Miss Harding. And I hope you find some man worthy of your love. For, by God, he will be a lucky man to win such a prize!"

Emma's eyes widened. She saw the momentary bleakness in his dark eyes before the shutters came down, masking the emotions she had briefly glimpsed there.

"My lord—" she began huskily.

"Come, Miss Harding, I think we have philosophized enough," Chadwick said briskly, gathering his reins. "Let us have done with such deep, brooding thoughts and turn our attentions to the day, for we are—"

"Chadwick! By God, do my eyes deceive me?" a lazy, masculine voice drawled. "Never say it is actually the Marquis of Chadwick I see riding in Hyde Park so early in the Season? I thought you were rusticating in the depths of the country, old man."

The owner of the voice was one of two occupants of a showy black-and-silver curricle drawn by a pair of perfectly matched, high-stepping blacks, which pulled up and drew to a halt level with them. Chadwick, turning to regard the new arrivals, inclined his head briefly and allowed a slow, mocking smile to curve his lips. "Adlington. I might have known I'd run into you sooner or later. Up for the races?"

"Is there any other reason for coming to London during the Season?" the younger man drawled, eyeing Emma with undisguised interest. "Apart, that is, from the pleasure of viewing its fair occupants," he added.

Chadwick purposely ignored the look. "Many would think so," came the dry retort. "Especially those in certain, shall we say, restricted financial straits?"

Lord Adlington smiled, but his good humour did not reach his eyes. "Ah, but have you not heard, my circumstances are no longer quite so restricted, Chadwick," the young peer informed him smugly. "Old Brewster gave up the ghost a few months ago. I am now the fifth Earl of Adlington."

His comment and the tone in which it was spoken were noticeably offhand, and Chadwick inclined his head. "No, I hadn't heard," he replied. Then he added sardonically, "Shall I extend my condolences, or my congratulations?"

Adlington affected an injured look and turned to address the Beauty beside him with mock chagrin. "Trust Chadwick to put a man in his place, eh, Letty?"

The lady thus addressed, resplendent in emerald-green silk, looked up at Chadwick with a good deal more than casual interest. "Lord Chadwick has ever been one to speak his mind, Rupert," the lady replied in a low, husky voice. "And personally, I have always found that to be an admirable trait, finding it so rare as one does amongst the gentlemen of the ton." She turned a pair of remarkable blue eyes towards the marquis and smiled warmly. "Good day, Lord Chadwick. It has been a long while since you last graced London with your presence."

"On the contrary, Letitia, it is your presence which does the gracing," Chadwick responded gallantly. "I'll wager there are many gentlemen happy to know that you are back in Society again.''

''If I may consider you but one of them, my lord, I shall be content,'' she replied smoothly.

Emma, listening to their exchange, suddenly felt terribly gauche and inexperienced. So this was Lady Thorold, whom Lady Hatton had mentioned the other evening. Emma could certainly understand why she would think her a suitable match for Chadwick.

At eight-and-twenty, Lady Thorold could still be deemed an Incomparable. She had married young, and been widowed young, and Emma had no reason to doubt that she was still a very desirable woman. Her skin was smooth and unlined, and her black hair glistened in the sun. She was clearly well versed in the subtle arts of flirtation: while her remarks were not exactly bold, neither was their meaning unclear. It was quite apparent that she was interested in Chadwick, though not blatantly so. She seemed quite content sitting in the curricle beside Lord Adlington, watching and listening. Emma received the distinct impression that Lady Thorold was more used to being the pursued than the pursuer.

As if suddenly recalling her presence, Chadwick turned to Emma, and introduced her to Lady Thorold and, more reluctantly, she thought, to Lord Adlington.

''Charming, Chadwick, quite charming,'' Adlington murmured, raising his quizzing glass, the better to observe Emma. ''You do seem to have a knack for finding the lovely ones before anyone else. I hope you don't intend to keep her all to yourself,'' Adlington said, his tone causing Emma's colour to rise uncomfortably. ''You should let some of us younger fellows have a chance, old boy.''

Chadwick smiled, but Emma noticed the tightness around his mouth. ''Miss Harding is well able to decide with whom she wishes to keep company, Adlington. And as she is here for the wedding of my cousin, I am sure she will enjoy the companionship of many gentlemen besides myself before the Season ends.''

His tone was unmistakably cool, and Emma thought she noticed an answering glint in Adlington's eyes. But it was gone as quickly as it came, leaving Emma to wonder whether she had merely imagined it.

"Shall we see you at Lady Fortescue's ball this evening, Lord Chadwick?'' Lady Thorold enquired in a voice that would melt butter.

The marquis nodded, and gathered his reins. "You shall. Perhaps you will be so good as to save me a dance, Lady Thorold.''

"I should consider the evening a loss if I did not," she murmured silkily, clearly pleased.

"And I hope you will also be attending the ball this evening, fair one," Lord Adlington said to Emma. "When I can converse with you away from the critical eye of his lordship.''

Emma blushed, and glanced uncertainly at Chadwick. Thankfully, he answered for her. "Miss Harding will be attending, Adlington, though whether her choice of partners extends to one such as yourself," the marquis said mockingly, "only the lady herself can say. Good day, Lady Thorold. Adlington.''

Emma smiled at the occupants of the curricle and then urged Antoinette forward, keeping her head high as she rode beside the marquis. She did not know why there were undercurrents running between the two men, but she had no doubt that there were. She could almost feel the animosity in the air. No doubt Lady Thorold had noticed it, as well, but being more used to moving in such circles accepted it as normal and dealt with it in her own way.

Emma could tell by the rigid set of Chadwick's back that he was annoyed, and wondered whether his anger was directed at her for some reason, or at the couple they had just encountered. It wasn't until they were outside the gates of the Park that he looked over at her and smiled a little sadly.

"Forgive me, Miss Harding. I have not been the best company this afternoon," he admitted. "Perhaps I should heed Lord Adlington's words and leave you to find more jovial company amongst those younger than I."

His voice was curiously flat, and it hurt Emma to hear it. "I cannot think, my lord, that younger company would be any more entertaining than yours. Indeed, I remember thinking before I removed to the country that a great deal of nonsense seemed to issue from the mouths of very young men. I have seen nothing in my visit thus far which has led me to believe that circumstances have changed all that much in the interim." Her voice was quite steady, and when Chadwick glanced at her, it was to see a mischievous twinkle in her eye.

"You are, in fact, quite correct, Miss Harding." He chuckled ruefully, relaxing. "Things have not changed overly much in that regard. And now, I had best get you home. Aunt Rachel will ring a peal over my head if I do not return you in plenty of time to dress, and heaven knows, I do not wish to incur that formidable woman's ire twice in as many days!"

CHAPTER EIGHT

THE BALLROOM at Lord and Lady Fortescue's impressive Elizabethan manor had been decorated to resemble the gardens of a French chateau, and indeed, many of the guests who had previously visited the Gallic countryside were heard to comment that for a moment, they had thought themselves transported there.

There were flowers everywhere, brilliant clusters of them all freshly cut and beautifully arranged, their heady fragrances blending to fill the room with sweet perfume. On the terrace, structures of white lattice-work over which leafy green vines had been draped imitated natural arbours, and provided the perfect place for lovers to meet. Along the paths, tiny lanterns lit from within by flickering candles illuminated the stone steps and mapped a magical route through the darkened lawns. Even a trickling fountain, the streams from which ran almost the full length of the ballroom, had been built to duplicate the lavish gardens of Napoléon's France.

Within the ballroom itself, several hundred candles flickered in wall sconces around the perimeter of the room and in the massive Venetian chandeliers overhead, illuminating the room with their brilliance and warming the air to an almost oppressive degree. Fortunately, the evening was fair, and the long windows giving on to the terrace had been thrown open to allow the balmy evening breezes to enter. By ten in the evening, Lady Fortescue was assured of success, the tally of guests amounting to something just over three hundred.

Lady Hatton and her party arrived at the socially correct hour: late enough to find the rout in full swing, but early enough to view the room in all its glory before the magnificent flowers began to wilt and the tall white candles to leave long trails of wax in their holders.

After dutifully greeting Lord and Lady Fortescue and the other members of the family comprising the receiving line, Lady Hatton and the girls slowly made their way into the ballroom where a glittering array of London Society was already mingling. Emma, catching her breath at the sheer opulence of the decor, hesitated on the threshold of the room and cast her eyes upward, marvelling at the beautifully painted frescoes on the ceiling. In doing so, she unwittingly drew the eyes of a number of the young gentlemen already assembled, who in turn marvelled at the sight of a startlingly lovely young woman in a gown of shimmering oyster silk, the low décolletage of which admirably displayed a creamy set of shoulders and a gentle swell of bosom. Matching satin gloves covered her arms to just above her elbows and, on her feet, the jewel-dusted toes of dainty golden slippers were just visible from beneath the slightly raised front hemline.

Lady Margaret and Lady Elizabeth were equally well turned out for the ball. Lady Margaret looked a vision in a gown of lavender watered silk, while Lady Elizabeth appeared demure and charming in a whisper-soft gown of white gauze. Lady Hatton, of course, was magnificent in black taffeta, a breathtaking diamond necklace displayed upon her ample bosom, the brilliance of the stones quite dazzling in the flickering candlelight.

Chadwick had gone ahead to speak with some friends, leaving the ladies to move forward into the throng. As expected, Lady Elizabeth was soon surrounded by several anxious young gentlemen all eager to secure a place on her dance card, while Lady Hatton, fondly watching her younger niece, shook her head, the diamond drops at her ears dancing.

"I am so delighted by the way Elizabeth has taken to all this," Lady Hatton murmured proudly to Emma. "I don't mind telling you, I was positively in despair of the girl last year. Hard to believe what a difference a year can make. I daresay there won't be a single spot left unclaimed on her dance card this evening."

"Yes, but I cannot help but think that the gentlemen offering for those places will more likely be hoping to converse with Lizzie than dance with her," Lady Margaret said with a giggle. "Poor dear. If only she could have learned the steps."

"I think you may be surprised to see Elizabeth dancing better this evening," Emma said casually, keeping her eyes on the floor. "I noticed her studying some notes in her room this afternoon."

In truth, Emma had managed to get Elizabeth alone long enough to show her a few basic steps, and was delighted at how well the girl had mimicked her movements. Emma felt sure that her young pupil would, with a few more lessons, be able to master the more difficult steps which had thus far eluded her. Unaware of this, however, Lady Hatton merely tutted, and shook her head kindly. "I fear it will take more than a few notes on paper to train those feet, my dear, but never mind. Elizabeth seems to do well enough talking to the gentlemen. Ah, there's Lady Horton. I really must go over and find out if that rumour about Annabel is true. Prudence!" she called, sailing away from the girls, and clearing the floor in her wake.

"She's quite impressive, isn't she?" Lady Margaret whispered in Emma's ear.

Emma smiled and nodded. "I don't know how I can ever thank her for everything she has done for me, Meg. And you. You have all been so very kind to me that I almost feel part of the family."

"You always were!" Lady Margaret assured her fiercely. "Which makes me all the more annoyed to find out that you were not telling me the truth about your . . . situation," she finished lamely.

Emma glanced at her friend uncomfortably. "What situation, Meg?"

Lady Margaret bit her lip, and was about to reply, when she was distracted by the sound of a murmur rippling round the room. Turning to see what had provoked such a reaction, Emma glanced towards the door, and in doing so, felt her heart plummet like a stone. Lady Thorold stood poised in the doorway, intent on surveying the milling crowd below, and looking absolutely breathtaking!

Like Lady Hatton, Letitia had also come to the ball wearing black, but that was where the similarity in their appearances ended. The gown Lady Thorold wore was specifically designed to draw attention to a figure still well able to attract it. Her voluptuous curves were accentuated by the skilful cut, and Emma felt sure her décolletage was lower than fashion decreed. And if the gown weren't enough to draw attention to the wearer, the flash of a magnificent ruby-and-diamond necklace against the translucent whiteness of her skin certainly was.

"Oh, my, Lady Thorold is certainly out to attract attention this evening," Lady Margaret commented, idly joining Emma in her study of the new arrival. "I wonder if Tristan has seen her yet?"

Emma endeavoured to ignore the unforeseen lurch her stomach gave in response to Lady Margaret's innocent question and purposely averted her gaze. "Is your cousin . . . interested in Lady Thorold?"

Lady Margaret wrinkled her nose, and shrugged delicately. "To be perfectly honest, I don't know. Tristan didn't actively court Lady Thorold before she married, even though I know she was dangling after him. And he danced with her a few times at various functions when her husband was still alive, but then, that doesn't really signify, either. Lord Thorold was never one for dancing. He was much older than she, you know. I think he used to like seeing Letitia enjoying herself. Still, as Aunt Rachel said, Lady Thorold is certainly beautiful enough to marry well again. And as her husband left her so nicely situated, I doubt her age will be viewed as much of an obstacle."

"I don't imagine her age would be much of an impediment to Lord Chadwick in any case," Emma heard herself reply with a touch more asperity than she had intended. "I received the distinct impression that he believes himself too old to consider taking a young bride."

"Yes, so I've oft heard him remark," Lady Margaret agreed, somewhat annoyed. "At times I could positively shake him for it. Listening to the way Tris goes on, you'd think him in his dotage, rather than being just eight-and-thirty. One need only look at him to see what wonderful condition he is in. As a matter of fact, Bertie told me that Tristan outlasts many of the younger bucks that go down to Gentleman Jackson's to exercise. And don't think that doesn't put them into high dudgeon!" Lady Margaret laughed.

Mortified to feel her cheeks blush as she recalled the trimness of the marquis's waist and the breadth of his chest and shoulders, Emma decided it was wiser not to comment, and turned to address a safer topic. "Oh, look, Margaret, there is Mr. Rowsbottom."

The gentleman so identified, at that moment catching sight of them, waved and strode through the crowd purposefully. Emma smiled when she saw the warmth in his eyes as he raised Margaret's hand to his lips, and turned away to allow them a few moments' privacy, even though in such a crowded room, privacy was a quantity almost unheard of. Unfortunately, in doing so, she also encountered someone she had been hoping to avoid.

Lord Adlington, who once having been told that he was exceedingly handsome by a woman whose lineage was remarkable, and whose desire to be Lady Adlington even more so, conducted himself with the airs and graces of a nonpareil. He was young, brash and obscenely wealthy, having been the sole heir to the riches of a vast estate, the monies from which would allow him to live in comfortable decadence for the rest of his life.

It was that inheritance which now funded his two main passions in life: horses and gambling; and which also made him, to his way of thinking, quite irresistible to ladies—especially to young, pretty girls such as the one he now addressed.

"Ah, Miss Harding, I had hoped to find you here this evening," Lord Adlington greeted her smoothly. "And how very charming you look, my dear. Too charming to be standing all alone."

Emma allowed the merest shadow of a smile to touch her lips, and opened her fan gracefully. "On the contrary, I am not alone, Lord Adlington," Emma informed him. "I am here with Lady Hatton and her nieces."

"But of course. And no doubt with crusty old Chadwick lurking somewhere nearby," Adlington remarked cryptically. "I hope, fair one, that you will grant me the honour of a dance this evening. Or am I too late to secure a place on your card?"

"There are still a few spots remaining, Lord Adlington," Emma replied, heartily wishing there were not. Adlington nodded, smugly assuming that no female would willingly turn him down. His sensual lips curved into a leering smile, while his outstretched hand left Emma little option but to present her card.

In spite of his expensive clothes and reasonably handsome features, there was something about Lord Adlington which Emma could not bring herself to like. It might have been the slight shiftiness in his eyes or the perpetual attitude of boredom he affected which repelled her. Lord Adlington viewed the world through watery blue eyes, the lids of which were frequently half closed. When he spoke, it was in the languid drawl so affected by the dandies of London fashion, as if apathy were a quality to be admired and emulated.

Whatever it was, Emma knew that she felt uncommonly ill at ease in his presence and consequently watched in dismay as he wrote his name down beside one of her earlier dances. She couldn't help but think that if this was the manner of the younger men Lord Chadwick had been referring to, she might just as well retire to the country now.

They made desultory conversation for a while, Adlington seeming ill disposed to relinquish her company. He kept Emma talking, pointedly drawing her attention back when it chanced to wander, and making her feel more uncomfortable by the minute. Hence, when she happened to glance over his shoulder and saw Lord Edgecombe approaching, Emma smiled at him with a warmth he could hardly fail to find flattering.

"Ah, Miss Harding, I thought I glimpsed you through the crowds," Lord Edgecombe greeted her. "How delightful to see you again. And Adlington," the earl said, his eyes cooling ever so slightly as he turned to address her companion, "I hadn't expected to find you about so soon. I hear you lost badly at Newmarket last week."

"Mildly so," came the laconic reply. "Nothing serious enough to keep me away from these fashionable diversions." Adlington's glance slid back to Emma. "Indeed, how untimely it would have been had I been forced to miss the opportunity of furthering an acquaintance with some of our lovely newcomers.''

"I'm sure we are all honoured by your presence," Edgecombe replied acerbically. "Miss Harding, would you care to accompany me to the refreshment table where I might procure a glass of punch for you?"

"Why, yes, thank you, Lord Edgecombe," Emma replied hastily, glad for the excuse to escape. "I do find it uncommonly warm in here."

"I say, Edgecombe," Adlington interrupted, clearly put out. "That's hardly sporting. I was about to offer the lady some refreshment myself."

"Ah, but you didn't, did you?" Lord Edgecombe replied calmly. "Adlington."

Ignoring the other man's gasp of outrage, Emma placed her hand on Lord Edgecombe's arm and allowed him to escort her away, purposely keeping her head high. She knew their exit had been a trifle precipitate, but really could not bring herself to feel remorseful. The man was quite odious, and she only hoped he would not be unpleasant during their dance.

Once clear of Lord Adlington, Emma sighed, and allowed herself to relax slightly. "Thank you, Lord Edgecombe. I do believe I am in your debt," she said, glancing up at him meaningfully. "I was beginning to find the company somewhat tedious."

Well aware of the intimation, Lord Edgecombe grinned, and handed her a glass of punch. "No thanks are necessary, Miss Harding. Adlington can be difficult to shake once he latches on to you. Rather like a physician's leech, I've always thought, if you will forgive the comparison," he added with a smile.

"Forgiven," Emma said, laughing up into his face.

"Well, good evening, Edgecombe, Miss Harding," Chadwick said, coming up behind them quietly. "You both seem to be in good spirits this evening. I hope I am not disturbing anything."

"Ah, there you are, Chadwick," Lord Edgecombe greeted him easily, seemingly unaware of the slight edge to Chadwick's voice. "Of course you're not disturbing anything. Where have you been, anyway? I have been looking for you all evening."

"I was down paying my respects to Lady Vyne," Tristan informed his friend ruefully. "Aunt Rachel swore she would ring a peal over my head if I did not speak to her."

"I suppose that means you've been cajoled into dancing with one of her daughters."

The marquis's eyebrow shot up. "How did you know?"

"Got roped into it myself earlier," came the amused response. "I do believe her ladyship is getting a tad desperate."

Unwittingly reminded of the conversation she and Lord Chadwick had had in the Park, Emma turned away to conceal a smile. She was well acquainted with the redoubtable Olivia, Lady Vyne, and with two of her three unmarried daughters. Consequently, she could well understand why desperation was beginning to set in. It was widely known that after three Seasons for the eldest daughter and two for the middle one, there had still been no offers of marriage. And now, with the last girl expected out this year, it seemed just too much for the poor lady to cope with.

Hence, with characteristic directness, Lady Vyne had taken matters into her own hands. Under the pretence of good-natured teasing, Lady Vyne inveigled every unmarried man she met to dance with one, two, or all three of her daughters. And short of causing a scene, there was very little a gentleman could do but accept.

And so, throughout the course of the evening, the three daughters would be dutifully escorted onto the floor, and then dutifully escorted back to their seats upon conclusion of the dance, the girls pleased at having been asked, the gentlemen relieved to be free of their obligation. It seemed a mutually satisfactory arrangement.

Emma, gazing at the occupants of the room over the top of her fan, suddenly noticed Lord Adlington advancing towards an unsuspecting Lady Elizabeth, who for some inexplicable reason was standing alone at the edge of the dance floor.

"Excuse me, my lord," Emma said, turning to Lord Edgecombe, "but I think there is another who will shortly be in need of your services."

Indicating Lady Elizabeth with her eyes, Emma was amused to observe the way Lord Edgecombe's face lit up. "Yes, well, you could be right," he said, glancing almost sheepishly at the marquis. "Chadwick, if you will excuse me but a moment."

Emma watched him depart with a hint of a smile hovering about her lips.

"Would you care to explain that remark about Lord Edgecombe's services, Miss Harding?" Chadwick murmured, trying to ignore the fact that the sight of his best friend laughing so easily with Emma had roused emotions he was ashamed to acknowledge.

"I refer, my lord, to his services as rescuer," Emma said, keeping her eye on Lady Elizabeth. "What Lord Edgecombe did for me, he is about to do for Elizabeth. Look."

They both watched as Edgecombe slowly made his way across the crowded floor towards Lord Adlington and Lady Elizabeth, stopping to chat with people along the way so as not to make his purpose too obvious. Adlington continued to monopolize Lady Elizabeth, his ingratiating smile clearly making her uncomfortable. When, as if by coincidence,

Edgecombe turned and found himself confronting the two, he chatted with them for a while, shortly after which he turned to Lady Elizabeth, no doubt making a similar offer to the one he had made Emma. Emma saw Elizabeth smile and nod in evident relief. Then, ignoring Adlington's protestations, Lord Edgecombe smoothly led a blushing Lady Elizabeth away, leaving Adlington to glare after them in frustration.

Now that he was wise to the game, Chadwick's mouth twisted ruefully. "Yes, I see the nature of the ploy. Adlington is not one of my favourites, either, and I am glad Edgecombe was able to rid you of his company. Especially if it was not desired."

The last was in the form of a statement, yet Emma knew there was a question behind it. She turned to look up into the marquis's face, and smiled. "It was not desired, my lord, be assured of that, any more than it was desired by Elizabeth."

She saw Chadwick nod briefly, and noticed that his features seemed to relax slightly. "Are you enjoying yourself, Miss Harding?" he asked, joining her in a study of the guests.

"Oh, yes, very much. I always find watching people to be of as much interest as dancing. You can tell as much about them by what they don't do, as what they do."

Chadwick turned a quizzical eye towards her. "Indeed. How so?"

Emma smiled, and glanced around for a good example. "Ah, there's a case in point. Do you see Mr. Chuzzleton over there, the thin bespectacled man standing by the potted palm?"

"Yes."

"And do you see the anxious look on his face, and the way he keeps fidgeting with his cravat?"

The marquis smiled. "Which he has nearly succeeded in destroying. Yes, go on."

"Well, if you will notice, the recipient of those frequent, anxious glances is Miss Harriet Brocklehurst, the rather plump girl sitting over there on the settee."

"The one in puce?" the marquis asked sceptically.

"The same. Now, if you notice, every now and then, Mr. Chuzzleton starts to take a step forward, and then hesitates. There, see. He just did it again."

"Yes, I see," Chadwick said, still wondering where all this was leading.

"And every time he does, Miss Brocklehurst sits up a little straighter and looks away," Emma continued. "There."

The marquis nodded, amused in spite of himself. "And what are you able to glean from these movements, Miss Harding?"

"I perceive, Lord Chadwick, that Mr. Chuzzleton would very much like to ask Miss Brocklehurst to dance, but that he is too shy to do so. And that she, being aware of his interest, tries to look nonchalant when he starts to approach, which only makes him think that she is not particularly interested in him."

Chadwick watched the two players for a while until he realized that Emma had them pegged perfectly. "And what do you foresee as the result of all this?" he could not resist asking.

Emma hesitated. "Well, any one of a number of things, actually. Mr. Chuzzleton may become so discouraged that he will eventually give up altogether and leave early. Or, Miss Brocklehurst will continue to keep up the pretence all evening and not be danced with at all. Or..."

"Or?" the marquis prompted.

"Or Miss Brocklehurst will eventually tire of acting nonchalant, and Mr. Chuzzleton will inadvertently creep up on her and ask her to dance."

"Well, thank goodness for that," the marquis commented, smiling down at her. "I hardly think I can bear the tension much longer."

Emma laughed along with him, aware suddenly of how much younger and more at ease he looked when he laughed. She found herself wondering what he had been like when he was her age, but found that she could not picture him looking any other way than he did now: handsome, worldly, slightly older, and slightly more wonderful than anyone she had ever met!

The sound of Lord Edgecombe's and Lady Elizabeth's laughter cut across her thoughts, and Emma came to with a start, abruptly aware that she had been staring again. Glancing away, she felt her cheeks glow warmly, aware that Chadwick also had noticed her study.

When the gentlemen had moved away to claim their respective partners for the next dance, Lady Elizabeth whispered, "Oh, Emma, what an objectionable man Lord Adlington is. I was just telling Lord Edgecombe how timely his arrival was when he informed me that you had sent him."

Emma nodded. "He did the same for me. I do not like Adlington overmuch myself, though I am not really sure why. He is handsome in a smooth kind of way, but there is just something about him that makes me . . ."

"Uneasy?" Lady Elizabeth supplied.

"Yes. That's it exactly. I do not think I quite trust Lord Adlington."

"It's his eyes, I think," Lady Elizabeth said. "I find them rather shifty. They are not trustworthy, like . . . well, Lord Edgecombe's, for example."

Emma carefully hid her smile, and nodded. "No, most definitely not. Lord Edgecombe's eyes are very trustworthy, are they not, Elizabeth?"

"Oh, yes, indeed they are." The girl sighed dreamily.

The next dance was a cotillion. Lady Elizabeth had been engaged by a pleasant-looking young man who blushed almost as much as she did. Fortunately, it was a relatively simple dance, and Lady Elizabeth quit the floor well pleased with her footwork. Or so it seemed to Emma, who stood watching her student with an almost maternal sense of pride.

"I wonder, Miss Harding, if you might have a dance to spare me?"

Chadwick had walked up behind her quietly, and when Emma turned round, it was to find herself only inches away from him. Bereft of words, she could only nod, suddenly finding it very warm in the room. Emma watched as Chadwick took her card and twice wrote his name in bold strokes, once for the supper dance, and again for a waltz.

Flustered, Emma shook her head. "I am...sorry, my lord, but I have not yet received my vouchers to Almack's and I do not think it would be socially correct to dance the waltz without the patroness's approval."

He saw the confusion on her face, but knew it was not unmingled with disappointment. "No matter, Miss Harding. Perhaps you might care to join me for a stroll along the terrace. Would that be more suitable?"

"Y-yes, I'm sure that would be fine," Emma said, her voice a trifle unsteady.

"Good. Now, I fear I must go and fulfil my obligation to Lady Vyne. If you will excuse me, Miss Harding."

With that, the marquis bowed and made his way to the floor. Emma watched, smiling as he led out Lady Vyne's eldest daughter, Euphadora, and partnered her through the dance, his exquisite skill as a dancer making her seem an accomplished partner. Though, to be fair, it wasn't that Lady Vyne's daughters could not dance; they all managed quite creditably. It was just that they were so plain of face that few gentlemen approached them, which was sad, given that their personalities really were not at all lacking.

Still, Emma acknowledged, no one had ever said the gentlemen of the ton were kind, and indeed, many a lady not blessed with pleasant features or an enviable portion had suffered the humiliation of being ostracized for no worse fault than that. Of course, such a fate would never befall such a person as Lady Thorold, Emma thought enviously, aware that ladies like her would always be desirable and eligible.

Emma watched as the Beauty glided across the floor, seemingly en route to Lord Chadwick. It appeared that they were promised for the next dance. Lady Thorold waited until the marquis had returned Euphadora to her mother before moving forward, a dazzling smile on her lips, as Chadwick took her lily-white hand and led her onto the floor.

As the strains of a waltz floated through the air, Emma bit her lip. The waltz was the most intimate dance Society allowed, and permitted a gentleman to hold a lady in his arms while they were dancing. Such close contact made some Society matrons gasp. To Emma, however, the idea of dancing so closely with someone you cared for was highly appealing. Now, as she watched the marquis spin Lady Thorold effortlessly about the floor, she could not help but notice what a striking couple they made, both so dark, both so good-looking. Others, watching them circling the room, were clearly of a like mind, and whispered comments amongst themselves Emma would have preferred not to hear. In response to something the marquis said, Letitia tilted her head back to expose the sensuous curve of her neck, and emitted a silvery laugh. Her skin was creamy white against the dramatic black dress, her lips as red as the rubies twinkling at her throat. She was breathtakingly beautiful, and with a sinking feeling, Emma turned away.

Who was she to think she could win Chadwick's affection? She, whom he thought of as little more than a "bath miss." How could she compete against the worldly Lady Thorold?

All too soon, Lord Adlington came to collect Emma for their dance. Seeing him approach, Emma fixed a smile on her face and dutifully kept it there. Fortunately, as the dance was one of the Scottish reels which had recently become so popular with London Society, Emma was not forced to endure his company throughout. But even so, when it concluded and Adlington returned her to her place, Emma could not prevent a shudder of distaste as the young peer bowed and brushed the back of her hand with his lips, his eyes lingering boldly on the shadowy cleft exposed by the low décolletage of her gown.

"Th-thank you, Lord Adlington," Emma said quietly, fighting the urge to pull her hand away.

The glassy blue eyes smiled back at her vacantly. "No, no, fair one. It is I who must thank you. Perhaps I could interest you in a stroll about the gardens?" he asked boldly.

"I think not, Adlington," Chadwick cut in peremptorily. "Miss Harding is engaged to me for the next round."

Emma turned, startled to see the barely controlled anger on the marquis's face. Adlington, however, seemed vaguely amused by it. "I say, old man, no need to cut up at me. I shouldn't think it healthy for a man your age."

Chadwick's eyes narrowed dangerously. "You might be surprised to discover what is healthy for a man my age, Adlington. Perhaps you would care to join me for a round at Mr. Jackson's rooms sometime."

Emma saw the young man flush and knew that Chadwick's barb had gone home. Pointedly ignoring Chadwick, Adlington muttered a good-evening to Emma and then hastily took himself off, no doubt looking for someone else to bother.

"What an objectionable man," Emma mused, echoing Lady Elizabeth's earlier sentiment. "Is he always like that?"

The marquis nodded. "Unfortunately. In fact, I was rather surprised to see him here tonight. He is barely received by polite Society anymore."

"Oh? What did he do?"

"Nothing," Chadwick replied, "other than be himself. Which, for Adlington, is reason enough to exclude him. Shall we walk, Miss Harding?"

Emma nodded, her smile tremulous as she put her hand on his arm and strolled out onto the terrace with him. Other couples were also enjoying the balmy evening air, strolling quietly and talking.

Chadwick found he enjoyed walking with Emma. In fact, he was beginning to find that he enjoyed doing almost anything as long as he was with her. The sound of her voice, the sight of that burnished-gold hair, continued to evoke feelings in him which he knew were wrong. He was not the one for her. He knew that instinctively. And yet, on the other hand, he knew that he was exactly right for her. She needed someone to guide her, someone who would love her and cherish her all the more for the special qualities she possessed.

"Are you cold, Miss Harding?" he asked her gently when they were far from the noise of the ballroom.

Emma glanced at him in surprise. "Cold, my lord? No, not at all. Why?"

"You were shivering."

"Was I? Dear me, it must be all this...excitement," Emma replied, casting about for a likely excuse.

"Yes, no doubt that is the reason," Chadwick replied easily. He laid his hand over hers, trying to ignore the feelings the lightest touch of her skin aroused.

They strolled along in companionable silence, their path lit by the flickering glow of the candles. The moon was a silvery crescent in the velvety darkness, and all around them were the gentle sounds of the night.

"How peaceful it seems when one is away from the crowds," Emma couldn't help remarking when they had seated themselves upon a stone bench. "It puts me in mind of the country."

"Do you enjoy the country, Miss Harding?" the marquis ventured, surprised to hear her say so.

"I do now." Emma laughed. "Though I certainly didn't when I first moved there. To be quite honest, I was dreadfully afraid of the dark. At least in London there were the gaslights. I didn't realize how used to them I had become until they were not there anymore. And then it was so very quiet in the country," Emma said, her voice dropping almost to a whisper. "I used to go outside the front door and gaze about, amazed that in all that huge countryside it could be so incredibly silent."

Chadwick, who was watching the beautiful, upturned face beside him, felt something move deep within his soul. "Yes, I understand that feeling," he admitted. "Many times I have gazed out at the stars in the night sky." His eyes lifted heavenward. "Looking for answers. Do you ever study the night sky, Miss Harding?"

"Yes, quite often, in fact," Emma whispered, almost shyly. "Though I firmly believe there are more stars in the country than there are here in Town."

"Yes, I do believe you are right," the marquis agreed. Then, to her surprise, Chadwick lifted his hand and brushed it gently against her cheek. "Though I fear, Miss Harding, that there is one star which I do not find in the country," he continued, against his better judgement. "One bright shining star which will always remind me of London."

Emma held her breath, and felt her heart skip a beat. She knew that she should look away, pretend not to understand what he was referring to, but she did not. "And this . . . star you speak of," Emma replied hesitantly, "does it shine brighter as the days go on?"

A rueful smile twisted his lips and his hand fell away. "Yes, I do believe it does. But I fear it wastes its precious glow on me, Miss Harding," he said, his voice so low that she had to lean forward to hear. "I am too old to be so blessed."

Emma swallowed, feeling a sudden pricking behind her eyes. "I think you judge this star too harshly, my lord. Does a star not have the right to shine its light on whomsoever it pleases?"

Chadwick turned a face alight with infinite tenderness towards her. "Indeed it does, Miss Harding. But what is the good of illuminating the way of one who has nowhere to go? It should shine down on someone who can use its guidance. I, alas, have seen much more darkness than this one precious star can irradiate."

Emma met his gaze, and then gasped, startled by the message his eyes were sending out. Chadwick was in love with her! It was there in his eyes, in his voice, in his very presence. It struck her forcibly, and with an intensity that left her in no doubt as to its validity. Yet, even as she rejoiced in it, Emma realized that it was an empty discovery, and one which would bring her no happiness. Chadwick would not acknowledge his love for her. He still felt himself too old.

"I think, my lord, that you underestimate the stars' power," Emma said quietly. She laid a gloved hand softly on his arm. "Though they appear to be little more than a tiny speck of light, you may be surprised to discover just how strong they can be."

Chadwick turned a puzzled face to her, and then caught his breath at the look in her eyes. By God, she was in love with him, just as he was with her. It was there, written all over her face.

"No! Emma...you mustn't!" Chadwick said in a tortured whisper, clasping the hand that rested on his sleeve. "This is...wrong!"

"Why? Why is it wrong?" she asked him.

"Because I am too old for you, Emma," he repeated dully. "You need someone younger. Someone more like you."

"So you keep saying, my lord," Emma replied drily. "And yet still you turn towards me. Still your eyes and your heart send messages to me."

"Would that they did not!" Tristan admitted, hanging his head. "You bewitch me, Emma. You did right from the start when I saw you in that room. When I think back now to what happened, to what might have happened, I think I could kill..." His voice was raw with emotion.

Emma shook her head, and placed her fingers lightly against his lips. "No, Tristan, there is no need to say such things. Thanks to you, nothing did happen, and no one is the wiser. My only concern now is you," she said, glancing at him from beneath lowered lashes.

He smiled wanly. "I do not know why. What is there for you to be concerned about?"

"Only that you are resisting me for no good reason," Emma told him plainly. "You are not too old for me, Tristan. Do you not recall my once saying that age does not matter so long as the heart and mind are true?"

"Yes, I recall your saying so, little one," the marquis whispered, aware that he had to make her understand before he—or she—fell any deeper. "And that is all very well to say, but there are other considerations. I have not been...without weakness in my life, Emma. I am a man, and I have enjoyed what the world has to offer."

"I am not condemning you for that, my lord," Emma told him, her eyes sparkling. "I would hardly have expected a man of your age to live the life of a monk. Indeed—" she chuckled "—I should have thought there something very wrong if you had."

"Emma!"

"Oh, please do not 'Emma' me," she scolded him quietly. "Why do you persist in treating me like some schoolgirlish miss, Tristan? I am all of nineteen years old!"

He could see the fire in those marvellous eyes, and felt the warmth of her hand under his. "Yes, you are all of that, little one. And I am twice your age. Only think what your Aunt Georgina would say."

Emma pursed her lips. "She would ask me if I were happy and then give me her blessing. Faith, Tristan, why do you persist in being so stubborn!" Emma cried, betrayed into strong feeling.

Chadwick hastily swallowed a laugh, and forced himself to look stern. "There, do you not see the bad influence I am already having on you? Need I remind you that a lady does not raise her voice?"

"Tristan, I . . ."

"No! Not another word," he said, pressing a finger gently against her lips. "We will not speak of this again, Emma. You will find another, more suitable man to love."

Emma laughed bitterly. "By 'more suitable,' I take it you mean younger."

"Yes, I mean younger," the marquis admitted. "And you needn't make it sound so arduous, my dear. There are more than enough gentlemen from whom to make your choice. Only think of it, Emma. When you are thirty, I shall be nearly fifty. When you are—"

"When you are dead, then so shall I be," Emma whispered fiercely. "Just as I shall be now if you do not accept my love. Oh, Tristan, please, please do not do this to me."

Emma implored. "To us! What we have is special, my love. It does not come to many."

Chadwick shut his eyes, as if to ward off the sight of her. "No, Emma! I will not hear of this! It is at an end." Abruptly, he rose, his breathing unsteady. "Do not speak of this to me again. I, in turn, shall endeavour to remain at a distance from you. The wedding is less than a week away. Until then, we must carry on as though nothing had happened between us. For Margaret's sake, if not for our own."

Emma shut her eyes, turning her back on the sight of him. It was all she could do not to fly into his arms. To beg with him, plead with him to listen. But she knew it was useless. Tristan would not be moved. She could see that now. He fully intended to let her go when all this was over.

"Very well, my lord," Emma said, her voice completely without emotion. "I shall do as you wish. If this is what you truly want. But I warn you," Emma continued, turning back to face him, the light in her eyes extinguished. "Do not try to matchmake for me, for I will not be a part of it. I shall leave here as I came, no matter what you or Margaret or anyone else tries to accomplish. If you will not accept my love, please do not force me to accept another in your place!"

With that, Emma picked up her skirt and quickly returned to the ballroom. She was dangerously close to tears, and kept her head down, praying she did not run into anyone she knew. If she was questioned now, Emma knew she would break down. She needed time alone to sort out her feelings, to sort out how to deal with the situation. Perhaps later she would chide herself for a fool. At present, all she could feel was the burning ache in her heart for a love that was not to be!

CHAPTER NINE

NOT SURPRISINGLY, the talk during morning calls the next day revolved around Lady Fortescue's ball. The consensus was that it had been a dreadful crush, the temperature too close to be comfortable, the food in sadly short supply and the musicians really quite mediocre. In short, it was judged a complete success.

Emma, upon being drawn into conversation by Lady Vyne, was asked if she was enjoying her return to London after spending a year in the country.

"Yes, Lady Vyne, I am," Emma replied mechanically, smiling as she accepted a cup of tea from Lady Horton. "It is, of course, quite a change from the peace and quiet of the countryside."

"Yes, no doubt you would find it so," Lady Vyne agreed, her nose quivering in a rather peculiar manner. "I positively wither when I am forced to remove to the country. I find it so dreadfully... bucolic." She caught a sardonic glance from Lady Hatton. "Now, Rachel, don't look at me like that. I realize that visiting the country has become the thing, but it doesn't suit me at all. I happen to like the selection of entertainments to be had in London, not to mention the shopping. I've always found the quality of merchandise in the smaller towns to be, well, rather inferior as a whole. And the company," she said, rolling her eyes. "Not a decent eligible gentleman to be had, unless you count the local squire, who's usually a frequent visitor to the inn, or the village vicar, who's too boring by half. And being the mother of three such delightfully marriageable girls, I feel it incumbent upon myself to present them to only the most eligible of gentlemen. As I did last evening." She glanced benignly upon her eldest, Euphadora, who was perched awkwardly on one corner of Lady Horton's settee, precariously balancing a delicate cup and saucer on her lap while trying not to allow the crumbs from the biscuit she was nibbling to fall into it. "Lord Chadwick was most attentive to dear Euphadora. Indeed, I don't believe I saw him appear more animated all night."

"Except perhaps when he was dancing with Lady Thorold," Lady Horton pointed out bluntly. She ignored the flush on Lady Vyne's face, and turned back to Lady Hatton. "I should not be at all surprised to see a match ultimately result there, Rachel. They suit each other quite well, don't you think?"

Lady Hatton shrugged in a noncommittal fashion. "Who can say? Tristan has always kept very close about his marriage plans."

"But you must admit he does seem to favour her," Lady Horton persisted. "I didn't see him spend as much time with anyone else."

"He did engage Emma for two dances," Lady Margaret pointed out, noticing the way Emma's face had paled during the discussion. "And he has in the past been particularly solicitous of her regard. Hasn't he, Elizabeth?"

Lady Elizabeth nodded, but Lady Horton just smiled and shook her head with a look that could only be called discouraging. "I would not put too much stock in that, my dear. It is well known that the marquis is looking for a somewhat . . . older bride. In which case, Letitia would be much more suitable. Would you not agree, Rachel?"

"I agree that she is older," Lady Hatton remarked drily. "But beyond that I cannot say that I have noticed Tristan singling her out for any undue attention. Nor anyone else, for that matter. Frankly, Prudence, I don't know that my nephew intends marrying,'' Lady Hatton stated flatly. "He seems quite happy as he is.''

"But surely Lord Chadwick must consider the matter of progeny,'' Lady Vyne observed pragmatically. "As the direct male heir, no doubt he will want a large family, and is Letitia not getting a little beyond all that? I should think a younger, stronger girl like Euphadora would surely be the better candidate. After all, it is not as though he need hold out for a love match,'' she stated disparagingly. "At his age, I should think he would be happy just to get on with it!''

If Emma could have been granted one wish, it would have been to be removed as far as was possible from that stuffy room at that particular moment. It was almost beyond bearing to hear Tristan discussed as though he were nothing more than a pawn in the marriage game, and his intended wife little better than a brood mare. How dared they discuss him as though he were some oddity, simply because he chose not to marry?

They were merely envious, Emma decided. Envious because they knew that he would never offer for any one of Lady Vyne's plain, unattractive daughters, and envious of Lady Thorold because she had been widowed young enough, and was still lovely enough, to attach his interest. Little did any of them know that there was already someone with whom Tristan Landover was in love ... though for all the good it would do her, Emma admitted bleakly.

Abruptly, Lady Hatton set her cup down and signalled to her charges. "Come, girls, I do believe it is time we were leaving.''

"Oh, dear, so soon, Rachel?'' Lady Horton and Lady Vyne cried in unison, obviously loath to give up the subject of Lord Chadwick.

"I'm afraid so. We have an appointment with Madame Broussard this afternoon for the girls to be fitted for their dresses, and there are still one or two other stops we must make before returning home. There are just that many things to attend to before a wedding. You understand.''

"Yes, of course," Lady Horton said, reluctantly accepting that nothing further would be gained by quizzing Lady Hatton. "Shall we see you and Lord Chadwick at Lady Amberly's tomorrow evening? I hear she has engaged a rather dashing Italian tenor to sing."

"Oh?" Lady Vyne looked up at her sharply. "You wouldn't happen to know whether the gentleman is single, would you, Prudence?"

Aware that they would soon be launched on another topic, Lady Hatton and the girls hastily said their goodbyes and left.

"Thank goodness we got out before they started on the merits of the poor Italian tenor," Lady Margaret commented ruefully. "Listening to them discuss Tristan was quite bad enough."

"Yes, as if Tristan would ever offer for Euphadora," Lady Elizabeth said, clearly put out. "Can you imagine?"

"No, I cannot," Lady Hatton said tartly. "But then, when you have three less than vivacious girls to settle, you tend to grasp at straws, Elizabeth. It takes very little encouragement from a gentleman towards any one of her daughters for Lady Vyne to become hopeful. And you know that Tristan always treats a lady with the utmost consideration."

Emma, sitting quietly beside Lady Hatton in the carriage, mulled over the significance of that comment. Was Tristan of the opinion that he was being considerate of her in trying to turn her away from him? That he was doing her a favour by pushing her towards "more suitable" gentlemen?

It seemed so, though how she was to convince him otherwise eluded Emma at present. She knew that she loved him, and that he loved her. All that remained was for her to convince him that she was serious in her intent.

"Emma, are you all right?" Lady Hatton enquired kindly. "You have been very quiet this morning."

Emma smiled, the corners of her mouth trembling ever so slightly. "I'm quite well, Lady Hatton, thank you. I think I must just be a little overtired from the ball last evening."

She caught sight of that lady's concerned countenance and hastened to reassure her. "Taking into account the events of the past year, I'm sure you can understand that it has been quite a while since I danced the night away."

"Yes, no doubt it has," Lady Hatton murmured sympathetically. "Though I guarantee it won't be the last. I noticed a lot of young gentlemen watching you last evening, my dear," she added, patting Emma's hand. "I predict you are going to be a very busy young lady over the next few days."

Emma kept the smile fixed on her lips, as was expected. She knew that Lady Hatton only had her best interests at heart. No doubt she assumed that Emma, like every other young lady of marriageable age, was looking for a husband. After all, was that not the express purpose of the Season?

"By the by, Emma," Lady Hatton continued, "I was going to wait until this evening to tell you, but I think now might be as good a time as any. I have received your vouchers for Almack's."

"Oh, Emma, how wonderful!" both Lady Elizabeth and Lady Margaret exclaimed together.

Emma gasped, and turned to Lady Hatton in surprise. "Almack's! I had no idea ..."

Lady Hatton waved her hand. "I spoke with Lady Sefton before you arrived and informed her that you were coming to London to stay with me until Margaret's wedding. When I mentioned that you were Diana Harding's daughter, and explained the situation, she was only too happy to assure me that it would be taken care of immediately. Though I didn't realize it at the time, your mother was a dear friend of both Lady Sefton and Lady Cowper. In fact, all the patronesses are quite anxious to see you."

It was an accolade of the highest degree, and Emma recognized it as such. "Thank you, Lady Hatton, I really do not know what to say. You have been so very kind to me."

"You have no need to thank me, Emma," Lady Hatton replied brusquely. "Think of you as one of the family, actually. I know we all do. Tristan included."

Emma nodded, her smile fading ever so slightly at the notion of Tristan's regarding her as a member of the family. The very idea made her blush, for her feelings towards him were hardly sisterly. Nor did she believe that his sentiments towards herself were of a brotherly nature, much as he might like to pretend otherwise!

DINNER THAT NIGHT was a quiet affair, with only Lady Hatton and the girls sitting down to table. Tristan had come home late in the afternoon, and advised his aunt that he would be dining at his club with Lord Edgecombe, after which they were engaged to play cards. He said little to Emma beyond enquiring after her health, and after nodding at her response, turned away, affording her no opportunity to converse.

Emma, however, was not left completely without hope. She did see the momentary bleakness in his eyes when Lady Hatton proudly informed him that along with the anticipated flood of cards for Lady Elizabeth, an impressive number had been received for Emma, as well as a charming posy of flowers from Lord Adlington. She compounded the damage by adding that Emma would no doubt be a busy young lady for the duration of her stay in London.

Chadwick mumbled something about the sensibilities of young men and then took himself off, leaving both Lady Margaret and Lady Elizabeth to stare after him in mute surprise. Lady Hatton, not unduly concerned by her nephew's peremptory manner, ignored his mumblings and continued to read her book. It was only when she turned to address a question to Emma, who was still watching Chadwick's retreating back, that she was startled out of her complacency. One look at the girl's expression told her everything she needed to know.

So that was the way of it, Lady Hatton thought, suddenly understanding the reasons for both Emma's recent silences and her nephew's tempestuous moods. She might have known. Indeed, she was not wholly surprised by the discovery of tender sentiments between Tristan and Emma. Emma was a jewel of a girl, and Lord knew, Tristan could do much worse. Nor did she harbour any delusions that Tristan would play fast and loose with the girl's affections. If Tristan were genuinely fond of Emma, it would be for the right reasons.

Whether Tristan viewed her as a likely candidate for marriage, however, was another matter altogether. Lady Hatton knew first hand how conscious her nephew was of his age. If he viewed Emma's youth as a serious impediment, only time would ultimately tell if he would be able to overcome it. Lady Hatton knew that love could move mountains; whether it could move Tristan Landover was another matter altogether!

NOT SURPRISINGLY, a similar question ran through the marquis's mind as he lingered over a second glass of brandy later that night. He and Edgecombe had partaken of an excellent dinner, and now sat relaxing in the deep leather armchairs and pleasant masculine ambience of White's. They were not expected at Lady Boothe's for a few hours yet. After all, a good card game could hardly get under way before the participants were well and truly sated on food and drink.

Amidst the low background hum of male voices, Chadwick swirled the reddish-gold liquid in the glass and stared morosely into its depths.

"Won't find the answer there, old stick," Edgecombe drawled, noticing the frown on his companion's face.

Chadwick started, and then smiled, guiltily aware that he had been lost in thought for some time. "Sorry I've not been the best company tonight, Jeremy. My thoughts have been...elsewhere."

"I didn't need a soothsayer to tell me that," the earl responded lightly. "So what's got you so blue-devilled, anyway?" Edgecombe's voice was mildly teasing. "Problems with the ladies?"

To this, the marquis laughed outright. "You always were too perceptive, Jeremy. And I fear the years have done little to diminish that shrewdness."

"Nothing shrewd about it." Edgecombe grinned and shrugged his broad shoulders eloquently. "Men get a particularly pained look when their problems concern a female. Either that, or gout. So what is it, my friend?" he asked, signalling a passing waiter for more brandy. "Is the fair Jane wearing you out, or could it be the lovely Letty pushing for something more permanent?"

Tristan chuckled. "Now there you have fallen a little short of the mark. The problem which concerns me the most has nothing to do with either of them, though what you say does have a grain of truth. Letitia, not unreasonably, I suppose, is starting to make veiled references to our similarly unwed state. It seems," Tristan informed his friend, "that we are viewed as a highly suitable and decorative couple."

Jeremy chortled. "Are you surprised? Only a blind man could fail to see how much she wants to become the next

Marchioness of Chadwick. And I can't imagine she would be such a bad choice, Tris, all things considered. She's certainly beautiful, and you wouldn't have to worry about her marrying you for your money. From what I hear, old Thorold left her pretty plump in the pocket."

Chadwick nodded, confirming his friend's assumptions. "So," Edgecombe continued, "if it's not the amorous Lady Jane, or the alluring Lady Thorold, what other female is causing you to stare into your drink?"

"The problem," the marquis said with a sigh, "is Miss Emma Harding."

"Emma Harding!" Jeremy repeated, plainly startled. "Now you are gammoning me. What manner of difficulty could you possibly be having with dear Miss Harding?"

Chadwick could not quite bring himself to meet his friend's eyes. "I believe the girl fancies herself...in love with me," the marquis muttered lamely.

"In love?" Jeremy replied, his mouth curving into a smile. "By Jove, that was fast. Even for you! She's only known you just over a week."

"Never mind the raillery." Chadwick grimaced. "I didn't try to make it happen. It just did."

"Well, what's the difficulty?" Edgecombe said, obviously not seeing his friend's dilemma. "She is a delightful creature, and quite a diamond, if I do say so. I am sure you must know how many gentlemen of our acquaintance would be only too happy to make such a claim?"

"Yes, I do. And that's just the point of it, Jeremy," Chadwick said in frustration. "Emma hasn't given any of them a chance to say such things. And we both know that I am not right for her."

"Yes, of course we do." Edgecombe nodded blankly. "Now would you care to tell me why not?"

"You know damn well why not," Chadwick growled. "I'm too old for her. My God, she's only nineteen."

"Yes, she is," came the calm rejoinder. "And probably one of the most charming and lovely nineteen-year-olds I have ever had the pleasure of meeting. And beg pardon for saying, but I still don't see your difficulty."

Tristan shook his head, suddenly regretting the impulse which had made him confide in Jeremy. It seemed he was just as stubborn as Emma.

"Look, Tris," Edgecombe said, observing that the situation was genuinely causing his friend grief. "What makes you think Miss Harding is in love with you, anyway? I find it difficult to believe that a young lady as proper as Miss Harding would admit straight out that she loved you without your first having given her some indication as to your own feelings."

As much as he regretted lying to his friend, Chadwick was not ready to confess his own part in the proceedings. "She hasn't come right out and said it in so many words," Chadwick equivocated. "But I know. Believe me, Jeremy, I know. And it is wrong. And I have told her as much."

"You told her!" Edgecombe said, his tone incredulous. "Good Lord, Tristan, that was hardly sporting. Poor girl. What did she say?"

"She told *me* in no uncertain terms that I was not to try to matchmake or push her towards any other gentlemen of my acquaintance, as she would simply refuse to entertain them."

"Good for her." Edgecombe laughed. "I always knew there was spirit in that young lady."

Tristan nodded ruefully and took a sip of his brandy. "Indeed."

"So?" Edgecombe sat back and grinned broadly. "What do you intend to do about this little . . . problem?"

"I intend to do exactly what Miss Harding has asked me not to," Chadwick informed his friend heavily. "I intend to introduce her to every suitably eligible gentleman I know. What else can I do?''

Chadwick's voice was noticeably devoid of emotion, and after glancing at his friend's face, Jeremy suddenly understood why. His good friend was in love with the very woman he was trying to marry off to someone else...and trying very hard not to show it.

"Well, yes, of course, I suppose it is the only decent thing to do,'' Edgecombe said, hiding the smile which threatened to expose his earnestness. "And to that end, I suppose we had best set our minds to thinking who might be available to escort dear Miss Harding. Unless you have already selected someone, that is.''

Chadwick sighed, and shook his head. "No. Given that I spend so little time in Town these days, I fear I am rather out of touch with the younger crowd.'' He glanced at his friend sheepishly. "I thought perhaps you might be able to recommend some suitable candidates.''

By not so much as a flicker did Edgecombe betray his amusement. He nodded with what he considered a fitting degree of solemnity, and appeared to turn his mind to the question at hand, even though inwardly he longed to laugh out loud at the absurdity of the situation.

They sat in silence for a moment. Then Edgecombe snapped his fingers. "I've got it. Why don't you introduce Miss Harding to Lord Crambie?''

"Crambie! Are you serious?'' Chadwick replied, clearly shocked at the idea. "That reprobate. The man is a boozer.''

"Yes, but he is very wealthy,'' Jeremy pointed out pragmatically. "In fact, one of the wealthiest, from all I've heard. Miss Harding would never want for anything.''

"Except for a sober husband,'' Chadwick muttered, fixing his friend with a baleful glance. "Care to try again?''

"All right,'' Jeremy said, undaunted. "What about Lord Taylor? Sober as a judge.''

"And about as boring," Tristan scoffed. "He put me to sleep during discussion in the House one morning. I wouldn't wish that on anyone."

"No, I suppose not. Well, then there's Edward Fitzhenry," Edgecombe suggested. "Not too old, reasonably entertaining..."

"And with pockets to let," the marquis informed him drily. "Whatever money Emma had would be gone in a trice once she married him."

"Yes, good point."

They sat and thought some more. Suddenly, Jeremy looked up. "Lord Brookeston?"

Chadwick shuddered. "Too fat. Freddy Ross?"

The earl looked sceptical. "I don't know that he likes ladies, if you catch my drift."

Chadwick's handsome features twisted in disgust. "Pansy! Who else?"

"Lord Wickenstead?" Jeremy suggested.

"Good Lord, he's older than I am. I'd like to see her take up with a younger man, not someone who's going to say 'I do' and then expire!"

"Well, then, there's only one other person I can think of who meets all of the exacting requirements you've set forth," Jeremy said casually.

"Oh? And who's that?"

"Me."

"You!"

"Well, yes, why not?" Jeremy said brightly. "I should think you would be happy to have me marry Emma. After all, I have all the necessary qualifications. I'm the right age, I have no particularly loathsome vices, nor am I bad-looking. I don't drink to excess, don't beat women or children, and have been known to be rather entertaining when the occasion demanded. Further, by marrying me, Emma would become a countess. I should think that would set your mind completely at rest. So, what do you say?'' Jeremy said with a remarkably straight face. "Shall I commence my courtship of Miss Harding at once?"

Chadwick for once was speechless. The knowledge that his best friend was not only willing but eager to begin his courtship totally unnerved him. And he knew why. Jeremy was exactly the type of man with whom Emma could fall in love. He was witty, urbane, charming and kind-hearted— everything Chadwick could have asked for in a husband for Emma.

Jeremy, seemingly unaware of the havoc he was creating, sat back and savoured his brandy, careful to maintain an outward expression of placidity. He knew instinctively that his arrow had found its mark. If, as he suspected, Chadwick really had no serious intentions of pushing Emma towards anyone, his plan could work out nicely.

The earl's plan was simple. He would visit Emma and pay court to her, being mindful not to overstep the bounds he set out for himself. He would take her out, but whenever possible, with Lady Elizabeth as her companion. That way, he would appear to be squiring Emma, while still being in the company of Lady Elizabeth. Then, when Chadwick finally came to his senses and decided he wanted to marry Emma himself, it would leave Edgecombe free to carry on his true courtship of Lady Elizabeth.

At the thought of that sweet, charming young lady, Jeremy's face softened. He could hardly believe how much she had changed over the past year. She was more beautiful than he would have imagined, and Jeremy had known himself lost that day in the library when he had held her in his arms. She had felt so soft and appealing, like a warm, lovable kitten. And when she had gazed up at him with those incredible green eyes, her breath coming quickly from between parted rosebud lips, Edgecombe had been utterly swept away. He had known then and there that it was only a matter of time before Lady Elizabeth Glendenning became his wife.

Chadwick, turning to address a remark to his friend, caught the hopelessly smitten expression on Edgecombe's face and felt his own spirits plummet even further. By God, the man was in love with Emma already. It was written all over his face.

Well, he had no one to blame but himself, Chadwick admonished himself pitilessly. It was he who had suggested finding someone else for Emma to love. Unfortunately, he hadn't thought the someone else would be a fellow as worthy as Edgecombe. His punishment now would be to sit by and watch as the woman he loved with every ounce of his being fell hopelessly in love with his best friend.

CHAPTER TEN

NOT HAVING ANY IDEA of the discussion which had taken place at White's between Chadwick and his closest friend, nor of the plan being enacted by Lord Edgecombe, Emma viewed the earl's sudden interest in her with a marked degree of confusion. When, on the following afternoon, Edgecombe was shown into the salon where Lady Hatton was conducting an at-home, Emma naturally expected his attentions to be directed primarily towards Lady Elizabeth. When they appeared to be focussing instead on herself, Emma glanced at Lady Margaret in mute surprise.

It was not that Lord Edgecombe had been blatant about it, Emma acknowledged later. He had started out by greeting them all in his usual courtly manner, and had, in fact, been especially charming to Lady Elizabeth, who had blushed prettily at his compliments.

The shift in attention had taken place a little while later. And it had been subtle, Emma admitted; so much so that she wasn't even sure Lady Elizabeth had noticed it, given the fact that a number of other people, Chadwick amongst them, had arrived at about the same time. But Emma knew she had not imagined the sudden warmth in Lord Edgecombe's voice when he had sat down on the settee next to her and engaged her in conversation. His remarks had been both flattering and attentive, and by the time he left after the requisite fifteen minutes, it was with the understanding that both Emma and Lady Elizabeth would drive out with him the following afternoon.

"Take both of you out?" Lady Margaret demanded with a giggle after the house had quieted down and Lady Elizabeth had reticently disclosed the information. "My word, Lord Edgecombe will have his hands full. Perhaps you should join them, Tristan. One man to two ladies is hardly equal odds."

Chadwick scowled. Since arriving home from the club, he had all but ignored Emma, and now seemed strangely loath to discuss his friend's generous invitation. He took himself off upstairs, grumbling.

"Heavens, I don't know what has come over that man." Lady Margaret sighed in exasperation. "When he's not looking daggers at someone, he's marching about the house muttering to himself. Hardly typical behaviour for our dear Tris...not typical at all."

There seemed to be a consensus on the subject. Only Lady Hatton refrained from making comment. When questioned, she flatly refused to speculate on the possible cause of her nephew's ill humour, knowing full well the real reason for his moodiness. And while Emma longed to speak to him and ease the pain in his eyes, she knew she dared not. Tristan had forbidden her to speak of it, and for the moment, she would obey.

Consequently, at Lady Amberly's musicale that evening, Emma, again wearing the elegant apricot silk, this time with her hair more artfully arranged in a tight cluster of curls, made a point of staying away from Chadwick. She took a seat between Lady Margaret and Lady Elizabeth, and seemed quite content to chat with them while Chadwick, sitting at the end of the row, cast frequent glances their way.

"Emma, have you noticed that Tristan keeps looking at us?" Lady Elizabeth whispered as Lady Margaret turned away to converse with a friend. "He seems terribly agitated tonight."

"Does he? I hadn't noticed," Emma said, keeping her voice light and her eyes purposely averted. "But then, it's hardly surprising. I don't imagine musicales are particularly entertaining diversions for gentlemen, on the whole. Men seem to get rather fidgety at these affairs. Personally, I've always felt musical evenings much more suited to female audiences."

"You could be right," Lady Elizabeth allowed dubiously. "Still, Tristan has always seemed comfortable enough at them before. I don't believe—oh!" Lady Elizabeth broke off. Glancing towards the door, she lowered her voice, "I wonder if *this* will improve Tristan's enjoyment of the evening."

Following her gaze, Emma saw that Lady Thorold had arrived and now stood poised on the threshold of the room, looking breathtakingly lovely in a gown of deep rose silk delicately trimmed with lace. This evening she wore around her slender throat a stunning pearl choker fastened with a diamond clip, with matching pearl drops dangling from her earlobes. Her thickly lashed eyes scanned the room, and upon spying her quarry, Lady Thorold moved with alacrity towards Chadwick, the smile on her lovely face warming noticeably.

Meanwhile, a murmur of anticipation rippled around the room as a tall, handsome gentleman entered through another door and went to stand by the pianoforte where he was immediately engaged in conversation by a fawning Lady Amberly.

"Emma. Look!" Lady Margaret said, drawing her friend's attention away from Lady Thorold. "That must be Mr. Puscaliaci."

"Oh, my, isn't he handsome!" Lady Elizabeth sighed. "Just look at those dark, brooding eyes!"

Indeed, Antonio Puscaliaci was a handsome man, and Emma soon discovered, much to her delight, that he had a voice to match. When the murmur of conversation died down and he began to sing, Emma felt herself lifted on the wings of his voice. He was a consummate performer, and held his audience captive, his rich tenor filling every corner of the room. So much so that, for a time, Emma forgot everything but the wonderful sound of the music.

When his performance all too quickly came to an end, there was a brief moment of silence before rapturous applause broke out. Emma, clapping along with the rest, felt the moisture on her lashes and glanced round, not surprised to see a number of other young ladies surreptitiously dabbing at their eyes.

"Oh, that was heavenly!" Lady Margaret said enthusiastically as the three girls rose and made their way towards the refreshments. "I simply cannot recall when I have heard a more magnificent voice. And to think Lady Amberly was fortunate enough to secure him. This will put her top of the trees for quite some time."

The girls moved into the dining-room, and were joined almost immediately by Lord Chadwick and Lord Edgecombe.

"Did you enjoy the tenor, Lady Elizabeth?" Lord Edgecombe asked, unable to curb his tendency to move towards her first.

His action was not missed by Lord Chadwick, who more casually directed his comments towards Emma. "He is, I think, a gifted singer. Would you not agree, Miss Harding?"

Emma smiled, the look tugging at Chadwick's heart. "Very talented, my lord. I admit I was quite moved by the performance."

"Yes. Lady Amberly is to be commended," the marquis continued. "So often the talent at these musicales is sadly lacking. Tonight, however, I believe we have seen true genius."

Emma glanced at him with a look that clearly bespoke her approval, and revised her earlier opinion that all men did not enjoy fine music. Clearly Tristan Landover did, and she was moved to admit that there were still many facets of the man's personality of which she was unaware.

"Ah, Lord Chadwick, there you are," Lady Thorold said, sailing over to join them. "I just *had* to speak to Signor Puscaliaci, I was so moved by his performance. He is giving a private audience for the Prince Regent and some friends at Carlton House in two weeks' time. We simply *must* go."

If Chadwick was amused by her assumption that they would automatically be invited to a function at the Prince Regent's opulent Town residence, he tactfully kept it to himself.

"It does not surprise me that the Prince has asked to hear him sing. Signor Puscaliaci is truly an *artiste*. But we all know how fickle the Regent can be. Those who enjoy great favour one day oft find themselves forgotten the next."

"But surely a talent such as Signor Puscaliaci's would not be glossed over so capriciously?" Emma protested.

Lady Thorold glanced at Emma in a vaguely patronizing manner. "Who can say what the Prince is likely to do? Those of us who know him well are used to his little idiosyncrasies and forgive them, whereas people from the country are not as likely to understand." She studied Emma as though she were some manner of foreign being. "Miss Harding, isn't it?"

"Yes," Emma replied quietly, well aware that Margaret, standing beside her, had bristled at the woman's condescending tone. Lady Thorold nodded and laid a faintly possessive hand on Chadwick's arm. "I daresay Miss Harding finds our Town entertainments vastly different from the type to be had in the country," she commented, fluttering her lashes at the marquis. "Whereas we, on the other hand, are quite used to such refined offerings, are we not, my lord?''

Her tone was so insufferably superior that Lady Margaret glanced pointedly at her cousin, hoping that he at least would say something quelling. But before anyone had a chance to respond, Emma, calmly ignoring the snub, turned one of her loveliest smiles on Lady Thorold.

''I agree that our country diversions may pale in comparison with the entertainments to be had in Town, Lady Thorold,'' Emma replied with equanimity, ''but I do not think I could ever hear a voice as fine as Mr. Puscaliaci's and remain unmoved, whether I were to hear it once a year or once a week. I believe I would appreciate it afresh every time.''

It was a wonderfully understated set-down, and suitably rebuked, Lady Thorold turned an unbecoming shade of red. Standing at Emma's side, Lady Margaret did not even try to hide her enjoyment. To make matters worse, Lord Edgecombe, having turned to join them after speaking with Lady Elizabeth, said, ''I fully agree with you, Miss Harding. One should never let oneself become so jaded by life that one's appreciation of the finer things begins to pall. To my way of thinking, certain things must always be admired. A breathtaking voice, a magnificent painting...'' Edgecombe paused, and glanced at her warmly. ''A beautiful woman...''

His remark elicited a number of different reactions amongst those gathered. Emma felt her cheeks glow at his compliment and hastily averted her eyes. Lady Margaret, glancing from Lord Edgecombe to Emma, said nothing but arched one eyebrow expressively. Across from her, Chadwick positively glowered.

''If you will excuse me...'' he said, abruptly turning and walking away.

Lady Thorold, still smarting from her dressing-down, seemed vaguely amused by Emma's discomfort, and after glancing disdainfully down her nose at both Lady Margaret and Emma, excused herself to catch up with Lord Chadwick. Lady Elizabeth had gone strangely quiet and seemed intent upon studying her reticule. Only Edgecombe seemed unaware of the stir he had caused. "I hope you ladies are looking forward to our drive tomorrow?" he enquired.

Emma murmured some kind of appropriate response while Lady Elizabeth merely nodded.

"Why don't you ask Tristan to go with you, Lord Edgecombe?" Lady Margaret suggested, well aware of the tension crackling in the air. "I do believe my poor cousin is already starting to feel the constraints of the city. He has been positively dour these past two days. Mayhap an outing will help cheer him up."

Edgecombe, who had belatedly noticed Lady Elizabeth's silence after his earlier effusions, hastily decided this might be a good idea. While he was determined to bring Chadwick to his senses where Miss Harding was concerned, he was well aware that he could not afford to do so at the expense of his own aspirations. He knew that if he were not careful, his actions might inadvertently drive Lady Elizabeth into someone else's arms. And then they would all be suffering, well and true!

"Yes, that's not a bad idea," he replied, brightening. "In fact, I think I shall put it to him right now. If you will excuse me, ladies."

Lord Edgecombe went off in pursuit of Lord Chadwick, rather hastily in Emma's estimation, and left the three girls to their own devices. Turning, Emma was about to comment on the strange state of affairs when she saw Lady Elizabeth's bottom lip begin to quiver. Lady Margaret, who had noticed it, too, remarked, "Why, Elizabeth, whatever is the matter, dear? You've gone dreadfully pale."

"It's nothing," Lady Elizabeth said, raising baleful eyes towards Emma. "I've just a touch of...the headache, that's all."

Perceiving that it had nothing to do with the headache, Emma slipped a comforting arm around the girl's slender shoulders. "Perhaps I should take Elizabeth upstairs for a moment, Meggie. It is getting frightfully warm down here."

Lady Margaret hesitated. She was reluctant to leave the room herself, but could certainly see that Elizabeth needed some air. "Yes, all right, Emma," she agreed gratefully. "I am sure it is just the heat. I shall endeavour to explain that to Aunt Rachel, should she ask where you are."

Emma nodded, and turned to lead the way upstairs. Lady Elizabeth, following meekly, seemed more in control of herself and only sniffed occasionally. Once they were in the privacy of the retiring room, however, her courage gave way and, covering her face with her hands, Lady Elizabeth burst into tears.

For a few minutes, Emma let her cry, comforting her as best she could. She knew what was troubling the girl; knew too there was very little she could say. She was too baffled by Lord Edgecombe's behaviour herself to know what to do about it.

"Oh, Emma, I'm so c-confused," Lady Elizabeth whispered when the wracking sobs were spent and she was finally able to speak more coherently. "I thought Lord Edgecombe l-liked me, and now he's t-turning to you! I don't...mean to be a wretch, but I just don't...understand," she said sadly.

"Now, listen to me, Elizabeth," Emma said gently, wiping away the girl's tears. "Lord Edgecombe is not attracted to me. It is you that he is interested in, I am quite sure of it."

"He s-said you were...beautiful," Lady Elizabeth spluttered between sobs.

"He didn't say *I* was beautiful, Elizabeth," Emma pointed out carefully. "He said a beautiful woman was a thing to be admired, like a fine work of art or a beautiful piece of music."

Lady Elizabeth dabbed her eyes with the handkerchief Emma had given her and shook her head. "He was looking right at you when he said it, Emma. We all knew he meant you. Tristan certainly did," she mumbled.

Seeing the wounded expression which momentarily dulled Emma's eyes, Lady Elizabeth moaned, and grasped Emma's hand. "Oh, Emma, forgive me, I should not have said that. It is just that, well, I think I . . . care for Lord Edgecombe more than I should. He really is the first man I have ever felt this way about." She raised red, tear-stained eyes to Emma's face. "Do you really think he still cares for me?"

"I am sure he does, Elizabeth," Emma said, albeit with a confidence she was far from feeling. "Besides," she added, deciding that the circumstances warranted making Elizabeth feel as secure as possible, "even if Lord Edgecombe were interested in me, I fear I could not . . . return his affection."

Lady Elizabeth stared, her hand arrested in the motion of wiping her eyes. "You couldn't?"

Emma shook her head sadly. "No."

"Is there . . . someone else?" Lady Elizabeth asked breathlessly.

Emma nodded, relieved to see a trace of colour come back into the girl's pale cheeks. "There is, but I want your solemn promise here and now, Elizabeth Glendenning, that you shall not utter a word about this to anyone. Nor," Emma added, "must you ask me who it is."

She watched Lady Elizabeth's face fall. "Oh, dear, that was to be my very next question. But why, Emma?"

"Because it is . . . unrequited love," Emma said, casting about for a likely answer and then saying the first thing that came to mind. "I shall . . . get over it and none shall be the wiser. Now, do you promise?"

"Well, of course I promise," Lady Elizabeth said, her voice a little bit brighter. "But are you sure it's a case of unrequited love?"

"Quite sure."

"Oh, my, how dreadfully romantic." Lady Elizabeth sighed. "Just like in my novels."

"Yes, and now that you know, you can understand why Lord Edgecombe holds no attraction for me. And why I must make that quite clear to him."

"Oh, but you mustn't hurt him," Lady Elizabeth objected, her frown returning. "Think how wretched the poor man will be."

"I'm afraid it simply cannot be helped," Emma countered, aware of how wretched her own situation was. "Besides, when Lord Edgecombe realizes that I am truly not interested in him, I feel quite sure that he will look at things . . . differently."

"And then do you think he will . . . come back to me?" Lady Elizabeth asked hopefully.

Emma smiled in what she hoped was an encouraging manner. "My dear, I don't believe he has ever left you. I think, if anything, he may be feeling a trifle sorry for me because I am newly returned to Town. That is all."

Lady Elizabeth gave this some consideration, and seemed willing to accept the explanation. Hence, after she had dried her eyes and repaired her toilette, the girls quickly returned back downstairs. When Lady Hatton made her way to them and expressed her desire to leave, she was met with a surprising chorus of agreement.

"Yes, Aunt, I think that would be a good idea," Lady Margaret said quietly. Her sentiments were quickly echoed by both Emma and Lady Elizabeth. Only Tristan, it seemed, was intent on staying behind for a while.

Emma saw Lord Edgecombe briefly before they left, and was frankly confused by what she saw. When he did not think he was being observed, Emma caught him watching Lady Elizabeth, whose attention was also diverted, with such a look of longing that it almost took her breath away. At that moment, she was convinced that it was, in fact, Lady Elizabeth with whom Lord Edgecombe was in love.

But then, no more than a minute later, the earl turned and smiled at her in such a way as to set Emma wondering whether she hadn't made a mistake. To make matters worse, Tristan intercepted the second look, but rather than glare at Edgecombe, as Emma might have expected, Chadwick seemed grudgingly to accept it, and slowly turned away. With a sinking heart, Emma watched as he walked back to Lady Thorold, whose flashing eyes and triumphant smile seemed to indicate that she was only too happy to have him near.

All in all it was a very confusing night, and one which Emma was glad to see come to an end. Unfortunately, she knew there was still tomorrow to face, and with it, her drive with Lord Edgecombe and Lady Elizabeth. She wondered whether Chadwick would agree to accompany them, and found herself hoping that he would. Perhaps all he needed was to see another man paying attention to her to make him sit up and take notice. Perhaps that would bring the recalcitrant marquis to his senses!

EARLY THE NEXT MORNING, well before the other ladies in the household were up, Emma rose and donned her old riding habit. It was one of the few items of clothing she had brought with her that was in any way flattering, and even though it could hardly be considered all the crack, Emma was reluctant to part with it. It was black and starkly unadorned, the deceptive simplicity of its styling lending it an elegance perfectly in keeping with London standards, and it fit her trim figure to perfection.

Now, setting the matching hat at a rakish angle, Emma picked up her skirts and quietly descended the main staircase. She had instructed a groom to have Antoinette ready for her early, and now as she settled her foot in the stirrup and took up the reins, Emma experienced a surge of exhilaration. How wonderful it would be to ride in the Park before anyone gathered. She might even be able to risk a gallop, given the very early hour.

With the groom following at a respectable distance, Emma put Antoinette to a trot and set off in the direction of Hyde Park. There were few people about this early in the day, other than the colourful street vendors and tradespeople who started their business early, and Emma trotted through the streets secure in the knowledge that she would be unlikely to meet any one of her acquaintance, for that segment of Society would hardly be abroad until much later.

Once inside the Park gates, Emma nodded to one of the grounds keepers and then urged Antoinette deeper into the leafy green interior. The crisp morning air, fresh and moist with the morning dew, felt wonderful against her skin. She breathed in the myriad smells of the Park: the freshness of the leaves, the mustiness of the damp earth, and the perfumed fragrance of the flowers. And for the first time since she had returned to London, Emma felt a sense of peace flow into her body.

She gathered up the reins and, pressing her heel gently into the mare's side, set off at a rolling canter before urging her that little bit more into a gallop. Emma thrilled to the exhilaration of galloping freely through the Park, unencumbered by the strictures of Society. She could feel the power of the mare under her and drew her own strength from it.

To Chadwick, obscured beneath the boughs of a large sheltering tree, she was a sight which quite literally took his breath away. There was his beloved Emma, riding like the wind, her face lifted, her eyes shining. There was such a sense of joy around her that for a moment, Tristan could almost feel it. He knew he should chide her for riding with such abandon through the Park at this early hour, but knew equally well that he could not. Had he not come here this morning for exactly the same purpose: to exorcise the demons which plagued his mind and body... the very demons *she* had unwittingly put there?

When Emma finally reined in her mare not far from where he stood, Chadwick slowly emerged from his cover. He saw her start as she glanced towards him and then quickly turned to see where her groom was. Tristan, recognizing the young lad, signalled him with a nod, to which the groom bobbed his cap and set his horse to grazing a tactful distance away.

"Good morning, Miss Harding," Chadwick greeted her evenly.

Emma stroked the dappled neck, and inclined her head gracefully. Her smile was like the sun itself. "Good morning, Tristan."

Chadwick blinked helplessly. "You should not address me with such familiarity... Miss Harding," he added belatedly. "'Tis not seemly."

"Perhaps not, but then, *you* should not ignore me," Emma countered boldly.

"Ignore?" he hedged, "I don't know what—"

"Please don't try to pretend you have not been doing so, Tristan. You all but run from the room when I'm there."

Chadwick had the audacity to grin. "I told you I was going to stay away from you."

"Yes, and you're doing a very creditable job of it. Still," Emma asked, her voice gentle, "I wonder is it making you happy, my lord?"

Tristan sighed, the sound expressing far more than he could possibly say.

"No, I thought not," Emma replied sadly. "Oh, Tristan, why do you persevere with this foolishness? It is not necessary! Can you not see that?"

"I see only that it *is* necessary, Emma," Chadwick reiterated as firmly as he was able. "I told you why and I see no reason to change that now. In fact," he continued slowly, "I think I was right to push you away. It seems that other interest has already been generated in you."

Emma looked at him blankly. "I beg your pardon?"

"I noticed Lord Edgecombe paying you particular attention the other evening," he said. "As he has done several times in the recent past."

"Yes, though for the life of me, I cannot understand why," Emma acknowledged, shaking her head. "I was so sure he was harbouring a tendre for Elizabeth."

The marquis glanced at her sharply. "Elizabeth?"

"Well, yes, surely you guessed." Emma looked at him frankly. "Did you not see the way he attended to her that day in the library?"

"No," Tristan admitted sheepishly. "In truth, I was too busy attending to you to notice much of what anyone else was doing."

Emma felt the colour creep into her cheeks, and her mouth twitched irrepressibly. "You are incorrigible, Tristan. First you try to discourage me and then you say things like that to me. How am I to know how to act with you?"

Chadwick shook his head, sadly she thought, and turned to gaze out over the Park. "There is no way for you to act with me, Emma, other than as you would to the cousin of your friend. I will not spoil your life by entering into it."

Emma checked the angry reply which automatically sprang to her lips, and strove for a measure of calm in her voice. She could not believe that he was still turning his back on her. "Then, I am afraid, sir, that you spoil it equally well by *not* entering into it. Good morning, Lord Chadwick."

Without another word, Emma turned Antoinette round and headed back in the direction from whence she had come. Her pleasure in the beautiful morning had vanished. She fought to hold back the tears which threatened to spill over and run down her cheeks. What had she to do to prove to Tristan that she loved him?

When Chadwick eventually arrived at the house, he was greeted at the door by a concerned Elizabeth, who informed him that Emma had returned early that morning and had promptly retired to her room with a touch of megrim, saying that in all probability she would not be well enough to drive with Lord Edgecombe.

"Do you think I should endeavour to get word to Lord Edgecombe to cancel the outing, Tristan?" Lady Elizabeth asked softly.

Somewhat distracted, Chadwick shook his head. "I think not, Lizzie. Leave things as they stand. Perhaps Miss Harding will be sufficiently recovered by the time he arrives to join you."

"And if not?"

"If not, you may drive with Lord Edgecombe yourself. After all, he did extend the invitation to both of you."

"Yes, he did, though I think he only asked me out of kindness." Lady Elizabeth sighed. "I think it was Emma he really wanted to be with."

The realization that his cousin was probably right did little to alleviate Chadwick's own annoyance. But, as he forced himself to admit, he had no one to blame but himself. He had told Edgecombe that he wanted someone to court Emma . . . and now he had it. But sitting back and trying to appear happy about it was asking more than even Chadwick was able to give!

BY HALF-PAST FOUR, Emma's headache had eased considerably, but she refused to let it be known. When Lady Elizabeth tapped on her door half an hour later, it was to find Emma still recumbent upon her bed, the curtains drawn against the bright afternoon sun.

"I feel so guilty that you are not coming, Emma," Lady Elizabeth said wretchedly. "Tristan told me I ought to go with Lord Edgecombe even if you do not, but I think I would rather just stay home. I know he will be terribly disappointed when he learns that you are not joining us."

Recalling the look she had seen on Lord Edgecombe's face the other evening, Emma did not agree, but tactfully refrained from saying so. "Lord Edgecombe will be delighted to drive with you, Elizabeth, and I will not hear of you cancelling the outing simply because of my headache."

Lady Elizabeth sighed, clearly of two minds as to what to do. She dearly wanted to go driving with Lord Edgecombe and was dressed for it, looking lovely in a deep blue driving gown, the colour making her eyes look brighter than ever. But Emma could see that she was still hesitant. "Promise me you will go, Elizabeth," Emma said firmly. "And then when you come back, you shall tell me all about who you saw and where you went. I know that will make me feel a good deal better."

"Are you sure, Emma?" Lady Elizabeth asked doubtfully.

"Of course I'm sure, silly goose," Emma teased, gently squeezing her hand. "Go and enjoy the day."

Half-heartedly, Lady Elizabeth nodded, and dropped a light kiss on Emma's cheek before she went out. A short while later, Emma heard Lord Edgecombe's carriage arrive, and quietly slipped out of bed. Hiding behind the curtain, she watched as Lord Edgecombe escorted Lady Elizabeth down the walk and then helped her to board, relieved to see that the besotted look was back on his face as they drove off. Yes, everything would be all right. Emma sighed, visibly cheered. She had not made a mistake. Lord Edgecombe was clearly smitten with Lady Elizabeth, regardless of the way he acted towards her.

But if that was the case, Emma pondered, why did he always seem to favour her? And at the worst possible times, too. He always seemed to wait until Tristan was there to—

The realization, when it hit her, caused Emma to gasp and stare at the window in dismay.

"Tristan?" Emma breathed, her eyes opening wide in shock. *But of course.* Tristan had put Lord Edgecombe up to this! Tristan had asked his best friend to court her, knowing that they had previously been acquainted, and convinced that he was the more suitable candidate.

The only thing Emma could not understand was why Lord Edgecombe had agreed to court one lady when he was so obviously in love with another.

Emma sat down at the dressing-table and stared at her reflection in the glass. She could hardly believe it was true, yet the more she thought about it, the more sense it all made. It explained why Lord Edgecombe only flattered her when Tristan was within hearing. It also explained the longing looks Lord Edgecombe cast Lady Elizabeth's way when he thought no one was observing him. He was pretending to court her while he was actually in love with Lady Elizabeth.

But now that she had discovered the plot, Emma was even more confused about what to do about it. What if she were wrong? What would Lord Edgecombe's reaction be if she accused him of courting her while being in love with Lady Elizabeth, if in fact he did not love Lady Elizabeth? And what would Tristan say if she erroneously accused him of manipulating his closest friend?

"Oh, dear, what a dreadful muddle this all is. And all because of you, Tristan Landover," Emma muttered aloud. "If only you weren't so blessed stubborn..."

MEANWHILE, Chadwick, sitting in the library in a brown study, heard Edgecombe's arrival and viewed his departure with Lady Elizabeth, noting that Emma did not accompany them, with a disturbing mixture of emotions. On the one hand, he was relieved that Emma was not about to spend more time in Edgecombe's company, falling prey to his not inconsiderable charm. On the other hand, however, Chadwick knew that he was being foolish. The sooner Emma was linked with someone, the sooner she would begin to forget him, and the sooner his life could resume some degree of normality.

Chadwick glanced at the lengthy legal document in front of him, trying to concentrate on the words which kept blurring before his eyes. He had promised his solicitor that he would look over the papers, which his own clerk had gone to the trouble of procuring the previous day, and return them to him promptly. But with an impatience entirely out of keeping with the matters concerning Messieurs Ridgely, Booker and Blake, Chadwick threw down his pen, heedless of the blotch of ink brought about by its precipitous landing.

Who was he trying to fool? His life would never be normal again...not if Emma had no part in it. He had never loved anyone the way he loved her. Chadwick steepled his fingers and drew a deep breath. He closed his eyes, as if by doing so he might shut out the truth. He sometimes wondered why Fate had intervened in his life, by bidding him to start out on his journey to London a full week before he had originally intended. What, except Fate, could explain his presence at that inn on the one day when Emma happened to be there and most in need of him?

Tristan rose, and restlessly crossed to the window. His plan to interest Emma in someone else was not proceeding as he had expected. Quite apart from the fact that it nearly destroyed him to see Emma receiving attentions from another man, even if it was his closest friend, Emma, by her own admission, seemed intent on foiling him. If Emma was determined not to marry anyone other than himself, nothing would induce her to change her mind. She would continue to turn down all suitors until either he gave in or she lost interest.

And then where would they be, Tristan asked himself miserably. No doubt they would both end up alone, Emma possibly doomed to spinsterhood and he to a lonely old age. The thought of Emma's glorious beauty and sweet, giving nature being thus wasted cast him deep in gloom. He could not allow it to happen. She had far too much life in her for that. She needed to be loved and cherished . . . to have children upon whom to lavish attention. She needed to be married!

Chadwick turned back to his desk, his expression suddenly grim. There was only one way he could convince her that there was no hope for them. He must force the issue. He must marry someone else. Surely, if Emma knew he was unattainable, she would reconsider her position.

But whom was he to marry? the marquis wondered with a complete lack of enthusiasm. Who was tolerable enough not to drive him to distraction, or worse, make insufferable demands upon his time? Most of the ladies already known to him were decidedly lacking in some area, he admitted ruefully. None of them could combine the qualities of beauty, intellect, charm and humour near so attractively as Emma.

Thinking further on his scheme, Tristan suddenly wondered whether simply announcing his intention to marry might not accomplish his end.

Chadwick ruminated on this for a while. It seemed a reasonable answer. At the moment, he had no desire to leg-shackle himself to anyone, but if Emma thought him betrothed, surely she would relent and marry someone else.

Deciding that it was the only feasible way out of a difficult situation, Chadwick nodded. Tonight at dinner, he would make the announcement that he intended to marry Lady Thorold. She was as likely a candidate as any and, considering their close recent association, the announcement would not be viewed suspiciously.

Also, since they were dining *en famille,* there would be less chance of the rumour getting out. Under no circumstances could Chadwick risk Rowsbottom's or Edgecombe's inadvertently spreading the news about Town. Once Emma retired for the night, he would quickly inform Aunt Rachel and the girls that they were to say nothing of this to anyone, as he had not yet spoken of it to Lady Thorold. No doubt they would be surprised at his temerity, but that was of little importance to Chadwick. His main focus was to convince Emma of his ineligibility. He would play out the ruse for as long as was necessary. After all, the wedding was only two days away. With everyone caught up in the final preparations, plans for his own engagement would hardly receive a second thought.

Yes, it seemed the only sensible thing he could do, Chadwick decided. But did he have the right to deceive Emma? He knew that if she found out, she would quite likely hate him. And he, in turn, would hate himself for having lied to her.

The marquis lifted the lid of the crystal decanter on the desk and poured himself a generous amount of brandy. What did it matter if she hated him, Chadwick reflected, downing the clear amber liquid in one gulp. It would be better in the end if she did. It would facilitate the parting. He had informed her in no uncertain terms that he was bad for her, and this would only confirm it. The fact that he would love her until the day he died could have no bearing on the matter.

No, his mind was made up. Tonight he would make the announcement. "And may God forgive me," Tristan said, dropping his head into his hands, "for tonight I lose the only thing which has ever meant anything to me."

CHAPTER ELEVEN

EMMA HAD NEVER BEEN one to suffer premonitions. There had been no evidence of clairvoyance in her family, nor had she any reason to suspect that she was so gifted. But for some reason, as she dressed for dinner that evening, she was aware of a growing prescience of disaster, and try as she might, she was unable to shake it.

Fiona, putting the final touches to her mistress's hair, remarked on her distraction, causing Emma to start, and smile ruefully. "Forgive me, Fiona. I'm afraid my mind is wandering this evening."

Emma glanced at her reflection in the mirror and nodded, well pleased with the Scottish girl's skill. Fiona had arranged Emma's rich, burnished-gold tresses in a style both unique and flattering to the perfect oval of her face. She wore again the pink gown Margaret had given her, this time adorned with her mother's pearl necklace and ear drops.

Emma descended to the drawing-room where the family was already gathered. She could hear the sounds of laughter and conversation before she reached the door, and hesitated on the threshold. When she heard Tristan's deep masculine voice, she closed her eyes, suddenly feeling an inexpressible weakness in her legs.

She loved him so much that it was like a physical pain, and she wondered abruptly if the strange feeling she had experienced earlier had anything to do with him. Then, quickly shaking herself to dispel the foolish notion, Emma opened the door and moved forward.

"Oh, good, there you are, Emma," Lady Margaret said brightly, coming towards her. "Come and give me your opinion. I say that we should have pink trim on the bride-cake, and Aunt Rachel says we must have silver. What do you think?"

Trying to enter into the spirit of things, Emma smiled and suggested that perhaps a touch of both colours would look very pretty, and asked if Cook might not be able to affix some silver beading and leaves along with a few pink roses.

"What a wonderful idea," Lady Margaret responded enthusiastically. "I cannot imagine why I didn't think of it before. Emma, what would I do without you? Tristan, don't you agree?"

Chadwick, who had been standing with one arm care-lessly draped over the mantel, looked up and met Emma's gaze. He was dressed in formal evening attire, the immac-ulate black coat over a snowy-white shirt and artlessly folded cravat accentuating his dark good looks. He seemed oddly distracted, however, as though other matters were upper-most on his mind.

"Indeed, Margaret, we are fortunate in having Miss Harding with us. I don't know what we shall do when she returns home after the wedding."

His voice was carefully bland, but his eyes glowed with an inner fire that burned into her very soul. Emma knew she was breathing quickly, and hastily looked away.

"Tristan, how can you even mention Emma's returning home so soon?" Lady Margaret shot back at him. "You know Emma is welcome to stay here as long as she likes, isn't she, Aunt Rachel?"

"Of course she is," Lady Hatton agreed placidly. "No doubt the house will seem uncommonly quiet after you and Mr. Rowsbottom leave on your wedding trip, and there will be no more wedding arrangements to attend to."

"I think that perhaps you speak too soon, Aunt Rachel," Chadwick said, his voice noticeably devoid of expression. "There may indeed be another wedding held before the year is out."

Lady Hatton could not resist stealing a quick glance at Emma, wondering whether perhaps her nephew had finally come up to scratch. But one look at the stricken expression on the girl's face convinced Lady Hatton that she had the wrong of it. Tristan's words were obviously as much of a shock to Emma as they were to the rest of them . . . mayhap more.

"Tristan, what are you talking about?" Lady Margaret enquired bluntly. "Who else is going to be married?"

The marquis glanced at Emma sadly. "I am," he announced without preamble. "I intend asking Lady Thorold to be my wife."

For a moment, there was a deathly silence in the room. Emma sat as if stunned, unable to move or think. Lady Margaret blinked, her mouth opening and closing ineffectually. Lady Elizabeth, glancing first from her cousin to Emma and then back again, looked utterly confused. Only Lady Hatton seemed to accept the announcement with any degree of composure.

"About time, too," that lady remarked casually. "But am I to assume from the way you phrase your announcement, Tristan, that you have not yet broached the subject with Letitia?"

"No, I have only just decided the matter myself," Tristan replied tonelessly. "As you say, Aunt, it is well past time I considered the succession, and rather than risk losing what remaining eligibility I have, I decided the time was propitious. And, given my own advancing years, a bride closer in age seems an intelligent decision." He paused to flick an invisible speck of lint from his jacket. "As Lady Thorold is hardly a blushing debutante and is quite clearly looking for a husband, I thought her the most suitable candidate.''

"I assume from this very perfunctory explanation of your choice that love plays no part in your decision?" Lady Hatton enquired.

"Love?" Tristan shook his head somewhat sadly. "No, I think not. No doubt Letitia and I shall . . . suit."

"Suit?" Lady Margaret squeaked, clearly shocked. "Is that the best you can say, Tristan? That you will *suit?*"

"What else would you have me say, Margaret?" Tristan said, his smile rueful. "That I am head over heels in love like some callow young pup in the throes of first love? Hardly," he drawled. "I gave up such aspirations long ago. This is a judicious match that will doubtless benefit both Lady Thorold and myself."

"But I thought..." Lady Elizabeth started, then stopped, her eyes widening in alarm as she glanced at Emma.

"Yes, Elizabeth?" Tristan asked, his gaze darkening ominously. "What did you think?"

Lady Elizabeth gulped audibly. "N-nothing, Tristan. I . . . must have been . . . mistaken."

Her voice faded away, and Tristan nodded tersely. He knew as well as the rest of them what Elizabeth had thought. Aware that something needed to be said, Chadwick looked down at Emma. "And will you not congratulate me, Miss Harding?" he asked lightly. "I had hoped someone might greet my news with at least a small degree of enthusiasm."

Emma slowly lifted her head, feeling as though her heart were encased in ice. She raised her eyes to the level of his chin and no higher. She would not meet his gaze. She knew exactly why he was planning to marry Lady Thorold. It had nothing to do with his age, or the succession, or with what Society thought. He was doing it to convince her once and for all that there could be nothing between them. He was sounding the death knell for her hopes.

"I wish you . . . happiness, my lord," Emma finally managed to whisper. "I am sure that you are quite well aware of what you are . . . giving up," she added, her breath catching in her throat.

Tristan looked at the head bowed before him, and inwardly flinched as the knife twisted in his heart. "Oh, yes, Miss Harding. I am . . . well aware of what I am losing," he replied softly. "Only too aware."

The arrival of Higgins to announce dinner put an end to any further discussion, and quietly, the family rose and filed in to the dining-room. It was, as expected, a subdued meal, with Chadwick and Lady Hatton carrying the bulk of the conversation. Lady Elizabeth's worried expression silently attested to her concern, while Lady Margaret kept glancing from her cousin to her best friend with more than covert suspicion. There was something here that wasn't quite right, Margaret felt sure, and not for the first time, she suspected that strong feelings existed between Emma and Tristan. But if so, why was Tristan acting like such a bufflehead? Why didn't he just marry Emma and have done with it?

The conclusion of the meal was greeted with relief by all parties. Emma, excusing herself as soon as was polite, hurried up to her room to escape the concerned eyes of the family below.

In truth, Tristan's announcement had devastated her. Emma had never expected him to take such a drastic step, and the knowledge that he was only doing it to discourage her sent a flash of red-hot anger through her heart. What fools men were, sacrificing everything for the sake of their noble pride. What good would his pride do him in the long, empty years to come, Emma wondered, for she had no doubt that was exactly the fate he had decreed for himself. Lady Thorold was a beautiful, wealthy woman, but instinctively Emma knew that there was little warmth in her soul. She would gladly marry Chadwick for his title and his protection, but once she was wed, her life would be a matter of her own concern. She would come and go much as she pleased, just as she did now.

Nor could Emma see her willingly bearing the marquis a nursery full of children. It was rumoured that Lady Thorold was not overly fond of children in general, and though she had agreed to give birth once as a necessary part of her marital obligations, under no circumstances would she consider undergoing the process again.

Well, if that was what Tristan wanted from his life, so be it, Emma told herself with a sob, angrily brushing away the scalding tears. Let him ruin his life if he chose to. It was no longer any concern of hers. If Tristan were willing to go to such dramatic lengths to prove he did not want her, clearly there was little choice left for her but to accept it. Once Lady Margaret was wed, Emma would leave London and return to Aunt Georgina, where she hoped she would never hear mention of Tristan Landover again!

IN THE DARKENED LIBRARY, Chadwick sat in his chair, blindly staring out of the leaded window, much as he had done earlier in the day. His hands cradled a generous glass of brandy. Beside him, the bottle stood nearly empty.

So much for heroics, Chadwick thought ironically. His announcement had been received with a marked lack of enthusiasm, and he hadn't even had the chance to inform his two cousins and his aunt that his betrothal was a sham. They had filed out, one after the other, almost immediately after Emma had left.

The memory of Emma's devastated face brought a fresh groan from the marquis, and he slumped forward in his chair. What had he done? Why had he thrown over the sweetest, most precious girl he had ever met?

Girl, he repeated miserably. That was exactly why he had done it. She was no more than a girl, and one who had as much knowledge of life as a sparrow.

And yet, what had he achieved by turning away from her, Tristan asked himself dispassionately. What, other than assuaging his guilty conscience, had he achieved in compelling Emma to look elsewhere for a husband?

Nothing. He had left her to Fate, he acknowledged bitterly. He had left her to the mercies of a man, possibly someone unknown, who would treat her in any way he deemed appropriate. He might beat her, misuse her or abandon her. Was that his noble idea of saving her?

"I thought I might find you here," Lady Hatton said, suddenly appearing in the doorway.

"Aunt Rachel!" Tristan exclaimed, surprised to find her still up. "What are you doing here?"

"Looking for you, actually," his aunt replied. She advanced into the darkened room and lit one of the lamps on the table. "I had a feeling I might still find you up. Well," Lady Hatton began in her usual forthright manner, sitting down in the chair next to her nephew, "would you care to explain that little fiasco that went on in the drawing-room earlier?"

Tristan looked at his aunt askance. "If you are referring to my announcement that I intend to marry Letitia, I cannot think what you mean," he grumbled. "Seems to me I made myself perfectly plain at the time."

"Oh, you made yourself plain enough," Lady Hatton agreed, her grey eyes full of humour. "What I am asking is why you are making such a cake of yourself?"

"A cake!" he sputtered. "Aunt Rachel, I . . ."

"Now don't 'Aunt Rachel' me, Tristan," she admonished mildly. "I've known you far too long for that nonsense." She glanced at her nephew shrewdly. "You don't wish to marry Letitia Thorold any more than I do. Nor, I think, have you any intention of doing so.''

His aunt's perspicacity startled him. ''I am a man of my word, Aunt Rachel. As such, I fail to see why you would doubt my intentions,'' Tristan replied stiffly.

''Yes, you are a man of your word, Tristan. Except this time, your word hasn't been given,'' Lady Hatton remarked. ''And I'll tell you why. For one thing, you love Emma Harding. No, don't even attempt to play the innocent with me,'' she said, holding up her hand even as he would have interrupted. ''I'm no fool, Tristan. These eyes may not be as sharp as they once were, but they still see what's plain. And your love for that girl, and hers for you, I might add, is quite as plain as the nose on my face.''

When he didn't reply, Lady Hatton nodded. ''Yes, I thought as much. So why all this shamming, Tristan? Why don't you just ask Emma to marry you and have done with it?''

Tristan sighed, the sound dragged up from deep within his soul. ''It is not that easy, Aunt. There are ... other considerations.''

''Considerations?'' she repeated, glancing at him sharply. ''What considerations? Are you telling me I have mistaken Emma's feelings?''

''No, I had thought to see her take up with Edgecombe, but—''

''Edgecombe? You thought there was something there?'' Aunt Rachel scoffed. ''Good Lord, Tristan, I thought you more perspicacious than that. Edgecombe is head over heels in love with Elizabeth. Has been for some time.''

''You know?''

''Fustian, of course I know. I don't go about with my eyes and ears closed. Besides, Elizabeth never was very good at dissembling.''

"No, I don't suppose she was," Chadwick replied dully. "I suppose I shall have to speak with Jeremy about it."

"Speak with him, by all means." Lady Hatton nodded. "But do you address his genuine interest in Elizabeth or his supposed one in Emma?"

Tristan shook his head. "Neither. You could hardly be expected to know, of course, but—" Chadwick drew a heavy breath "—Edgecombe made me . . . an offer, I suppose you could call it. He volunteered to court Emma himself after I informed him that I intended to look for someone else for her."

"You did *what?*" Lady Hatton replied, aghast. "You knowingly encouraged Edgecombe to court her?"

"Well, no, not exactly," Tristan hedged. "I begin to think now that he was playing merry with me all along. I think he saw that deep down I didn't want anyone else to marry Emma, and thought that by putting himself forward as a candidate he was protecting her from the advances of other, less acceptable suitors."

"But didn't you think it would make his courtship of Elizabeth difficult?"

"To be honest, I did not know that he was interested in Elizabeth," Tristan confessed. "I wasn't made aware of that until recently. If I had known, I would never have condoned his approaching Emma."

Lady Hatton shook her head. "Faith, Tristan, what machinations you have gone through to avoid the girl. Would it not have been simpler all round just to marry her yourself?"

"But that's just it, Aunt!" Tristan replied, rising agitatedly. "I am too old for Emma, as I have told her, times without number. What use can I be to her? She deserves someone young and fresh-faced. Someone who isn't wearied of life."

"You poor old devil," Lady Hatton said, and then, to his amazement, burst out laughing.

Completely taken aback by her unexpected reaction, Tristan looked at her in vexation. "Would you care to explain what you find so amusing, Aunt?"

"Oh, Tristan. I never thought to hear such noble gibberish coming from you, of all people," Lady Hatton said, clearly enjoying herself. "Pour me a glass of that brandy, will you?"

"Brandy?" he said, raising an eyebrow as he nevertheless complied with her request. "I didn't know you drank."

"I don't in company," Lady Hatton agreed placidly, accepting the glass. "But Minnie knows to keep a bottle in my bedside table for those occasional nights when sleep eludes me. Learned it from your late uncle, actually."

Tristan chuckled as he watched his aunt take a mouthful of the amber liquid and close her eyes, obviously enjoying it. "Ah, that's better. Now, where were we?"

"You were in the middle of roasting me over my noble sentiments," the marquis informed her drily.

"Yes, so I was. You were telling me some Banbury tale that now that you are old and decrepit, you couldn't see yourself as a suitable husband for a mere slip of a girl."

"I didn't exactly say decrepit, Aunt," Tristan corrected her in a tone of droll amusement.

"No? I must have assumed it from your tone of voice, then," came the crisp reply. "You were also saying that Emma needs someone young and fresh-faced. Someone who hasn't . . . experienced the, er, indulgences of life to the extent you have." She glanced at him keenly. "I take it that was what you were referring to?"

"Yes, I suppose I was."

"So what you meant to say," Lady Hatton said slowly, "is that you want Emma married to someone who will no doubt dabble in gambling, horses and loose women *after* he marries her rather than before.''

Tristan's dark brows drew together ominously. ''I meant nothing of the kind!''

''Well, that's what you're saying, dear boy,'' Lady Hatton pointed out. ''Why would you believe that any young man who moves within the ton would escape the lure of things which have attracted men for years? The very things you admit to having already experienced.''

''I didn't mean that he might not experience them,'' Tristan explained patiently. ''I merely thought that if he were married to Emma, it might dissuade him from becoming too heavily entangled with them.''

''Oh, Tristan, how terribly naive. Has the presence of a wife ever stopped any gentlemen of your acquaintance from indulging in such pastimes before?''

Tristan thought about that for a moment, and ruefully shook his head. ''No, I don't suppose it has.''

''Of course it hasn't. Nor has it any of mine,'' Lady Hatton pointed out, her eyes twinkling. ''And that includes your late uncle.''

''Uncle Mortimer?'' Tristan ventured, his voice revealing his surprise. ''I don't believe it.''

''Your uncle was no different from the rest,'' Lady Hatton informed him. ''Horses were his particular weakness. He was always popping down to Newmarket to view the field. Especially when he heard rumours of a particularly promising new filly. I can't tell you how many times he came home pockets to let. It's just fortunate we had the wherewithal we did or we might have been in dun territory today.''

Tristan gazed into the fire, an odd half smile playing about his lips. ''I never would have guessed. Uncle Mortimer always struck me as being the archetypal uncle. Kind, absent-minded, humourous. A...gentleman.''

Lady Hatton shook her head a touch sadly. "And he was. Make no mistake about that, Tristan. Your uncle was as good a husband to me as they come, and I can honestly say I did not want for anything while he was alive. But at heart, he was still a gambler. With a gambler's love of risk."

Tristan continued to look amused. "He did not seem the type."

"Oft-times they don't," Lady Hatton said quietly. "A man's vices are not stamped upon his forehead for all to see, my dear. Nor are his virtues. No one can see what lies within. But as for you," she said, holding out her glass to be refilled, "I don't suppose you realize that you're about to take the biggest gamble of all."

Tristan tilted the decanter and regarded his aunt sceptically. "Me? A gamble? How?"

Lady Hatton shrugged eloquently. "By condemning Emma to look for love elsewhere."

Tristan looked surprised. "I hardly see that as being a gamble."

"Why not? She may never find it."

"No, that I cannot credit," Tristan objected firmly. "Emma is a warm and engaging young lady. She will marry and..."

"Silly boy. I didn't say she would not marry," Lady Hatton interrupted. "No doubt she will, and possibly quite well. But whether she will be lucky enough to find the kind of love she feels for you again, therein lies the gamble. You should remember, Tristan, that love is not a guaranteed thing," Lady Hatton told him softly. "And not all men are like you. Too often men seek merely to marry for position or money, and then begin to search for love, or whatever you wish to call it, outside the marriage. I need not tell you how commonplace a thing that is."

Chadwick hung his head, knowing full well how true it was. There were plenty of beautiful, successfully married women looking to enjoy a discreet *affaire de coeur* with a handsome younger man. How many times had he himself been approached by wives all too obviously bored with their husbands and looking for a diversion. It was done all the time. Lady Jane was a case in point. And as long as it was done with tact and discretion, Society turned a blind eye to it.

"Then I've lost her, haven't I?" The marquis sighed, his eyes bleak. "She certainly won't have me now, after what I did tonight."

"I wouldn't be so sure," Lady Hatton said, beginning to feel the edifying warmth generated by the two glasses of brandy. "Emma is not like most young ladies. Her feelings run deep, and love so truly felt is not easily dismissed. Whether she will forgive you this subterfuge regarding Letitia Thorold, however, is another matter altogether."

"She must forgive me!" Tristan whispered fervently. "She is everything to me, Aunt Rachel. Everything I have always wanted in a woman."

"Dear me, I do believe that is the first intelligent thing I have heard you say all evening. And," she added, her eyes sparkling, "the first time I have heard you address her as a woman."

Slowly, Tristan smiled, admitting it for the truth. Emma was every inch a woman in his eyes. A warm, beautiful, loving woman whom he wanted to marry more desperately than anything he had ever wanted in his life.

"And I thought you never noticed what went on in this house." Tristan chuckled. "What would I do without you, Aunt Rachel?" he said, warmly brushing her cheek with his lips.

"Oh, no doubt you'd muddle through," Lady Hatton observed. "Though what a botch you'd make of it, I shudder to think."

They rose together, and after extinguishing the lamp, Chadwick escorted his aunt up the stairs. At her door, she turned and smiled up at him affectionately. "I take it we shall hear no more about Lady Thorold's becoming the next marchioness, then?"

Chadwick looked momentarily sheepish. "Rest assured you shall not."

"Good. Never did like the idea of being related to Letitia," Lady Hatton grumbled. "Bold as brass, that one. Well, good night, dear boy. Sleep well. And remember. Tomorrow is another day."

Yes, another day and a fresh chance, Tristan thought. And the first thing he intended to do was make a clean breast of it with Emma. She deserved his honesty. She was too good and innocent to be toyed with.

What was it his aunt had said? If love was truly felt, it wasn't easily dismissed. Chadwick could only hope it were true!

THE WEDDING of Lady Margaret Glendenning and the Honourable Bertrand Rowsbottom took place at eleven o'clock in the morning. It was a lovely ceremony, attended by a small group of family and close friends who smiled their pleasure as the beautiful bride and her adoring young husband solemnly whispered their vows.

Margaret looked radiant in a high-waisted gown of silver gauze over white lace. Her happiness was plain to see, and under the headdress of delicate white rosebuds which held in place a shimmering length of silver gauze which floated down around her as soft as a whisper in the mist, her eyes glowed with love and contentment.

During the ceremony, Emma, who acted as chief bridesmaid, held the bride's posy while Bertrand placed the ring on Margaret's finger. Emma only half listened to the moving words of the marriage service, painfully aware of

Chadwick's presence close by. Over the past few days, she had taken great pains to avoid Tristan. Today, she had been particularly careful to avoid his eye, even though she knew that he had been casting frequent glances her way all through the service.

And then, it was over. The newly married bride and groom, along with their retinue and family, repaired to Eaton Square, where a host of invited family and guests joined them for a sumptuous nuncheon. There was food and wine aplenty, and champagne flowed in endless supply as the happiness of the young couple was toasted again and again.

After the ceremony, Emma helped Margaret change out of her wedding finery and into her travelling clothes. When she was almost ready to go, Margaret turned to her friend, and smiled at her with eyes which were suspiciously bright.

"Oh, Emma, I am going to miss you. I don't know quite what I would have done without you here these past few weeks."

Emma smiled and gently shook her head. "You would have been fine, dearest. And now you are a happily married lady, about to embark on a whole new life. And you know that I wish you every happiness, don't you, Meggie?"

"Yes, I know," Margaret whispered tremulously. Impulsively, the girls exchanged a quick hug. "You will be here when I get back, won't you, Emma?" Margaret whispered, looking searchingly into her friend's eyes. "There will be ever so many things which need attending to and I know that I shall forget something. And of course, I shall be longing to tell you all about my trip to Italy."

Emma forced a note of brightness into her voice. "I cannot promise, Meggie. I have been gone awhile as it is, and no doubt Aunt Georgina will be anxiously awaiting my return. There is so much to do on the farm."

"Oh, bother the farm," Meggie replied, her nose wrinkling. "Your aunt has done without you this long. Surely a few more weeks won't matter."

She hesitated a moment longer before glancing at Emma uncertainly. "I hope Tristan's announcement the other evening did not...discompose you too much, Emma. I must admit, I was rather startled by his declaration. It was unexpected at best."

Emma shrugged with studied indifference. "Why should I be discomposed, Meggie? It is not for me to be pleased or displeased by Lord Chadwick's choice of a wife. He may marry as he sees fit. And it is evident that he considers an alliance with Lady Thorold efficacious."

"Mayhap, but I had begun to wonder whether there might be a tendre developing between the two of you," Margaret admitted quietly.

Emma hid her pain admirably well. "I cannot imagine what would have induced you to think so. Lord Chadwick has never been anything but polite in his dealings with me, and has never given me cause to believe that he saw me as anything other than your friend."

Margaret sighed. "Pity. I had secretly hoped to see the two of you form an attachment, but it is clear now that such is unlikely to happen. I cannot, in all honesty, say that I welcome Lady Thorold as a member of the family, but it seems that I am to have no choice. Still, as you pointed out, Emma, no doubt Bertie and I shall see little enough of them once we are settled in our new home and Tristan is likewise riveted. Perhaps we shall see you and Lord Edgecombe instead," Margaret said more hopefully.

Emma smiled, but did not deign to reply. She could hardly tell Margaret that, like Tristan, Lord Edgecombe's intentions lay in another direction altogether.

By the time Margaret and Bertrand finally left for their wedding trip, it was early evening, and Emma's nerves were strained almost beyond bearing. She had smiled and laughed the day away, never once giving way to the tears which at times trembled so dangerously close to the surface. Not even when she had seen Chadwick conversing with Lady Thorold at the wedding nuncheon had she broken down.

But now that it was over, all Emma wanted to do was finish packing. She still had much to do before returning to her aunt's farm tomorrow.

Emma had asked Fiona to see to booking passage on the first stage back to Brighton the morning after the wedding. She had also asked Fiona to accompany her, not wishing a repetition of her earlier journey. Once the house emptied of wedding guests, Emma intended to retire to her chamber, pleading a touch of the headache, no doubt brought about by the excitement of the day, and remain there until the early hours of the morning when she and Fiona would quietly slip out to the curricle waiting to take them to the station. All that remained now was to finish a few letters.

At best, they were difficult to write. The note to Elizabeth was perhaps the easiest, filled with sincere wishes for her future happiness. To Lady Hatton, Emma expressed her warmest appreciation for that good lady's generosity, and to Margaret, Emma apologized for not being present upon her return, saying that she simply could not prolong her stay owing to her aunt's pressing need of her. She finished by wishing Margaret every happiness for the future, adding that she hoped that they might continue to correspond occasionally.

But her letter to Tristan had been another matter altogether, and more than one sheet of parchment had ended up in a crumpled heap on the floor. How did one go about saying goodbye to the most important man in one's life, Emma pondered wretchedly. How could she explain her reasons for leaving, other than by saying that to stay would only intensify her suffering, rather than lessen it? How could she convince Tristan he was making the gravest error a man could make?

She could not, Emma admitted wearily, and eventually, she gave up trying. In the end, her letter to Tristan had been brief, polite and emotionless . . . just as she intended her parting to be.

Sealing the letters, Emma went to pull the bell rope for Fiona, and then stopped, belatedly remembering that the servants had been given the evening off to enjoy their own private celebration of Lady Margaret's wedding. She had no choice but to deliver the letters herself.

Fortunately, she knew that Elizabeth and Lady Hatton had retired early and were likely to be fast asleep after the excitement of the day. She also knew that Tristan had left for his club immediately after Margaret and Bertrand had departed, and that he had informed Higgins that he would not be returning until the morrow. All Emma had to do was slip quietly into each room and leave the letters where they would be seen in the morning, by which time Emma and her maid would have already left.

Slipping her shawl over her nightdress, Emma picked up the letters and made her way down the darkened corridor. She delivered Margaret's letter first, propping it against the jewel box on her dresser. She prayed that Margaret would understand why she had to leave. Perhaps in a few years they might even be able to laugh about it, but now, the pain of it all was far too fresh to allow her that luxury.

Elizabeth's room was next. After quietly opening the door and peeking inside to see that Elizabeth was asleep, Emma carefully tiptoed in and set the letter on her bedside table. The delivery of Lady Hatton's letter was no more difficult. Opening the door, Emma saw that the bedside candle was still lit, but that Lady Hatton seemed to have fallen asleep. Her eyes were closed, and a novel lay open across her chest.

Lord Chadwick's room was her last stop. His was at the opposite end of the hall from the rest, and even though Emma knew Tristan was out, she could not prevent her hand from trembling ever so slightly as she turned the handle and went in. It was the first time that she had been in a gentleman's chambers, and the realization that this was where her beloved slept made her feel rather weak at the knees.

But, forcing herself to be sensible, Emma moved forward and, after surveying the room for only a moment, decided to leave the letter on top of the chest of drawers, next to the now-wilted flower which Margaret had given him from her bride's posy.

Impulsively, Emma touched the flower which had briefly adorned Tristan's lapel. How handsome he had looked today, she recalled wistfully. And how very proud as he stood and watched his dear Margaret speak her vows. Would that he could have looked that way upon her, Emma thought sadly.

Abruptly aware that such thoughts were leading her nowhere, Emma turned and started towards the door. But when she heard footsteps in the hall, and the sound of a man humming quietly under his breath, Emma gasped, too horrified to move.

Tristan was home! And he was about to retire to his room for the night—blissfully unaware that she was in it!

CHAPTER TWELVE

TRISTAN OPENED THE DOOR and stepped into his room, surprised at finding it in near total darkness. Odd that Parker hadn't left the lamp burning, the marquis thought, shuffling towards the desk. But then, why should he have? Had he not told Higgins himself that he would not be returning home until the morrow?

"Damn!" Tristan swore thickly as he stubbed his toe on the corner of the dresser. His fumbling fingers soon located the lamp and, after lighting it, placed it atop the chest. In doing so, he noticed Emma's note.

Quickly breaking the seal, Chadwick read the few brief lines inside. In the semidarkness, his face paled, and he drew in his breath in a sharp gasp. Emma was leaving early the next morning. Her note, brief and impersonal, wished him well in his marriage with Lady Thorold and expressed her hope that they would be happy together.

Tristan flung down the letter, and ran a hand through his tousled curls. Damn and blast his stupid plan to pretend he was to marry Lady Thorold! If he hadn't concocted that half-witted scheme in the first place, none of this would have happened. He had been unable to see Emma alone since his conversation with Lady Hatton, but he had assumed there would be time to speak to her after the wedding. Thank God he had come home, Chadwick realized belatedly. If he had stayed out all night as his cronies had wanted him to do, he would have returned home in the morning only to find Emma already gone. And doubtless he would have had little luck in persuading her to return once she had reached the farm.

Thankfully, now that he knew of her plans, he could attempt to stop her. His future happiness depended upon it! He had to tell her that there was going to be no marriage to Letitia Thorold, and that the only woman he wanted to marry, or had ever wanted to marry, was her own dear self.

Tristan glanced at the ormolu clock on the mantel. It was still early. The first stage did not leave Piccadilly until a little after five in the morning. He had plenty of time. No doubt Emma intended to slip away in the early hours without waking anyone. He would wait in the library, from where he could see the stairs. And when she came down, he would confront her and tell her that she had no reason to leave. Then, he would ask her to marry him—as he should have done last week!

Satisfied that his affairs were perhaps finally about to be resolved, Chadwick turned, and in doing so, set in motion a comedy of errors which would not have been out of place on the theatre stage. Stumbling over the edge of the carpet, Chadwick fell forward into the wardrobe, knocking over a small table in the process. The force of his landing against one side of the wardrobe knocked the other door open, and at the sound of a cry, Tristan glanced up, astonished to see Emma cowering within.

"My God! Emma!"

Unfortunately, the noise of the table falling over, compounded by the thump of his landing heavily against the wardrobe, only served to wake Lady Hatton and Lady Elizabeth, both of whom suddenly appeared in the doorway to his room.

"Tristan, what on earth is going on in here?" Lady Hatton demanded. "We heard a crash and—oh! Upon my word!" Lady Hatton gasped, her eyes widening as the flickering candlelight revealed the sight of Emma standing *en déshabillé* inside the wardrobe. "Emma! What on earth are you doing in Tristan's wardrobe?"

Blushing furiously, Emma gathered her shawl more tightly about her shoulders. "Lady Hatton, I can explain—"

"Aunt Rachel, it isn't what you think—" Tristan began quickly, picking himself up off the floor.

"Considering that I am not sure what to think, I shall reserve judgement on that for the moment," Lady Hatton interrupted drily. "Perhaps it would be best if you were to return to your room, Emma. We shall speak of this in the morning."

Belatedly recalled to the presence of her other niece, who was staring at Emma dumbfounded, Lady Hatton declared, "That goes for you, too, Elizabeth!"

"But—"

"Immediately, young lady!"

Her tone brooked no argument, and after darting one last curious glance at her friend, Lady Elizabeth quickly returned to her room.

"Lady Hatton, please, I can explain . . ." Emma began, but was once again cut short.

"I am sure you can, Emma," Lady Hatton said, a touch more gently. "But I hardly think now is the time. It is late. We shall speak of this in the morning."

Aware that there was nothing further to be gained by trying to explain, Emma lowered her eyes and reluctantly went back to her room. That settled, Lady Hatton turned to regard her nephew, a small smile tugging at her lips. "Well, Tristan. This is a pretty kettle of fish you have landed yourself in. I had assumed that you were going to set matters to rights, but I hardly expected you to move so quickly—nor in quite such a manner. You know, of course, that you have no recourse now but to marry Miss Harding."

Tristan continued to stare at his aunt in a slightly bemused fashion. He was unable to forget the sight of Emma as he had seen her in the wardrobe, her gold hair floating down around her shoulders in glorious disarray, her magnificent eyes gazing up at him in the dim light.

Then, remembering himself, he shook his head. "As a gentleman, I would consider no other option. However," he added with a smile, "since that was exactly my desire, I shall be only too happy to comply."

"I am delighted to hear you say so."

"By the by, Aunt," Chadwick added in a more serious tone, "do not hold Emma in any way responsible for what just happened. Her being in my room was quite accidental. I suspect she was in the middle of leaving this letter for me when I inadvertently stumbled into the room."

"A letter?" Lady Hatton asked suspiciously. "And what was the nature of the information contained in this letter, if I may ask?"

"You may, since I venture to say that you and the girls have similar notes waiting for you in your respective bedrooms." Tristan glanced at the note and smiled wistfully. "Emma was saying goodbye. No doubt she intended to slip away on the first stage back to Brighton in the morning."

His aunt blinked, and then glanced at him in amusement. "Poor girl. No doubt her haste to flee had something to do with your rather startling announcement the other evening."

"Alas, I fear you may well be correct, Aunt. But as I assured you last night, I have every intention of setting the matter to rights."

"That's all well and good, my dear," Lady Hatton said, smiling ruefully. "But I hope you realize that if Emma was fleeing because of the proposed marriage between yourself and Lady Thorold, you may have set yourself a rather difficult obstacle to overcome."

"An obstacle? How so?"

"Because if you propose to Emma now, as we all know you must, she may believe that the offer is motivated by your sense of obligation rather than by your feelings of devotion."

"Obligation has nothing to do with it," Chadwick replied fervently. "I love Emma, and I intend to tell her so!"

"I understand that, Tristan." Lady Hatton nodded. "But look at it from her perspective. Emma doesn't know that your proposed marriage to Lady Thorold was nothing but a sham. She only knows that her virtue has been compromised and that as a gentleman, you have no recourse but to offer her marriage. And knowing that you will have to break off your plans to marry Lady Thorold in order to do so will not sit well with Emma, not well at all. She will feel that she has forced your hand, and that will be an anathema to her. Your task now, my dear," Lady Hatton said with a sigh, "will be to convince Emma that you truly *wish* to marry her rather than you feel obligated to."

EMMA WAS UP long before the rest of the house was stirring. She watched the sun make its slow, majestic journey over the tops of the houses until it finally cast its pale golden light through her window, chasing away the shadows of the night. Strangely, as she waited for the onset of daylight and with it, her meeting with Lady Hatton, Emma was surprised to find herself remarkably calm. She took breakfast in her room, and then, in response to Lady Hatton's eventual summons, made her way down to the blue salon. At the threshold, she tapped lightly on the door.

"Enter."

Emma drew a deep breath and advanced. She found Lady Hatton seated at her writing desk and smiled tentatively. "Good morning, Lady Hatton."

"Ah, good morning, Emma. Come in, my dear. Have you had breakfast yet?"

"Yes, thank you," Emma replied quietly, then belatedly noticed that the tray Lady Hatton's maid had just brought in contained two cups. "Though perhaps I might take a cup of coffee with you," she added quickly.

Lady Hatton signalled to the maid, who quickly poured two cups of coffee and handed one to Emma. "Thank you, Minnie," Lady Hatton said. "That will be all for now."

The maid bobbed a curtsy and hastily withdrew, leaving Emma alone with Lady Hatton. "Well, Emma," Lady Hatton began in her usual forthright manner, "it has certainly been an eventful few days, capped off by a rather eventful night." She glanced at the girl with interest. "I don't think I need tell you how surprised I was to find you in my nephew's chamber last evening. Would you care to explain how you came to find yourself there?"

"It was really quite innocent, Lady Hatton. I was leaving a . . . letter for Lord Chadwick," Emma replied quietly.

"Ah, yes, the letter," Lady Hatton said. She picked up a note and held it towards Emma. "Similar to the one you left in my room, I assume."

"Yes, Lady Hatton."

The older woman nodded thoughtfully. "I am sorry you feel the need to leave us so soon, Emma. I understood that Margaret had asked you to remain until she returned from her wedding trip."

"She did, Lady Hatton, but under the present circumstances, I thought it better that I leave as soon as possible."

"The present circumstances," Lady Hatton repeated, smiling. "Meaning my nephew's marriage to Lady Thorold?"

Emma blushed to the roots of her hair. "I am sure Lord Chadwick's marriage is of no concern to me, Lady Hatton."

"Then why were you in such a hurry to leave, Emma? And without telling anyone?"

Emma breathed a heavy sigh. "I . . . thought it best. Now that the wedding is over, I must return to the farm. I simply thought it would be easier to say my goodbyes on paper."

"Ah, I see," Lady Hatton said, carefully hiding a smile. "Hence the letters in our rooms. In particular, my nephew's room. And your untimely unveiling as the deliverer."

"I only delivered the letters because the servants were away," Emma said quickly. "Had a footman been on duty, I would have left the letters with him with instructions to deliver them first thing this morning."

"But not until *after* you had departed for Brighton?" Lady Hatton surmised.

"No, Lady Hatton," Emma agreed quietly. "Not until then."

The silence lengthened between them, and not for the first time Emma cursed her bad luck at having been discovered. Had she not lingered in Lord Chadwick's room, she would be on her way home now, with her memories of London, and Tristan's love, behind her. Instead, she was forced to remain to face Lady Hatton's ire, and to try to explain why she had felt the need to leave so impetuously.

"Well, Emma, I am relieved to hear that your reasons for being in my nephew's room are justifiable, and certainly above reproach."

"Thank you, Lady Hatton."

"However, the fact remains that Elizabeth did see you there, and that she may draw the wrong conclusions."

"But I am sure that if you were to tell her otherwise, Lady Hatton..." Emma began, anxiously.

"I may tell her, yes, but she is an impressionable young woman at best, and may well prefer to draw her own conclusions." Lady Hatton momentarily suspended their discussion at the sound of a knock on the salon door. "Come in," she replied.

"Good morning, Aunt Rachel, Miss Harding," Lord Chadwick greeted them cheerfully.

"Ah, Tristan, come in. Your timing could not have been better," Lady Hatton said, glancing at Emma's painfully flushed cheeks. "I have just been talking over the events of last evening with Emma, and telling her that certain things must be put right. And since you play a very large part in doing exactly that, I think I shall leave the two of you to, how shall we say, settle matters between yourselves.''

''But Lady Hatton . . . !'' Emma began in alarm.

Lady Hatton rose, and then, to Emma's surprise, stooped to place a gentle kiss upon her cheek. ''I shall be back directly, Emma. If my nephew does anything even remotely ungallant, you have but to call.''

Emma blinked, too surprised for words. After Lady Hatton left, Tristan turned to regard her, a faint smile hovering about his lips. ''By the shadows under your eyes, Miss Harding, I would hazard a guess that you did not enjoy a restful sleep last night.''

Emma fixed Chadwick with a baleful stare. ''No, my lord, I did not. And it is entirely your fault.''

''My fault?'' Chadwick replied, clearly taken aback. ''How is it my fault?''

''Because you, sir, were not supposed to return home last evening.''

''Ah, yes, so I recall,'' Tristan agreed, having difficulty hiding his smile. ''And because I did, you now find yourself in the uncomfortable position of having been compromised.''

''I hardly call being discovered in someone's wardrobe being compromised,'' Emma corrected him. ''Your aunt does not hold me responsible for what happened.''

''Ah, but you were in my room, Emma. And in your night attire, I hasten to point out.''

Emma met his gaze without flinching. ''I was respectably covered, Lord Chadwick.''

''Unfortunately, yes, you were,'' Chadwick replied audaciously.

''Lord Chadwick! I would thank you to remember yourself!''

"I am remembering myself," Chadwick continued, ignoring her heated response, "and whether you choose to admit it or not, Emma, you were compromised by my return. And that be the case, I must now come up to scratch, as it were."

Unhappily aware that Tristan intended to offer her a proposal of marriage in order to salvage her reputation, Emma threw back her head in a touchingly defiant gesture. "I hardly think such desperate measures are called for, Lord Chadwick. You know that the circumstances which led to my being in your room were entirely innocent."

"*I* do, yes. But my dear cousin Elizabeth may not understand," Tristan hastened to point out. "Only think what conclusions she may be drawing even now."

"I feel quite sure that Lady Elizabeth is sensible enough to understand that what she saw last evening was...was..."

"Was what, Miss Harding?" Tristan asked when Emma's words trailed away uncertainly. "A rendezvous?"

"Certainly not!"

"A light-hearted game?"

"Not in the least!"

"Then what, Miss Harding?" Tristan said in that same quietly infuriating tone. "What would you call your being in my wardrobe last evening, if not a game or a meeting?"

"A very foolish undertaking, I'm sure," Emma muttered under her breath.

Unfortunately, Tristan heard her. "A foolish undertaking, indeed, Miss Harding. And one which, as a gentleman, I feel obliged to rectify. Therefore, I am asking you to marry me."

"Marry you!" Emma replied, looking at him through pain-clouded eyes. "You offer me an insult, my lord, not a solution. How can you possibly offer me marriage when you have already made your choice of a bride well known?"

"Ah, yes." Tristan sighed. "Lady Thorold."

"Yes, Lady Thorold," Emma replied tightly. "Or have you forgotten the announcement which you made scarcely two nights ago?"

"Forgotten it? I am hardly likely to forget an announcement which caused my cousins to abandon me in disgust and my aunt to give me a right set-down before elucidating a few truths I had been too stupid to realize."

"She did?" Emma said, looking up at him in surprise.

Tristan nodded and walked towards Emma until they were no more than a few inches apart. "Indeed. She told me in no uncertain terms that I was a fool to let you go, and that I was neither too old, nor too reprehensible, to approach you. And," he added, sitting down on the love-seat next to her, "she told me that if I did not marry you myself, I deserved the living Hell my life would probably turn out to be."

Emma, who was having trouble concentrating on his words, given his disturbingly close proximity, allowed herself a brief, nervous smile. "And why did she envisage that, my lord?"

"Because she informed me that if I were not the man to marry you, I would never know if the man who eventually did would love you as much as I. And that I would have to suffer another man's doing this—" Tristan slowly ran his hand along her cheek and cupped the pointed little chin between his thumb and forefinger "—and this . . ."

Emma closed her eyes as Tristan's mouth slowly came down on hers, exulting in the glorious sensation which coursed through her body as their lips touched. She felt his arms go round her, pulling her closer until she could feel the tumultuous pounding of their hearts beating together. Never had her blood surged through her veins in such a way. Truly, if this was what it was to be loved, it was worth the sacrifice of her reputation. For Emma knew suddenly, and with blinding clarity, that if she did not marry Tristan Landover, she would not marry at all!

Abruptly recalled to her senses, Emma gently pushed Tristan away, well aware that her cheeks were burning. It was a few minutes before she was calm enough to address him. "That is all well and good for you to say now, Lord Chadwick," she said finally, "but it still does not explain why you suddenly came to the realization that everything I have been telling you all along was true."

Chadwick grinned ruefully. "It wasn't sudden, my dear. Not in the least. I have been in love with you from the moment I picked you up and held you in my arms after you fainted at the inn. And I have been fighting it since then, too. You don't know how hard it was for me, Emma, seeing you try to hide your fear and uncertainty that day, watching that beautiful, proud little face, and knowing that all I wanted to do was to take you in my arms and hold you, and tell you that everything was going to be all right. To tell you that I wanted to look after you for the rest of my life."

Emma gazed up at him with ingenuous eyes. "You knew all that, even then?"

"Even then," he admitted.

"Then why were you willing to let your good friend Lord Edgecombe court me?"

Chadwick flinched, and did not meet her gaze. "I did not...let him court you," he answered evasively. "The man was quite naturally interested in you. I could hardly stop him from seeing you, could I?"

"Fustian!" Emma murmured, her lips curving in a reluctant smile. "Lord Edgecombe was in love with Elizabeth, and had been long before the two of you concocted that silly plan to make me think otherwise."

Chadwick glanced at the lovely young woman with barely concealed surprise. "You knew?"

"I guessed," Emma said quietly. "There were too many contradictions in Lord Edgecombe's behaviour for me to believe he was genuinely interested in me. On the one hand, I saw the way he gazed at Elizabeth when he thought no one was looking. And when I saw the way he looked at me when you *were,* it didn't take very long for me to realize that Lord Edgecombe only paid attention to me when you were present. And the fact that you just seemed to accept the situation and allow Lord Edgecombe to proceed finally made me guess that the two of you were doing it by mutual agreement.''

Chadwick drew a heavy breath. "I did not intend to hurt you, Emma. I only had your welfare at heart. I thought I was doing what was best—for you."

"And I suppose you thought it best for me that you weave some Banbury tale about intending to marry Lady Thorold?" Emma couldn't resist asking.

"That!" Chadwick uttered the word as a grunt. "That was an action motivated purely by desperation. I was sure that if you thought me betrothed, you would turn away from me. That you would look elsewhere for love."

"But why Lady Thorold?"

Chadwick grinned sheepishly. "Would you have believed me had I said I intended to marry Euphadora Vyne?"

Emma carefully hid her smile. "No, I don't suppose I should have. Although Euphadora does turn a very nice leg."

"Yes, and Miss Harriet Brocklehurst looks very well in puce, but that doesn't mean I want to marry her, either!"

The thought of the illustrious Marquis of Chadwick marrying either lady was quite inconceivable to Emma, and she hastily turned away to hide her smile. But she was not quick enough.

"Yes, well you may laugh," Chadwick said, looking somewhat abashed. "No doubt a number of people have. But it seems that Aunt Rachel, like you, was quite correct," Tristan admitted, his expression suddenly becoming serious. "I love you, Emma, with all my heart, and I don't care how old—or young—you are. God knows, I was miserable enough just seeing you in the company of another man, let alone knowing that you were going to marry one eventually.''

"Oh, Tristan," Emma said softly, shaking her head. "I think you know I would not have married. How could I have married another while my heart was so full of you?''

"But do you still feel that way about me now?" Tristan asked hesitantly. "Even after I have admitted that I never had any intention of marrying Lady Thorold, and that I did indeed condone Jeremy's plan to court you? Can you forgive me for trying to deceive you?''

"I can forgive you anything, my lord—as long as you tell me here and now that you wish to marry me only because you love me.''

"As if there could be any other reason," Chadwick whispered, pulling her into his arms. "Yes, I want to marry you, my darling girl. And *only* because I love you.''

"And you are quite sure it has nothing to do with saving my reputation?" Emma teased him blissfully. "Because if it does—''

The rest of Emma's words were lost as Chadwick's lips came down upon hers, his kiss effectively sweeping away any lingering doubts she might have had. In that instant, Emma no longer doubted that Tristan loved her. She knew it for a certainty. And she knew that nothing would ever change that—not Lady Thorold, not Lord Edgecombe—not even Tristan Landover himself!

So caught up were they in their mutual enjoyment, that they were unaware of having company until the sound of a startled gasp and an embarrasssed "ahem" diverted their attention. "I say, does this mean my attentions to Miss Harding are no longer required?" Lord Edgecombe drawled, smiling down into the startled face of Lady Elizabeth at his side.

"Jeremy! Elizabeth!" Chadwick greeted the newcomers, reluctantly releasing Emma from his embrace. "You've come just in time to hear our news.''

"I don't know that we need hear anything," said Edge-combe, laughing. "Your actions speak loudly enough." He glanced at Lady Elizabeth somewhat enviously. "Lucky devil!"

Lady Elizabeth coloured at the meaning behind his words and ran forward to Emma. "Does this mean that everything is all right after . . . last night?" she asked shyly.

Lord Edgecombe looked puzzled, but as Tristan turned away to hide a smile, Emma laughed prettily. "Yes, Elizabeth. Everything is just fine. And this is not as a result of last night."

"No? Oh, good! Then I assume that also means, Tristan, that you were never seriously considering Lady Thorold as a wife?"

At Tristan's somewhat startled nod, Lady Elizabeth beamed and hugged Emma affectionately. "Thank goodness. I am so very delighted to hear that. I thought Tristan's announcement rather silly at the time, but I assumed he must know what he was doing. Tristan normally does."

"Your faith in me is flattering, Elizabeth," Chadwick said good-naturedly. "I begin to think I was the only one who did *not* see my suitability as a husband for Emma."

"Indeed. I, for one, never doubted it," Jeremy said. "That was why I offered to court Miss Harding myself."

Lady Elizabeth gasped in dismay. "You told Tristan that you intended to court Emma? But why?"

Lord Edgecombe smiled in his most charming manner. "Simple, really. I knew that he did not want anyone else to pay court to Emma, so by offering my own services, I was able to keep other would-be suitors away while Tristan came to his senses."

Lady Elizabeth shook her head. "That was very decent of you, I am sure, but how did you know your plan would not go awry? You could just as easily have . . . fallen in love with Emma as anyone else."

"No, I think not," Chadwick interjected. "Though I didn't realize it until later, Jeremy was the perfect choice. He was really no threat to me at all."

"But why not?" Lady Elizabeth repeated.

"Because, my dear, dear Lady Elizabeth," Lord Edgecombe said quietly, lifting her hand to his lips, "my affections had already been captured by another thoroughly delightful young lady whose beauty allowed me to see no other."

Lady Elizabeth gazed up at him, her large eyes opening wide. "They had?"

"Indeed they had. And perhaps if I could persuade you to join me for a stroll through your aunt's lovely rose garden, I could enlighten you as to her identity."

Lady Elizabeth, suddenly at a loss for words, hastily lowered her eyes. But not before Lord Edgecombe caught a glimpse of the joy shimmering in them. "Chadwick, may I have your permission to escort Lady Elizabeth to the garden?" Lord Edgecombe requested formally.

"With my blessing." Chadwick beamed, tightening his own embrace on Emma as the other two slipped away. "Now, my dear Miss Harding," he whispered against her lips, "where were we?"

"Put that young woman down, Tristan!" said Lady Hatton, abruptly re-entering the salon. "I saw Elizabeth and Lord Edgecombe come in and I won't have you setting another bad example for—" Lady Hatton looked around in puzzlement. "But where are Elizabeth and Lord Edgecombe?"

"If I don't miss my guess, Aunt Rachel—" Chadwick laughed "—they are well on their way to becoming the third wedding this house shall see this year. If, that is, they—and we—have your blessing."

The obvious delight in Lady Hatton's eyes was answer enough. "Well, thank heaven *that's* all sorted out," she said, glancing pointedly at her nephew. "I hate misunderstandings, and goodness knows there have been more than enough of them here lately. Of course you *and* they have my blessing. And in light of two engagements in one day, I believe I shall instruct Higgins to bring up some of your uncle's finest champagne for a celebratory dinner this evening." She smiled her delight at the young couple. "We can scarce let such a momentous day slip by without commemoration!"

As soon as Lady Hatton departed, Chadwick drew Emma to his side and the two of them slipped away through the French doors onto the sunny terrace. Amongst the flowering rose-bushes, Tristan took Emma in his arms and kissed her quite thoroughly.

"Tristan, your aunt..." Emma protested, blushing heatedly, nevertheless loving the feel of his arms around her waist.

"My aunt will excuse us for a moment, my darling girl," he whispered against one dainty ear. "Besides which, I needed to see you alone."

Emma's lips curved alluringly. "Alone, my lord? Shall I hide in your closet as I did last night?"

Tristan chuckled, the wickedness of it invoking the most unladylike thoughts in Emma's mind. "The next time I find you alone in my bedroom, young lady, you shan't escape quite so easily," he informed her. Chadwick's arms tightened round her and when he touched his lips to hers, it was with a passion that thrilled Emma to the core. When eventually he drew back, they were both breathing a trifle unsteadily.

"Baggage!" he mumbled huskily, delighting in the knowledge that his future marchioness was neither cold nor inhibited. "Now, I did bring you out here for a reason." As Emma watched, Chadwick reached into his pocket and drew forth a small, black velvet box. "This is for you, my darling. I hope you like it."

Emma looked down at the box in his hand, and then gasped, her round eyes opening wide as he flipped up the lid. "Oh, Tristan!" she exclaimed, catching sight of the magnificent square-cut amethyst set amidst a cluster of brilliant white diamonds. "I never thought to own anything so... breathtaking."

"It was the only stone that came anywhere near to matching those bewitching eyes of yours," the marquis explained. "But if you don't like it, I shall take it back immediately."

Watching as he reverently slipped it onto her finger, Emma shook her head, her eyes misting. "You shall do nothing of the kind. I love it. Almost as much as I love you," she added shyly.

Pulling her into his embrace, the marquis sighed. "Well, my dearest, you are mine until the day I die. And while I know that may not be as long as if you had caught yourself a young buck, I hope it will be long enough."

Emma closed her eyes and nestled against the warm strength of his chest. "If I could be married to you but for a day, it would be enough, my love, and never think otherwise. Besides, I like the idea of being married to an older man. You won't be so inclinced to go out at night looking for... diversions," she said, flashing him a mischievous smile.

"My darling girl," he murmured before his lips lowered to capture hers once more, "I get the distinct impression that having such a delightfully wanton youngster for a wife will leave me precious little time *or* energy for anything else. And to be honest, I cannot think of any way I would rather have it!"

ROMANCE IS A YEARLONG EVENT!

Celebrate the most romantic day of the year with MY VALENTINE! (February)

CRYSTAL CREEK
When you come for a visit Texas-style, you won't want to leave! (March)

Celebrate the joy, excitement and adjustment that comes with being JUST MARRIED! (April)

Go back in time and discover the West as it was meant to be . . . UNTAMED—Maverick Hearts! (July)

LINGERING SHADOWS
New York Times bestselling author Penny Jordan brings you her latest blockbuster. Don't miss it! (August)

BACK BY POPULAR DEMAND!!!
Calloway Corners, involving stories of four sisters coping with family, business and romance! (September)

FRIENDS, FAMILIES, LOVERS
Join us for these heartwarming love stories that evoke memories of family and friends. (October)

Capture the magic and romance of Christmas past with HARLEQUIN HISTORICAL CHRISTMAS STORIES! (November)

WATCH FOR FURTHER DETAILS IN ALL HARLEQUIN BOOKS!

CALEND

Harlequin is proud to present our best authors, their best books and the best for your reading pleasure!

Throughout 1993, Harlequin will bring you exciting books by some of the top names in contemporary romance!

In February, look for *Twist of Fate* by

JAYNE ANN KRENTZ

Hannah Jessett had been content with her quiet life. Suddenly she was the center of a corporate battle with wealthy entrepreneur Gideon Cage. Now Hannah must choose between the fame and money an inheritance has brought or a love that may not be as it appears.

Don't miss **TWIST OF FATE** ...
wherever Harlequin books are sold.

BOB1

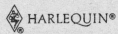

HARLEQUIN®

my *Valentine*

1993

The most romantic day of the year is here! Escape into the exquisite world of love with MY VALENTINE 1993. What better way to celebrate Valentine's Day than with this very romantic, sensuous collection of four original short stories, written by some of Harlequin's most popular authors.

ANNE STUART
JUDITH ARNOLD
ANNE McALLISTER
LINDA RANDALL WISDOM

THIS VALENTINE'S DAY, DISCOVER ROMANCE
WITH MY VALENTINE 1993

Available in February wherever Harlequin Books are sold.   VAL93